A DEMON'S DUE

LATTER DAY DEMONS SERIES, BOOK THREE

CONNIE SUTTLE

To Walter, Joe, Larry, Lee, Dianne, Sarah and Mark.
Thank you.

And to Carmel, Norm and Judy for the best tour of Adelaide anyone could ask for, great food, plus a treasure trove of research information and materials on caving and underground passages.

Also to Sharon and Rupert in Perth, for an evening in King's Park, a magnificent tour of the city, wonderful food and the Southern Cross.

Thank you, too, to all the amazing people in Sydney, Melbourne and Adelaide who took time from their busy schedules to meet with me.

I had a wonderful time.

ACKNOWLEDGMENTS

As always, this book is the result of collaboration. If it weren't for the support of my editor, my cover artist and my beta readers, it would be less than it is. All mistakes, as usual, are mine and no other's.

About the Author:
Connie Suttle lives in Oklahoma with her husband and a conglomerate of cats. They have finally banded together to make their demands, which has proven disconcerting to all humans involved.

You may find Connie in the following ways:
Facebook: Connie Suttle Author
Twitter: @subtledemon
Website and Blog: subtledemon.com

Blood Destiny Series:

Blood Wager

Blood Passage

Blood Sense

Blood Domination

Blood Royal

Blood Queen

Blood Rebellion

Blood War

Blood Redemption

Blood Reunion

Blood Destiny Series Boxed Set (Books 1-10)

Blood Recall

Blood Alliance*

Legend of the Ir'Indicti Series:

Bumble

Shadowed

Target

Vendetta

Destroyer

Legend of the Ir'Inditi Boxed Set

High Demon Series:

Demon Lost

Demon Revealed

Demon's King

Demon's Quest

Demon's Revenge

Demon's Dream

God Wars Series:

Blood Double

Blood Trouble

Blood Revolution

Blood Love

Blood Finale

Saa Thalarr Series:

Hope and Vengeance

Wyvern and Company

Observe and Protect*

First Ordinance Series:

Finder

Keeper

BlackWing

SpellBreaker

WhiteWing

~

R-D Series:
Cloud Dust
Cloud Invasion
Cloud Rebel

~

Latter Day Demons Series:
Hot Demon in the City
A Demon's Work is Never Done
A Demon's Due

~

Seattle Elementals Series:
Your Money's Worth
Worth Your While*

~

BlackWing Pirates Series
MindSighted
MindMage
MindRogue
MindMaster*

~

Black Rose Sorceress Series
The Rose Mark

Rose and Thorn

Black Rose Queen

Queen of Thorns and Roses

Future Wars Series

Buffer Zone

Black Zone*

Other Titles from SubtleDemon Publishing:

Malefactor

Transgressor

Underhanded*

by Joe Scholes

*Forthcoming

CHAPTER 1

A mterea
Morwin Quiffilis

"Are you sure you won't reconsider?" Jerwill, my commanding officer, dropped onto a chair beside my desk.

"I've had enough of the military life. It's time I went home to help my father with the family business." I didn't add that serving three stints in the Amterean military was more than enough, when only one was required by law.

Besides, attempting to teach younglings how to serve their planet wore me down—more than I liked to admit. I wanted to teach other things. Instill a desire to learn and search for truths instead of teaching blade and pistol skills, in addition to memorizing drills and firing patterns for battles.

And I wanted to grow my eyebrows—to indicate that I came from one of the best scholarly families Amterea produced.

I didn't say that to Jerwill. He was military and would always be so. His eyebrows were the prescribed length and would always be kept that way.

"Well, I still have almost a moon-turn to convince you," Jerwill offered a half-smile and slapped his knee before standing. I watched him saunter away before turning back to my father's latest communication.

Father was excited about his most recent commission; a stranger had come, asking him to research tales and myths on an isolated world the inhabitants called Earth. Father could barely contain his excitement—the thing the stranger asked him to research was called the Metal Library.

How interesting.

According to the tales, it held the power to relocate itself.

If this thing were real, I wanted to see it for myself.

The stranger claimed that the Metal Library had recently relocated, from a position he could pinpoint on a map of Earth. Father had sent me his research—and a copy of the map, along with his speculation as to where it may have moved.

My fingers itched to hold a research-quality comp-vid to study it myself. The mystery of it had helped me decide to leave the military. If such secrets were still waiting to be discovered in the universes, I wished to find them.

Father, I tapped into my military-issued device, *I will be home in less than a moon-turn.*

~

San Rafael, California
Kordevik

Lexsi's pale-blonde hair covered most of my claiming marks. I could still see one indention clearly as she slept in my arms.

I wanted to touch it.

Kiss it.

Reverently.

Li'Neruh Rath had supervised my smaller Thifilathi as I claimed my mate the night before. Her wounds had healed swiftly, once I removed my fangs from the back of her neck and kissed the marks gently.

I was more than grateful she slept through the whole ordeal and would wake with no recollection of the pain. I had to wait patiently for her to wake on her own—I couldn't wake her early—Li'Neruh was very firm on that.

As if she felt my eyes on her, Lexsi stirred in my embrace. "Kory," she breathed softly and snuggled closer.

If I died at that moment, my life would be complete. Who wouldn't want a lover's first word to be their lover's name, whispered while still asleep?

"Kory," she said again before pulling away from me. "I'm hungry."

"Baby?" I said when sky-blue eyes opened to blink at me.

I was hungry, too, but not for the same thing.

Sure, all I had to do was kiss her again. My fire would light hers and we'd be all over each other.

She was hungry.

For breakfast.

"Baby, I'll feed you," I said, leaning in to rub her nose with mine.

Sex could wait.

Lexsi

I couldn't explain how I felt—least of all to Kory. I wanted our first time to be private, in a private place. Not with a houseful of people just outside our door, knowing, in all likelihood, what was going on between us.

I guess I wanted a honeymoon.

I had no idea how to tell Kory that.

Therefore, he and I were in the kitchen of Aunt Bree's house, putting ham and eggs together as if we'd been married for years instead of hours.

At least I felt all right. My neck didn't hurt and I felt hungry instead of sick. I wanted to touch the back of my neck, to feel the indentions there. I forced myself not to do that.

"Do my eyes deceive me?" Anita, wearing house slippers, scuffed across the kitchen tile. She was wrapped in a long, fuzzy robe while

Kory and I, dressed in pajamas (well, Kory only wore the bottom half of his), wove our way past each other to make breakfast.

"Why would they?" I stopped to ask. "Want coffee?"

"The last time I saw both of you, you were unconscious," she shook her head. She couldn't hide her concern—she'd thought we were half dead, at least.

"We're fine," Kory gruffed. He pulled a coffee cup from the cabinet and poured for Anita. Her cup was set on the island while she continued to gape at us.

"Something's different," her eyes narrowed.

"What's different?" I turned away from her to pull a pan of biscuits from the oven. Gran made the best biscuits and she'd taught me her recipe when I was young.

"Something's different," Anita repeated.

"I don't know what you're talking about." I set the biscuits on top of the stove.

"Lie," Anita said.

"You taking over where I left off?" I turned toward her. I saw she was grinning, so she was teasing me.

"Check the back of Lexsi's neck," Kory said, thumping a stack of plates onto the island. "Drink your coffee, too, before it gets cold."

"Eeeeeee," Anita screeched before hurling herself in my direction. I had no idea until she wrapped me in a hug and twirled around the kitchen that the screech was a happy one.

"What the fuck is that unholy racket," Watson growled as he walked in, raking fingers through mussed hair.

"Oh." He blinked dark eyes as his gaze traveled from Kory to me. Anita set me down and straightened my pajama top, which had shifted and settled somewhere above my breasts.

That wasn't embarrassing.

"Breakfast. Take it or leave it," Kory breathed smoke when he caught Watson staring at what had previously been uncovered.

"Yeah. Breakfast. I'll take it," Watson said.

"You, sit," Anita snapped at Watson.

"Not a dog," Watson grumped, but as breakfast was being served, he sat anyway.

Other people wandered in as the four of us sat at the island to eat. Opal and Kell, first, then Sandra and Mason, followed by Zaria and Klancy.

I blinked when Esme and Yoff walked in together.

"I hear a toast is in order," Zaria raised her glass of orange juice. "To Kory and Lexsi, because it's about damn time."

Kordevik

I thought Lexsi and I would be in bed, copulating like a pair of fluffy, Amterean gudgings after breakfast.

We weren't. Something was making her uncomfortable and she wouldn't talk to me about it.

Instead, she did laundry, cleaned the bedroom and wrote a grocery list.

Fucking hell.

My Thifilathi wanted to skip to a hilltop and roar its dissatisfaction when she and Anita disappeared to go to the market.

"Ahem," Zaria interrupted my fist clenching, smoke-breathing reverie at the kitchen island.

"What?" I turned toward her so fast she jumped.

"She, uh, doesn't feel comfortable with so many familiar people around," Zaria began, before placing an envelope in my hand. "Because she thinks we'll know what she's, well, that will take care of it," she pointed to the envelope I now held.

"What is it?" I asked, lifting the flap.

"An all-expense paid trip to Australia and New Zealand. You're going on a cruise—for your honeymoon."

My hand stilled while the papers inside the envelope were only halfway out. "A honeymoon?"

I said the word as if it were foreign to me.

"This is their summer," she pointed out. "You'll have ideal weather and sixteen days of cruising around Australia and New Zealand. You won't know anybody and don't have to get to know them if you don't want to. If you want to spend the whole time in your cabin, that's your choice."

I pulled the papers out of the envelope then, and studied the date. The cruise started in three days. "If you leave today, you can spend two nights in Sydney before getting on the boat," Zaria grinned.

"But what about," I began.

"Let us worry about those things. You'll have your cell phone and mindspeech, if we need you. You can skip back and forth, if necessary."

She was right, plus it could be the only way I'd get sex in the next month or so. Yes, my cock was doing the talking. Hell, it would do the walking, too, if I let it. If Lexsi insisted on being a shy flower, then I'd do whatever it took to get her in my arms and her lips on mine.

The linking would take care of the rest.

~

Amterea

Morwin

My trunk and satchel were already packed and waiting; I only had two more days to fill out the necessary forms and arrange for transportation to Kinvalles, Amterea's second-largest city.

My father waited there for me, and was more than excited that I'd decided to join him. He'd uncovered many fascinating legends and tales from Earth, and felt he'd only touched upon a fraction of what was available.

There are many races, not just one, he'd sent in a message. *They all have their tales and myths. It is like a treasure mine for me.*

What about the stranger's request? I'd returned.

Yes, I have more information on that, too. I will send you what I have.

He'd sent it, but I postponed reading the whole of it until I boarded transport for home. It would occupy my time and keep the memory fresh when I saw Father again. I looked forward to discussing the research with him.

"Morwin?" Jerwill strode into my small office, with two guards behind him.

Those two guards wore full dress uniforms.

Why would they do that? One only dressed like that if one had official information to convey.

I went still.

"What is it?" I asked, keeping my voice calm and steady.

"Bad news, I'm afraid," Jerwill sighed.

One of the dress uniforms stepped forward and handed a comp-vid to me.

When I read the news of my father's violent death the night before, I went still from the initial shock.

Then the anger came.

~

San Rafael

Lexsi

My breath caught when Kory waved cruise tickets in front of my face.

Australia.

Who doesn't want to go to Australia?

And two days in Sydney? That was even better.

My mind became so crowded with all the things I wanted to do and see there, that it overwhelmed me.

"Sydney Opera House, here I come," I crowed, snatching the tickets from Kory's hand.

"Bed?" Kory murmured softly.

I blinked at him for a moment before my cheeks heated.

"No worries," Kory said, failing to produce the proper accent while pulling me into his arms. "We'll work it out. Come on, onion, let's pack."

~

Two hours later, Kory and I stood in line to check in at a hotel in The Rocks, which had a wonderful view of Sydney Harbor. That view included the Sydney Opera House. I was so excited, I almost vibrated with joy.

I get to see it for myself, instead of in photographs!

Slow down, onion, we'll get to that, Kory's voice sounded in my mind. Until then, I hadn't realized I'd sent my thoughts as mindspeech. Somehow, too, Zaria had picked the perfect place for our honeymoon.

Honestly, I shouldn't have been surprised. Kory's hands gripped my shoulders from behind, as if he worried I might float away in my excitement.

"ID and credit card?" I almost didn't realize our turn had come at the front desk. A clerk smiled at us as Kory handed over our passports and a credit card. Somehow, Zaria had accomplished what would have taken weeks to do; she'd secured visas for both of us—for Australia.

New Zealand didn't require a visa application made in advance; I was grateful because we had a few stops to make there on the cruise.

"Sign here," the clerk set an electronic pad in front of us. "Here are your room keys," he handed Kory two key cards. "Fourth floor; the elevator is just past the desk and down the hall."

We pulled our bags toward the elevator, but the moment the doors closed on us, Kory skipped us to the fourth floor. Our room was only a short distance down the hall, and we were inside it quickly, thanks to a second skip.

"Kory," I poked him in the chest when we landed in a rush inside our suite.

His mouth was on mine immediately.

I can't begin to describe the furious bout of heated sex that came after that.

CHAPTER 2

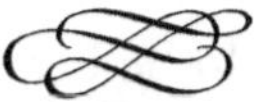

*mterea
Morwin*

My father had so many notes written on paper; he'd only consented to keep records on a comp-vid in the past three sun-turns —after I'd convinced him to do it.

Still, he'd drawn his maps and musings on paper before transferring them to his device.

That same device was now missing, amid brown-stained piles of papers. Yes, those brown stains were my father's dried blood. The constabulary had done its investigation and taken robotically detailed images to place in its files, in an attempt to track down the murderer.

Father had never given me the stranger's name, so I had nothing to offer the authorities, not even a description.

They shrugged when I said my father was studying Earth—only one had barely heard of it and didn't think it worthy of their research.

My assumption was that whatever my father found caused his death. I had the records he'd sent to me; the constables accepted copies with reluctance, sure that they'd had nothing to do with my father's murder.

Perhaps they were correct; perhaps this was a war between houses

9

of research. After all, to Amterean Dwarves, information is more treasured than gold, and is often sold for precious metals, jewels or other valuable compensation.

I'd never asked my father how this fee would be paid, or how much he would charge for the information.

For me, and where I'd been in the military for the past thirty sun-turns, it mattered little.

What mattered now was that my father's killer had escaped.

I had an idea where he could be heading, too. I merely had to find passage to Earth to catch up with him.

Sydney, Australia

Lexsi

"No," I placed a hand between Kory's mouth and mine. It was after eight the following morning, after what surely must have counted as a marathon of sex the night (and previous day) before.

Not that the sex wasn't awesome and everything I could have hoped for.

The truth was, I was starving and I still hadn't seen the Opera House.

"Seventeen times isn't enough," Kory muffled into my palm before kissing it.

"You're not hungry?"

"For you," he pulled my hand away from his mouth.

I was beginning to view his mouth as a very dangerous weapon; one that could make my blood boil and my fingers struggle to remove clothing or any other barriers between us. The truth was, his kiss made me forget everything else, and that could be perilous in the extreme.

"We can have eighteen, nineteen and twenty after dinner. For now, I want breakfast, the Opera House, lunch and then whatever else there is to see," I tapped his nose.

"All right." Kory's mouth curled into a smile, letting me know that we'd had enough sex for the moment. Maybe he did want breakfast after all. "Did I hurt you?" he asked.

"I don't remember," I confessed. "It was just—so consuming."

"I just remember how good it was," Kory grinned. "Come on, let's get in the shower and then find breakfast."

At least I took my shower alone; if Kory had come with me, we may not have left the room. We walked out of the hotel an hour later and had brunch at a small restaurant nearby. Tables were scattered throughout an open courtyard at the back, all shaded by a large, flowering tree.

Small, pale plumeria flowers with yellow centers would drop occasionally from the tree; two landed on our table while we ate. I lifted one and toyed with it while sipping the last of my flat white coffee—a favorite drink for Australians.

"It's perfect," I held it up for Kory to see.

"And yet it fell," he pointed out, lifting his cup of coffee.

"Isn't that a rather depressing way to look at it?" I asked.

"It fell for you. How's that?" His dark eyes held mischief as he sipped from his cup.

"Gag," I grumped. "Groan," I added.

"Are you still hungry? I can get you another omelet," Kory said, ducking his head to hide a smile.

"Trying to put me in a better mood?"

"Maybe."

"I saw there's a restaurant of sorts at the Opera House. I say we take the tour and then have lunch there."

"If that's what you want."

"What do you want?" I asked. His eyes narrowed and a light appeared in them. "Okay, forget I asked," I held up a hand. "I'm going for another flat white. I sort of like them," I said and rose from the table.

"Want me to get it?" Kory asked.

"I can do it. Want anything?"

"Ice water? With actual ice, this time?"

"All right."

I made my way through the crowd of small tables to reach the back door of the restaurant. I still had to go to the end of the customer line to put in a new order, though. I was there, waiting near the front door when I watched him walk past.

Except for the buzzed haircut and normal-looking eyebrows, the four-foot-tall man could have been Master Morwin.

A much younger Master Morwin, I decided, who'd likely have no way of reaching Earth in this day and age.

Perhaps my lack of sleep caused my mind to play tricks on me. Nevertheless, I shivered in the late-morning heat of a summer day in Sydney.

"Here," I placed the glass of ice water in front of Kory. "I made them fill it with ice, first," I explained before taking my seat across the table.

"Big line?" Kory asked. "You were gone forever."

"Yeah. It's worse, now," I said. "I guess we chose a popular place with the locals. You'll never guess what I saw, too," I added. "I saw a man who could be Master Morwin, if he were hundreds of years younger. Well, except for the eyebrows. And the long hair."

"Not Morwin, then," Kory said and drank his water. "I've seen him. If you cut off his braid, he'd kill you. Shave his eyebrows and you'd be tortured before you died."

"I don't think it would be that extreme," I said, sipping my fresh coffee. "It doesn't matter anyway, because it wasn't him."

"He spent thirty years in the Amterean military before he took over his father's business, did you know that?"

I blinked at Kory. I only remembered Morwin as the tutor and master scholar he was. "Amterean military?" I croaked. Amterean Dwarves excelled in two things; fighting and obscure knowledge. The RAA had several platoons of Amterean Dwarves in their ranks, with others sprinkled here and there.

Kory shrugged at my question. "How do you know this?" I asked.

"I met your dad, remember? We talked about your schooling, and how he'd been taught by Morwin, too. I met Morwin when I visited your grandmother's palace once. Formidable intelligence."

"So, Daddy never told me that—about Morwin being in the military," I grumped. "I'd have asked plenty of questions if he had."

"I doubt Morwin would be happy to answer them," Kory pointed out.

"I wonder if he was an expert in something?" My mind explored the possibilities.

"No way to know, but most Amtereans are only required to spend around ten years in the military. He tripled that."

"How nosy were you?" I was now back to my dad, and any secrets he'd told to Kory.

"Just basic, non-invasive stuff," Kory sounded hurt. "Your studies, hobbies, that kind of thing. Don't you think it would be a good idea to know your intended as well as possible before—well."

"Hmmph." We were back to the old argument of female High Demons being handed out like candy to reward the males.

"Baby, I realize now how stupid the system is," Kory held up both hands in surrender as I frowned at him. "If I ever hold a seat on the Council, I'll stand with Dad and protest the whole thing. It needs to change. There ought to be some choice in the matter—on both sides. All that aside," his dark eyes softened as he gazed at me, "I would have chosen you from a million others—or as many as there could possibly be. You are my treasure, m'hala."

"Queen Glinda is the only female who has any influence with the Council," I sighed, although I was secretly pleased with Kory's compliment. "There are no others to stand in support of females. Glinda will only slap King Jaydevik's hand if she disagrees with him on anything."

"Jayd is old school, as they say in the States," Kory grinned at me. "Most of his Council is, too. It'll be a long road to change minds, but I'll stand with Dad to see if we can't point things in the right direction, at least."

As my husband, he was entitled to a seat on the Council—in the future. Here we were, though, stuck in the past. "I appreciate the thought, and I'll appreciate it even more when we get back to where we came from."

"Yeah. Sometimes I miss Kifirin," he sighed. "Veshtul, especially," He said, referring to the capital city where the royal palace stood.

"I miss gishi fruit and oxberry wine," I said. "And the cheese we get on Avendor."

"Sounds like an amazing meal," Kory grinned. *After sex*, he added in mindspeech.

"You realize that we come from the only two planets that can produce gishi fruit?" I asked, ignoring his mindspeech.

"Match made in heaven, or close enough," he laughed.

Sydney, Australia

Morwin

The trip to Earth was longer and more uncomfortable than I wanted it to be, even compared to military standards. The smuggler's ship was patched debris, in my opinion, and only operated on hope and regular threats from its crew.

I felt fortunate that I arrived on the planet merely half a continent away from my intended destination, intact and with my trunk at my side.

I had a communicator with me, but had my doubts whether the ship would hear my call to take me home again. I imagined I could end up dying here in the search for my father's killer—my father hadn't gone down easily, as evidenced by the disarray and amount of blood in his study.

My quarry was formidable, but I intended to challenge him anyway.

There was a difficulty, however.

There were few of my stature on Earth, thus marking me as an item of curiosity and making me more visible to an enemy. This had to be dealt with, and in such a way that I would no longer draw attention. If I failed to do so, the murderer would find me easily enough. I wanted to catch him unaware, instead.

Standing out on Earth made me more than vulnerable. My hearing is quite good; I heard many things behind me as I passed those considered normal on the streets. The first time I was called a midget behind my back, it made me angry. Not just on my behalf, but for those who were born here who'd been called such a derogatory thing.

As if I—and they—were less than others, and not merely in stature.

I had to find a way to make myself less noticeable, but had no idea how to accomplish that feat. My steps drew me closer to the walkway leading to the Opera House; it was a magnificent study in architecture, and one my father would have loved to visit.

He would have been fascinated by it, as was I. Perhaps I should take a tour, and lose myself with the others who gathered there—to be led through the structure and soak in the stories a guide could tell us about its creation.

~

Kordevik

I wasn't as fascinated by the Opera House as Lexsi was, but she wanted to see it. If it made her happy, then I'd see it with her. We stood in line to pay admission for a midday tour; other groups were being called and led away while we waited.

Kory, Lexsi's mindspeech invaded my preoccupied brain, *There's the man who looks like Morwin, sixth in line behind us.*

Casually I turned, as if gazing about at the lower level leading into the Opera House. A railing wasn't far away, where tourists stood to watch ferry boats in the harbor. The Opera House is surrounded by the harbor on three sides; today the sky was nearly cloudless while sunlight dappled the water.

Without drawing attention, I turned farther to see the man Lexsi spoke of, sure that she was wrong about this.

I stilled. Make his eyebrows longer, his red hair longer and his face older, he'd be Morwin.

Actually, he would probably look exactly like Morwin in this timeline. Stuffing hands in the pockets of my cargo shorts, I turned back to gazing at the water.

I wasn't really seeing it, this time.

How in hell could this one look so much like Lexsi's tutor?

~

San Rafael
Zaria

Zaria? Lexsi's mindspeech was tentative, as if she were afraid she'd be disturbing me, somehow.

What is it, sweetheart? I returned.

I—there's this man here, who looks exactly like Morwin, except he's younger than the one I know.

Yes, my heart kicked into a higher rhythm. *Where are you?* I sent. *Never mind, I can tell. Give me a minute, I'll be right there.*

Thank you. Her mindspeech expressed relief that someone was taking her seriously.

I was dressed warmly in sweats, sitting at the kitchen island with Klancy, sharing a dish of ice cream. "Hon, would you like to go to Australia?" I asked him.

Klancy blinked at me—he really enjoys ice cream, a treat he'd never had before he'd met me, actually.

"I've never been," he admitted. "If you wish to take me, I will be quite happy to go."

"Awesome." I leaned forward to get an ice-cream flavored kiss. "I'll dress us appropriately and we'll go. Then, we'll find out how they do ice cream Down Under."

"I look forward to it." He gave me a rare smile.

"Have you ever worn shorts?" I asked him. "It's hot there, right now."

"I will attempt to retain my dignity," he sighed.

~

Sydney Opera House
Lexsi

"Buy four tickets—Zaria and Klancy are coming," I whispered to Kory as we stepped toward the ticket counter.

"Huh?" Kory's eyes widened.

"I'm sorry," I hunched my shoulders. "I—just want Zaria to look at Morwin's twin, that's all."

"I don't care that they're coming," Kory squeezed my shoulders in large hands. "I'm sort of creeped out by this, too. He just looks—too damn familiar, you know?"

"Yeah."

"Buy five tickets," Zaria shoved a wad of Australian currency into Kory's hand. She'd appeared from nothing, Klancy right beside her. I drew in a breath; nobody around us acted as if two people hadn't just arrived from nowhere.

"Why five?" Kory began.

"Because that's Morwin," Zaria snapped. "He's in danger, so he's coming with us."

~

Morwin

I'd barely noticed those in line ahead of me, unless it was to take a step or two closer to the ticket counter.

Until the dark-haired woman and her mate left the counter and walked straight toward me.

"Morwin Quiffilis," she said, as if she could see my name written across my skin, "Come with us. We have your ticket here."

If she hadn't pulled herself to her full height as a Larentii, with sky-blue skin and riveting blue eyes, I'd have thought I was in more danger than originally imagined.

Here was a Larentii, telling me that I should come with her.

I went.

"My Larentii name is Corinnelar," she explained as I followed her to our designated waiting area. It would be an hour before our group for the tour was called. "People here call me Zaria, when I am my other self."

She shrank into the woman I'd first seen—the one with dark hair and bright-blue eyes. "This is Klancy, a former vampire," she added, introducing me to the tall man at her side.

"Quite pleased to meet you," Klancy dipped his head respectfully.

"A former vampire? I can't recall meeting one before," I said, attempting to hide my excited curiosity.

"There are a few of us," Klancy smiled. "Zaria had a great deal to do with that, as you may imagine."

"I've heard the Larentii are quite powerful, but seldom intervene," I observed.

"That is correct," Zaria agreed. "I will explain more later. Please, come meet Lexsi and Kory—neither know yet that I am also Larentii," she added.

"Why should I meet them, then?" I asked.

"Because they may be your best hope for destroying your father's killer," Zaria replied, her words cryptic.

That aroused my curiosity.

Greatly.

"I see I have much to learn," I mumbled and followed Zaria toward Lexsi and Kory.

Kordevik

"We're High Demons," Lexsi explained to a much younger Morwin than the one she'd known in her earlier life.

I could tell immediately that he'd never met any of our kind, before. Questions formed in his mind—there was a gleam in his eye that was easily recognizable—a thirst for information was forming and wouldn't be quenched until he was satisfied.

We sat at a table in the restaurant that took up much of the lower level of the Opera House while we waited for our tour to begin. Zaria had ordered tea for Morwin and Klancy; the rest of us had either soft drinks or water.

"How do you know about my father?" Morwin ignored his curiosity on the High Demon front and turned to Zaria, instead.

"It's difficult to explain," Zaria shrugged. "My condolences, by the way."

"Thank you." Morwin's eyes dropped to his hands; he held the cup between fingers calloused from handling swords, rifles and other weapons.

Morwin is fresh out of the Amterean military, Zaria explained to us in mindspeech. That explained the short hair and shaved eyebrows—those were military cuts. He looked like a human as a result—a little person human.

On Amterea, he wasn't considered little. In fact, he was above average height for his race. In the Alliances, he'd be recognized and given due respect for his heritage. Here, he was an oddity.

I could see Lexsi was already concerned for him in that way. She loved him—that was easy enough to see—as you loved a dear teacher who'd shown you the world in fresh and enlightening terms.

Her father, Torevik, had nothing but love and respect for Morwin, too. I never thought to see Morwin in such circumstances—grieving for a murdered father and set on revenge against his father's killer.

I knew I'd never stop looking for the murderer if my father died in such a way.

"Why did you come here?" I asked the obvious question. "What makes you think your enemy is here?" I had no idea why he'd chosen Earth, and Australia in particular.

"Because of this," Morwin drew an ancient version of a comp-vid from his pocket and set it on the table between us. "My father was doing research for a client—on a mystical place called the Metal Library. That client, I believe, is also my father's killer."

Perth, Western Australia
   V'ili

"This information is incomplete," I dropped the comp-vid on the table. Deris was angered by my words, that was easy to see.

His anger should have been directed at himself, for botching this in the beginning. Instead of making sure that he had all the pertinent records, he'd taken the comp-vid offered by the scholar, then killed him before obtaining all the information needed to track the Metal Library.

The Amterean scholar had withheld important information, too, and there was no way to determine where it lay.

Morgett would demand that someone return to Amterea to look for the missing pieces to this puzzle. I worried he'd send me, when I had no desire to visit that planet. The obvious choice would be Deris, but as he'd fucked up the mission initially, I imagined Morgett would send someone else.

Morgett and I knew better than to send Daris. If she left Deris' side for too long, she became mentally unstable.

Morgett knew the family curse as well as anyone; his niece, Daris' grandmother, had borne that illness when she died, although it hadn't killed her.

According to Morgett, Helsa died by the worst of spells—cast by Grey House wizards.

He refused to say more than that, and Deris and Daris never spoke of their grandmother's death.

It mattered not to me that those two were related to Karathian royalty. I had my own goals and plans; they merely had a part to play in this portion of them. Revenge was my ultimate objective; revenge for my home planet, destroyed long ago by the blue-skinned devils called Larentii.

"V'ili, you must rectify this mistake," Morgett strode into the room after his bi-weekly feeding. At least he'd cleaned the blood from his teeth before speaking to me. "Go to Amterea and look for this confounded information—the scholar had to hide it somewhere."

"As you say." I dipped my head while silently cursing.

Zaria

"What are you going to do?" Lexsi asked, her blue eyes pleading with me to do something for Morwin. After we'd read the information and looked at the maps Morwin's father sent to him, the more confident we'd become that Morgett and the Blackmantle twins were behind this.

They were still looking for the Metal Library.

It fit well enough that Deris or Daris had approached Morwin's father for information on where the Metal Library may have relocated. In turn, Mardin had searched through many myths and legends on Earth to determine the likeliest places. He'd settled on legends from Australia, with Uluru dominating his attention.

With Deris' penchant for making his victims suffer before they died, and with the amount of blood and evidence of a struggle in the scholar's study, I'd bet money the twisted asshole had done the murder himself—for the pleasure it brought him.

I'd know it for sure if I saw him again—I'd read the evidence of it easily in him. As for V'ili—he had to be earlobe-deep in this somehow.

Morgett, V'ili and the Blackmantle twins. A more than deadly combination. "I can disguise Morwin," I said absently. "Although I'm not sure how much good that would do. Besides, he may object; his strategy may be to draw the perpetrator to him, instead of hunting him in secret."

Lexsi and I had excused ourselves and gone to the ladies' toilet for a private conversation; the others were still sitting with their drinks in the restaurant.

They're calling our tour group, Kory's mindspeech reached Lexsi and me.

"We'll work this out," I hugged Lexsi. "Somehow. Now, let's go see the Opera House."

"What if they go back to Amterea to hunt for anybody who may have information about this—to get rid of evidence?" Lexsi whispered as we walked out of the toilet and headed toward the rest of our group.

"There's a thought," I acknowledged. "I'll go after the tour—just to set up a disturbance spell—in Morwin's father's study and in Morwin's old quarters. If anybody shows up, I'll know about it."

"That sounds really good," Lexsi breathed a sigh.

"You're right," I said, although she hadn't voiced her fear aloud.

"Huh?"

"About this not being in the original timeline," I said. "Therefore, we have to keep this ripple as small as possible. Really terrible things can happen if we don't."

I watched as she hunched her shoulders. *Honey, don't worry until it's warranted,* I sent. *Enjoy your day. You have some strong people on Morwin's and your side. Never forget that.*

"Yeah."

Lexsi

Eventually, as the tour took us through the Opera House, I let my misgivings slide while I watched Morwin's face; we took in the views, the stages, colors and sounds of the Opera House, its architecture and its decoration.

It was everything I'd hoped it would be—made sweeter by the fact that Morwin was enjoying it with me.

Kory had come because I'd wanted to see the Opera House; Morwin came because he loved the learning and the experience of it.

Sometime in the future, I hoped he'd recall these moments. It was something else we could share that hadn't taken place in a teaching environment.

I couldn't get Zaria's words out of my mind, however. They lurked there, rising to the surface often, while I repeatedly shoved them down again.

She'd said I was right—*about this not being in the original timeline.*

To me, that meant one thing; this history had already happened once.

How many other times had it happened?

I was afraid to ask, because I was afraid she'd have the answer. Our enemies were changing the timeline, and this time, they'd killed Morwin's father. I wanted to curse about how little I knew of Morwin's personal life, but Kory was correct on that front. Morwin wouldn't want to tell me those things in the future.

It made me sad.

I'm working on getting Morwin on the boat with us tomorrow, Zaria informed me as the tour guide led us toward the Opera House gift shop—our last stop of the tour.

Oh, thank goodness, I replied. *I was worried.*

I know. Will you mind if a few other friends join us? she asked.

Not now, I admitted. Morwin was in danger. That fact took precedence over any embarrassment I might feel.

Good. I've sent for Opal, Anita and anybody else who wants to come. If Morgett, V'ili and the twins are here, we may need as many allies as possible.

We don't need another Peru, I agreed.

Or even halfway like Peru.

CHAPTER 3

*S*ydney, Australia
    Opal

I decided to stop worrying about how Zaria had pulled strings—or when she'd pulled strings—to get us all on the boat.

Regardless, those of us who could come were now standing in line to deliver our bags to the collection area, so they could be loaded onto the boat.

Farin and Tibby stood in line ahead of Kell and me, while Anita waited with Watson, Esme, Yoff, Sandra and Mason behind us.

Zaria had also sent mindspeech, telling me she'd transported herself to Amterea shortly after the authorities were finished searching Mardin Quiffilis' home and study.

She'd laid a shield—and a spell—about his home—and about Morwin's former quarters with the military, so she'd know if anyone breached those spaces. If the killer or anyone else came through, she'd identify them immediately.

It was my hope that Mardin had withheld some information until payment was made, and it clearly wasn't. It was an old Amterean habit —not to provide the full record or research until money had changed hands.

24

Surely Morwin knew that, too—that his father may have held something back. He also had information sent to him by his father, but there was no way to tell whether Mardin had sent him everything.

Poor Mardin—in the previous timeline, he'd lived for another two hundred years, as Earth measured time. Amterean dwarves were notoriously long-lived, and Mardin had already reached nine-hundred-eighty years before his death this time.

They'd gone to him because he had one of the best reputations on Amterea for scholarly research. He'd died for it, too.

"I've never been on a cruise," Farin's excited voice broke into my thoughts. I turned to Kell, who lifted an eyebrow at me.

I didn't tell her much, I sent to Kell, who nodded.

She can't help but be bubbly, he agreed.

Lissa calls them Triple-Ps, I said. *Perpetually perky people.*

Kell stifled a laugh.

~

Lexsi

"They're all on lower decks," I said. "Except for Morwin, Zaria and Klancy. They're two cabins down from ours and across the hall from each other," I told Kory. Zaria had left me with a list of everyone joining us on the ship, and where their cabins were located, in case of emergency.

"She probably had to settle for what she could get," Kory leaned over my shoulder to look at the list.

"Yeah. At least Morwin is close enough that we can protect him if necessary."

"I hope he's close enough that we can nullify the evil twins' spells," Kory breathed before pulling my hair back and kissing my neck. "If they show up."

"At least evil Laurel, evil Dervil and evil Berke are in the slammer," I said. "I hope Jamie knows not to leave the San Rafael house without Jorden or Mason."

"Evil Hannah is dead, don't forget that," Kory breathed against my neck before placing another kiss.

"You have to thank Anita for that," I said.

"Yeah—we were sort of missing in action there," Kory agreed, his voice soft.

"Your mouth is a lethal weapon; you know that?" I turned toward him, making it easier for his lips to connect with mine. I wanted to avoid the conversation regarding *why* we'd been missing in action—and the pain that accompanied it. At least we were in the privacy of our cabin when heat and desire overtook us.

Rose Hiboux

We were late arrivals, barely reaching port before the gangway was removed and the ship readied for sailing out of Sydney Harbor.

That meant we were the object of many stares and conversations from passengers standing at the ship's rails. They thought their comments were witty—and unheard by my family.

Sixteen of us. Safety in numbers—or so you might think.

"It's the seven dwarves—times two, at least," someone at the railing above us joked. My mouth tightened; I gripped my cane harder and strode toward the doorway, passport in hand and my handbag slung over a shoulder.

At two-hundred-seventeen, I'm not as agile as I once was. Were I younger, I might have considered shitting on the jerk's head later.

"I'm shitting on his head later," my oldest son, Jim, grumbled behind me. I didn't bother hiding my smile.

Morwin

"I was going to offer to disguise you—as a taller person," Zaria set a drink in front of me. She, Klancy and I had met in the bar before going to dinner. "But there's a problem with that, now."

"What's the problem?" I asked, before sipping the amber-colored liquid in my glass. "Very nice—what is this?" I held up my glass.

"Scotch," she replied absently. "The disguise was to lead the enemy away from you, should they show up here," I said. "The problem is this; including you, there are now seventeen potential targets for the enemy to hit on this ship."

"Seventeen?"

"Sixteen others who are close to your stature, are on board. Those sixteen can be mistaken—by those who don't give a damn—as people from your world."

"So the enemy may think I formed a hunting party, instead of coming on my own?" I downed the rest of my drink in a single gulp.

"That's my guess," Zaria sighed.

"I will stay as I am, then. I have no desire to place others in danger," I held up my glass, signaling to a wandering server to bring a refill. I had to provide the card given to me when I boarded the ship, so he'd know the drink was already paid for—by Zaria's generosity.

"Yeah," Zaria hunched her shoulders at my words. I could see that this presented a problem for her—already she'd vowed to protect my life. That protection had just stretched to cover sixteen others.

Sixteen who had no idea what was happening and were completely innocent in all this.

I silently cursed my father's killer.

Again.

~

Lexsi

"I'm starving." My stomach rumbled to indicate the truth of my statement. Kory, who'd fallen asleep with his arms around me, stirred.

"Baby," he pulled me tighter against him.

"Kory, please take me to dinner before we, uh, get back to it."

One eye cracked open. An eyebrow lifted. A smile curved the edge of his mouth. He kissed my bare shoulder before pulling away.

I sat up and stretched. I had no idea sex could be so pleasurable—

or so tiring. If I hadn't stopped Kory after the sixth time, we'd probably still be at it. "Who gets the shower first?" I asked.

∼

"I have six sisters and two half-brothers," I said as a plate of food was set in front of me. We'd shown up at the hostess stand without a reservation, and were now eating at a table with two other couples.

Two curious couples, actually—one couple came from Brisbane, the other lived in London.

"So, newlyweds?" One of the men smiled at Kory and me.

"Yes." I struggled to keep my face from heating.

"How many brothers and sisters do you have?" the man's wife asked Kory. He coughed into his hand while crafting a reply.

"No sisters," he said truthfully. "I've lost count of how many brothers I have."

They thought he was joking.

He wasn't.

One-half of the House of Weth consisted of his brothers. His parents were very old and quite prolific, if the history I'd read was correct.

"We went to Greece on our honeymoon," the other woman said. "It was wonderful."

"What made you decide to come on this cruise for your holiday?" her husband asked when I couldn't decide how to respond to his wife's statement.

"It was a gift," Kory answered for me. "A very generous gift."

"And so it was," the man smiled. "Here's to the newlyweds," he lifted his glass of wine to us.

∼

Veshtul, Kifirin
  Li'Neruh Rath

"You sent mindspeech?" I'd arrived as my smaller Thifilathi, choosing to meet with Queen Glindarok in her outer chamber.

I'd surprised her—as I'd intended. She'd attempted to contact me nearly a moon-turn earlier. I'd waited until now to reply—by arriving in person.

She was dressed according to her station—in rich fabrics that enhanced her beauty. That meant nothing to me. She took a moment to gather her thoughts—she never imagined she'd be speaking to me in person, or at all, judging by her demeanor.

"I, ah, wanted to ask for something," she said, moving toward a tall window that overlooked the palace walls—and beyond them to the city of Veshtul. Dusk had fallen; twinkling lights began to appear across the vast city.

"What do you want?" I folded arms across my chest.

"I want children."

"You have two daughters of your own," I pointed out. "And six others, that were not your own. Yet you took them anyway. Are you upset that Lexsi wasn't handed to you without her mother's consent, as Lexsi's sisters were?"

"Kifirin did that," Glinda attempted to defend herself.

"Yet all along, a small voice kept telling you it was wrong, what you and Jayd did."

"Yes." She hung her head.

"This is your punishment," I said. "You will not have more children."

When she lifted her head, I saw her cheeks were wet with tears. "I'm sorry," she wept. "Please, there must be something I can do to atone for that wrong."

I frowned at her for a moment, while my mind worked. "There may be something," I said.

"Please—whatever it is, I'll do it."

"You have no idea what it is, yet you agree?" I asked, while smoke curled from my nostrils.

"I want children," she croaked, her voice rough with emotion. "I'll do anything, although I ask for your mercy."

"In two moon-turns, I will come to you again," I said. "To tell you what you must do. The choice will be yours at that time. If you say yes, I will grant you and Jaydevik children. Say no, and you will be barren for the rest of your life."

Glinda sobbed as I folded away.

~

Australian Waters

Lexsi

"You don't talk about your sisters much," Kory said as we sat in the bar later, having a glass of wine.

"I know." I hugged myself at the thought. "You've probably seen more of them than I have. They never think of Mom and me."

"I know Glinda and Jayd overstepped their bounds, forcing your mother to allow them to live at the palace," Kory said. "I still remember the rants my father had about it when he and I were alone. That was before your birth, m'hala. Before I knew I'd be your chosen."

"Mom doesn't like talking about those days," I said. "Uncle Teeg told me her living conditions were awful—all while Jayd and Glinda kept my sisters in luxury at the palace and Mom almost killed herself planting gishi fruit groves to save Kifirin."

"I remember my father's specific rant about that," Kory grimaced while the barest curl of smoke drifted from his nostrils. "I think he wanted to grab Jayd by the scruff and shake sense into him."

"Which would have gotten him killed," I pointed out.

"It would have gotten us both killed, because I wanted to do the same," Kory's arm came around me and pulled me close. "I wish your sisters understood what it is that they missed—with your mother. And with you and your brothers. I see them at the palace often, though. More often than Glinda's own daughters, actually."

"It's a mess," I sighed and leaned my head on Kory's shoulder. "I'm so glad I married you," I confessed.

"You have no idea how glad I am that you married me," he chuckled. "Because I don't deserve you."

"I disagree," I said, turning in his arms to grin at him. "I'm not sure I deserve you."

If we hadn't been in public, he'd have kissed me right then. We both knew what would happen. That's why we almost ran for the elevator, and, since we were on it alone when the doors closed, Kory kissed me and skipped us to our cabin immediately.

~

Rose Hiboux

"Mum, look," my daughter Emma touched my shoulder.

I turned to see what she had, and found myself blinking in surprise. We weren't the only little people on the ship—another was sitting down to dinner across the dining room. He was joined by two others; both much taller than he.

It appeared they knew one another, and weren't mere strangers thrown together by the ship's crew.

"I wonder where he's from," my granddaughter Chloe asked.

"He's a ginger. Chloe likes gingers," her sister Georgia snickered.

"I do not," Chloe retorted. Yes, they were grown.

Did they act like it?

Not always.

"He's human," I pointed out.

"Hmmph," Chloe expressed her displeasure. "We could at least try to meet him."

"Chloe likes gingers," Georgia teased.

"Somebody wants an eye full of feathers," Chloe retorted.

"That's enough," Jim growled at his daughters. His other two children, Tim and Sarah, were glancing at the stranger across the way, but hadn't joined the argument with their siblings. Their cousins, Jessica, Ellie and Hayley, had watched the teasing with interested enthusiasm, wondering who'd win.

Jim put a stop to it, thank goodness, before the waiter arrived at our table.

~

Morwin

"They're wondering where you're from, and the grandmother says you're human. At least for now."

I hadn't failed to notice the interest from the table across the way —the sixteen Zaria had promised to protect along with me. Zaria was now explaining what she saw in them. I couldn't stop my curiosity about Zaria's gifts—they appeared formidable.

I wasn't familiar with Larentii, however. Perhaps they could all do what she did. "What do you mean, at least for now?" I thought to ask.

"They're not human," Zaria informed me. "No, they were born here," she held up a hand before I could ask. "They're a family of shifters. Owls, actually. The grandmother will know you're not human either, if she gets close enough to you. She has a sense about these things."

"Should I be concerned?" I asked.

"I doubt it," she shrugged. "What we should do, beginning tomorrow, is go through all the information your father sent you. I imagine he withheld vital information until payment was made, and payment was never made."

"That was his habit—in cases where the client was new and unfamiliar," I agreed. "It's expected of the best scholars on Amterea."

"It's my hope that the killer didn't get that last bit of information, and didn't know he didn't get it," Zaria said. "I worry that he may learn what he doesn't have, however, and come looking for anyone connected to your father, to see if they have it."

"Which will lead them in my direction." I couldn't help but turn my head toward the family of sixteen across the dining room. They were laughing, talking and enjoying themselves, even if a few eyes were occasionally turned in my direction.

"I will do research on owls native to this continent," I said aloud.

"Good idea," Klancy smiled. "I hear one of them likes gingers."

~

Lexsi

It took two days for the ship to reach Picton, New Zealand, our first stop. It rained the entire day. Kory and I would have stayed in our cabin, but Anita and Watson came looking for us.

"You've been hiding for two days; time to poke your head out of this cabin," Anita said the moment she and Watson walked in after Kory answered their knock on the door.

"Their cabin is a lot bigger and nicer than ours," Watson gazed about the room.

"Because they're on their honeymoon, furball," Anita grumped. "Come on," she turned back to me, "Come to Picton with us. It's time to put your feet back on solid ground."

"It's raining," Kory pointed out.

"You think your ass will melt off?" Anita's fists went to her hips.

"It could," Kory grinned.

"Not likely," Watson snickered.

"Fine. We'll go. How should we dress?"

"It's in the fifties right now, unless you're measuring in Celsius," Anita struggled to hide her smile.

"I'll bring a jacket and my favorite High Demon," I said. "Give us a minute, okay. We haven't had coffee, yet."

"Have you found the coffee shop on deck five?" Anita asked.

"There's a coffee shop?" Kory was interested already.

"Dude, you really have shut yourself in the hen house," Watson huffed. Anita elbowed him in the ribs for the inappropriate comment.

"You know how fast fur burns?" Kory blew a curl of smoke at Watson.

"Just teasing," Watson held up a hand. "Get your shirt and shoes on, man. Let's get coffee and get off the boat."

"Let me find my shoes and a jacket," I said when Kory went to the small closet to find a shirt. At least I was dressed in jeans and a pullover already; Kory's muscles bulged as he sorted through what I'd hung in the closet.

"Jacket, baby," Kory flung a zippered hoodie over his shoulder in my direction. I caught it before kneeling beside the bed to look for my athletic shoes.

It embarrassed me that one shoe was under the bed, the other across the room. I didn't recall whether I'd done that or Kory had, we'd been so anxious to remove clothing the night before. When the linking overtook us, the elimination of barriers between our bodies became a top priority.

At least Anita was polite enough to duck her head as I stuffed the second shoe on my foot. Grinning at your best friend who'd unmistakably been engaged in several rounds of hot sex the night before can be embarrassing for the recipient.

"Ready?" Kory now had a suitable shirt pulled on and shoes on his feet. He hadn't been forced to hunt for his shoes—they were together near the closet. Maybe it was his military training that did that—teaching him to place his clothes and shoes where he could find them easily enough.

My lower lip extended in a pretend pout; he grinned, reached for my hand and we followed Watson and Anita out the door.

~

Zaria

"The others are going out; we can go with them," I told Morwin. He'd figured out how to use the outdated phone system aboard ship and had called my room. I considered giving him mindspeech, but that could wait.

He wanted to see as much as he could of our destinations—the curious scholar in him demanded it. So far, at least the enemy hadn't breached the invisible barriers I'd placed in his father's home and his former quarters.

That could change soon enough, but for now, they probably didn't know he'd come to Earth to hunt them.

I hadn't told him exactly what we were up against, either—I disliked frightening people unless there was no other choice. Morwin deserved more than a break—his father had died a horrible death, at the mercy of Deris' Fifth-level warlock's powers. If seeing the beauty of Picton helped put that out of his mind, so much the better.

"It's a bit chilly outside," I said. "Dress accordingly."

"I have already checked this ancient thing called a television monitor," Morwin teased. "It has given me the temperature in both Celsius and Fahrenheit."

"Then get your pants on and let's go," I teased back. He chuckled.

"I'll be knocking on your door soon," he replied.

Amterea

V'ili

I sat at a table outside the tea shop, drinking the richly-flavored, milk-and-sugar-and-cinnamon tea so many Amtereans favored.

Across the street lay the lane entrance that would lead me to Mardin Quiffilis' home. If there was hidden information there, I intended to find it. If the local constabulary had confiscated it, I would take it from them. Lastly, if Mardin had given the information to his only son, who, according to records was in the Amterean military, well, I'd have it from him quickly enough.

Unlike Deris, I'd done my homework, rather than blundering along blindly and accepting incomplete information before torturing the scholar to death.

The fool.

He and Daris were Morgett's kin before he became Ra'Ak and his commands prevented me from placing obsession on either. Morgett held my life in his hands, after all. He was Ra'Ak, extremely powerful, and could kill me with barely a thought.

He was also well-placed in the Ra'Ak hierarchy, and had the favor of the Prince. I didn't need or want the enmity of that entire race, merely because I wanted to follow my own whims where Morgett's nephew and niece were concerned.

All Ra'Ak were immune to my obsessions, and I'd cursed that fact many, many times. Serving Morgett—at least for now—fell in with my plans, so I was forced to do his bidding. I would find a way to extract myself from his clutches eventually, when a more suitable master appeared.

"A refill?" The half-tall Amterean server approached my table with a teapot.

"Of course." I pushed my cup toward him, so he wouldn't spill anything on me. Mardin's home wasn't going anywhere. I'd have more tea.

~

Picton, New Zealand

Morwin

"Hat." Zaria stuffed the felt-based contraption on my head to keep the rain off. It had a wide brim, worked well enough and probably made me look like an idiot.

The tender boat ride from the ship had been wet enough, but now rain was pouring on the town of Picton. At least my military-issued boots kept my feet dry, and the jacket I'd brought kept my shoulders and body dry, but my head and hair were drenched.

A souvenir shop was Zaria's first stop after we'd left the tender boat. The walk to that shop ensured we were all wet. I imagine Zaria could dry us off well enough with power, but to do so would make us stand out among the other passengers who'd come to visit Picton.

Many had plastic rain sheaths draped over them; others had umbrellas, but those blocked out the view of the sky and hills surrounding the town, so that wasn't an option, in my opinion.

The family of sixteen had gotten off the boat, too, although I only saw fifteen of them inside the shop.

When we walked outside, I saw the reason.

Against the odds, an owl flew overhead, his wings graceful as they dipped and rose expertly in the rain. Only a few noticed the creature;

certainly not the man who was the recipient of the raptor mute—or defecation—of the owl.

The man stood in the street, cursing as the mute splattered his head and shoulders, although the rain washed it away quickly enough.

The owl, finished with his business, flew over a nearby building and disappeared. Zaria, who stood beside me, struggled to quell laughter.

When I opened my mouth to question, she explained in a soft voice that the man had insulted the family when they first boarded the ship. He'd just gotten payback for his short-sightedness, and the pun was most certainly intended.

Soon enough, I saw the family of sixteen again, all intact and laughing at their private joke. I wanted to give a nod to their ingenuity, but that would be too much, I think. No need to worry them with the knowledge that I knew their secret.

Shifters are generally secretive on worlds where they aren't able to reveal themselves. Here, they'd be seen as something dangerous, I think, and some would actually believe them to be abominations.

Earth was far, far behind the Alliance in these matters. In the Alliance, shifters, power wielders and all sorts were accepted and protected by Alliance laws. It was a stipulation each world agreed to upon joining the Alliance. My shoulders drooped when I considered how much time it would take before Earth saw shifters and others as their fellows instead of curiosities or something to distrust.

"They have a long way to go." Zaria, who understood my thoughts, rubbed my shoulders to comfort me. Klancy, standing beside her, nodded his agreement. He, as a modified vampire, understood that as well as anyone.

"Excuse me," someone walked up to me. I almost jumped at the interruption.

"Hello." I turned toward her. An impish smile rewarded my greeting.

"Hi. I'm Chloe," she held out a hand. "Grandmother asked me to invite you to dinner with us tonight, at eight in the deck six dining room."

Blonde curls, damp from the rain, framed a lovely face. I took the offered hand and smiled at her.

Go ahead, Zaria sent mindspeech.

"I would be happy to join you," I smiled at her. "Shall I meet you there?"

"Sure. Just ask for the Hiboux table. They'll know where we are."

"I look forward to it," I bowed slightly over her hand, which caused her to giggle.

"You have a dinner date," Zaria said as Chloe walked away from me to rejoin her family.

"I have a dinner date," I breathed.

~

Lexsi

We'd walked through a large portion of Picton before lunchtime. We stopped at a restaurant along Wellington Street to eat, all of us soaked to the skin by the unrelenting rain. That's where we caught up with Morwin, Zaria and Klancy; they wanted lunch, too.

I could tell Watson wanted to change to wolf and shake off the dampness—mostly on Anita, who wanted to keep slogging through the rain. We'd seen the maritime museum she wanted to visit, along with other things that Kory *could read about someplace dry*, but I didn't share that mindspeech with Anita.

"Esme, Yoff, Tibby and Farin went back to the ship," Anita informed Klancy, who asked about them while servers pulled another table up to make room for us. "Opal and Kell never got off."

"They wanted some time alone," Zaria said. "Besides, neither are fond of heavy rain."

I noticed she, Morwin and Klancy looked quite dry and warm. *Hold on,* she informed me, *I'll do something about your cold, wet clothing after the servers take our order.*

Probably a good idea, but I was shivering already.

Soon enough, our orders were placed, and that's when the warmth and dryness came, courtesy of Zaria's power. I was so grateful I leaned against Kory's shoulder and sighed in blissful relief.

"Thank you," Watson mumbled.

"Oh, no," Zaria whispered.

I pulled away from Kory immediately.

Someone just entered Mardin's study, Zaria sent to all of us.

CHAPTER 4

a mterea
  V'ili

No scrap of evidence to be found anywhere. I began to wonder if the scholar had merely pretended to have complete information for Deris.

I sent mindspeech to Morgett, telling him as much.

Find his son, Morgett replied. *I've searched the comp-vid. There may be evidence that information was sent along with regular communications to his son, Morwin Quiffilis. I've discovered a military address there, and plenty of messages.*

Smart, to send information to a family member hidden inside a normal message. Perhaps the scholar was craftier than I thought, although it wouldn't take much to outmaneuver Deris.

Give me the address, I replied. *I will pay a visit to the Master Scholar's son.*

New Zealand Waters
  Zaria

"There's been a hit on Morwin's information," I told Opal and Kell. "It won't take much brain power to follow Morwin's trail. I think the smugglers who brought him here will be tracked soon enough."

"How much interference will happen if we intervene?" Opal asked. "Are those smugglers' lives worth saving?"

"Too much interference, I'm afraid. Lives are lives, but these," I shrugged. There really wasn't a good reason to save them, and Opal was just as unhappy as I was at that news. Plus, in this case, V'ili's survival was essential to the future, to keep it on track. Opal was aware of that, too. Morgett, on the other hand—we'd wait and see about him.

"So Kory and Lexsi will have to carry the load this time," Opal sighed. She and Kell had come to my cabin when I sent mindspeech— after Klancy and I were back onboard.

"With Anita, Watson and the others," I agreed. "We can keep them safe enough, but beyond that, we may be hauled in front of a few folks."

"Not a good thing, either," Opal said. "I know what happened when they let Jayson have it."

"Jamie's brother?" Kell asked. "I've heard Jamie mention him several times," Kell held up a hand.

"Only Jayson's drubbing wasn't for interference—it was for not doing his job. He's still in the dog house over it, too," Opal informed her mate.

Kell's love for her shone in his eyes, although he kept his expression neutral. I wondered how long it would take for Kell to propose, but decided that wasn't any of my business.

"We wait and watch, then," Opal sighed. Kell placed an arm about her shoulders and pulled her against him. I understood what it felt like to be attacked and close to death as a result, with no promise of help coming.

It is a terrible and lonely way to die—even for smugglers.

My love, Klancy send mindspeech, *let us leave these two alone.*

Yeah. I took Klancy's hand and folded us to an empty corner of a bar near one of the ship's swimming pools. The area was shaded and cool as we made our way to the bar and ordered drinks.

~

Morwin

"You look fine—stop fidgeting," Kory said, dropping a hand on my shoulder. He'd accompanied me to the deck six dining room, where I was to meet the shifter family for dinner.

The clothing was Earth-style—a knit shirt and slacks, as Zaria called them. It was a far cry from the monochromatic clothing I'd worn as recent ex-military from Amterea.

The shirt was pale yellow, the slacks dark brown. Zaria said the colors suited me. Until now, I'd never worried about the colors I wore. Suddenly, all of it became important.

"Hello." Blue eyes met mine. I couldn't stop the smile; it insisted on spreading across my face and likely obliterated my other features.

"Good evening, Chloe," I took her hand and lifted it to my lips.

She giggled.

Her grandmother approached me, then, cane in hand as she stepped deliberately in my direction. I went still, recalling Zaria's words. She could tell I wasn't human. I tensed for a moment.

My eyes widened as her cane lifted, but instead of poking me with it, the tip went straight to Kory's midsection.

"Not human," she hissed at him.

Kory's low chuckle surprised me. "Not human," he nodded, agreeing with her. "Certainly not human, Mother Owl."

"Are you winged, fanged or scaled?" she asked.

"Yes," Kory chuckled.

Lowering her cane, she lifted an eyebrow at him. "Are you joining us for dinner?"

"Not tonight," Kory said. "My new bride is waiting for me at a restaurant upstairs."

"Is she human?" the grandmother asked.

"She is what I am," Kory dipped his head respectfully.

"If trouble comes," the words tumbled from my lips, "Stay close to Kory."

"My name is Rose," she held out her hand to Kory, who went to one knee to accept it.

"I am most pleased to meet you, Mother Rose," Kory said.

"Good. You and I will talk later," Rose said. "Now, you," she turned in my direction. "I'm still wondering what it is you are, but you can explain that over dinner."

"Of course, Mother Rose," I bowed formally to her.

She laughed.

"Have fun," Kory slapped my shoulder and stood before striding away.

"He's handsome," one of Chloe's sisters whispered as she watched Kory leave.

"Do you know what he is?" Chloe asked.

"I'll let him tell you," I said, although another smile turned the corners of my mouth. "Shall we? I hear there is salmon on the menu, tonight." I held my arm out for her to take. She giggled again before threading her arm through mine.

I sat between Mother Rose and Chloe at dinner, although Chloe's father, Jim, watched me carefully from across the table. Two others separated Jim from Chloe's mother, Leisa. Chloe had already whispered that her parents weren't together any longer, although Leisa was included in most family outings.

"You say everyone is like you where you're from?" Chloe still couldn't believe my words. I'd been honest with them; Zaria never said I shouldn't be truthful.

"Yes. On occasion, a very tall Amterean is born. As we are well-acquainted with taller races, it's much easier for them to be accepted, although they do have a difficult time with normal chairs and tables."

"I hear that," Mother Rose said. "Although it is reversed, here."

"I dislike the bathroom in my cabin," I said.

I had no idea that everyone at the table would find that so humorous, until Mother Rose patted my hand. "Dear," she said, "there isn't a person on this boat who doesn't dislike their bathroom."

"Ah. It becomes clear, now," I said. "I thought it was only my preference not to bump into walls or wear a shower curtain while I bathe."

"You are wide in the shoulders," Chloe patted my arm.

"Military training," I shrugged.

"You're in the military?" Jim asked.

"I was until recently. I retired after thirty of your years, or a good equivalent. I spent the last twenty or so training new troops."

"They have a military," Chloe breathed as she leaned around me to blink at her grandmother.

"The Amterean Army is admired by everyone in the Alliance," I said. "We provide entire cohorts to the RAA."

"What's the RAA?" Jim asked.

"Regular Alliance Army, although our troops are elite squads."

"You belong to an Alliance?" Leisa asked.

"More than four hundred member planets," I said. "I've met all kinds as a military officer."

"Oh, tell me about the most unusual race you've met," Leisa said. "I've always wanted to meet aliens."

"Dear lady, I will introduce you to Zaria," I said. "I cannot reveal who or what she is, but to me, she is marvelous."

"Which one is she?" Mother Rose asked.

"The dark-haired woman with bright-blue eyes," I explained. "That is Zaria, although I think she may have other names, too."

"Meet me on the upper deck after dinner." Zaria and Klancy were suddenly beside me at the table. Several of my dinner companions gasped softly, but none spoke. "I'm Zaria," Zaria said, then disappeared with Klancy.

Chloe and her family looked about them, concerned that others in the dining room would surely notice two people who'd appeared and disappeared in moments. Diners at tables nearby acted as if nothing had happened.

"Zaria, ah, has the ability to conceal herself and others, and to, ah, fold space," I mumbled.

"Tell me why you are here," Mother Rose commanded. "Should we be worried?"

"Not directly," I held up a hand. "I came here because my father was murdered," I admitted with a sigh. "The one or ones who killed him may now be on your world. I intend to stop them before they can harm others."

"I'm in a science fiction story," Leisa breathed.

She didn't sound disappointed.

Lexsi

Zaria sent mindspeech, asking Kory and me to meet her on the upper deck after dinner. Kory and I had chosen the ship's steak and seafood restaurant for our evening meal, instead of going to the regular dining room, which was huge.

This was quieter and more intimate, as we'd spent the day the with others. This was our time together.

"I hope we get to go to Veshtul someday," Kory said after we'd placed our order. "There's a restaurant there that serves steak and other specialties. Not as good as your mother's or uncle's restaurants, but still good," he smiled at me. "And it has a good view of the palace from the upper floor."

"I've only been there when I was tiny, and I don't remember any of it," I said. "I wish I could have seen you then—all serious and military-like," I teased.

"I was approached not long after that—Jayd sent a message through my father, saying he wanted a meeting. I had no idea what he wanted," Kory shrugged and lifted his glass of Scotch. "I think I forgot to breathe when I was told that they'd selected me for you. I still have no clue what I'd done to deserve that."

"Kory," I reached out to touch his hand under the small table. "I'm glad it was you. I don't want anybody else."

"Onion, I'm happy that this worked out for us. More than happy. But think on this—what if we have a daughter someday? I don't want her going through the fear and uncertainty that you did. The laws need to be changed, so the females have a voice, too."

"I want the same thing," I squeezed his fingers before letting go. "I hope your father still has the strength to fight the crown over this. I'll stand with him all the way."

"Gardevik is old school, and you can bet he'll back Jayd on this."

Gardevik was King Jaydevik's older brother, and Prime Minister for Kifirin. His voice carried a lot of weight in the Council Chambers. Garde was also one of Gran's mates, and even she argued with him about these things. He usually ended up blowing smoke and skipping away.

I'd only seen it twice; both times when I was visiting Gran and hiding in the library when the arguments took place. I never felt like a real person around Uncle Garde; I always imagined that he saw me as property to be given away.

At least Jayd and Glinda had stayed away when I visited Gran; I may have shouted at them when I was old enough to form coherent arguments regarding arranged marriages.

I'd never really wanted to involve myself in High Demon politics. With Kory at my side, and what we'd gone through together, that was no longer true. Some things certainly needed changing.

We'd have to go through regular, accepted pathways to make our arguments heard. Those paths could be blocked easily by an unwilling King and his brother, the Prime Minister.

Glinda could help us, but she would allow Jayd to speak for both of them, instead. My shoulders sagged at the thought.

"Don't let it trouble you, onion," Kory said softly. "We will stand for what's right. Just because we face defeat doesn't mean we should allow bad laws to go unchallenged."

"You're right," I sighed and lifted my wineglass. "It's an uphill battle, and we'll get knocked down. We'll have our say, regardless."

"And that's how it should be," Kory smiled.

"We just have to deal with Morgett and his unholy alliance, first," I chewed my lower lip for a moment.

"Yeah. I won't even go into how we were so close to them last time, and then the Library happened."

"I don't want to talk about that, either," I whispered. All I could remember was the pain of it. I think Kory and I could have taken all of them down, if we hadn't been attacked by the Library.

Morgett and his crew had gotten away, shortly after the Library itself disappeared. Kory and I were left unconscious, crumpled on the rock floor inside an exploding volcano.

Zaria had taken us away from the eruption; if she hadn't, we could have been crushed beneath the weight of a collapsing cauldron.

Baby, stop thinking about it, Kory tapped the table with a finger. *It's done. Let it go.*

Kory, I can't help but think we're in the middle of it, still, I returned. *I can't say why that is, but I do.*

Our food's here, he drew me back to the present. *Eat, baby. Let's enjoy our meal together.*

You're right.

Our server set plates in front of us and asked if we needed anything else. "Refills on drinks," Kory said. "Everything else is fine."

"I'll drink to that," I said, emptying my wineglass as the waiter left our table.

～

Rogue Planet Akkl

V'ili

"I need transport to Earth," I said.

The Phogann, whose lumpy face revealed his race and planet of origin, studied me with small, speculative eyes. His seldom-blinking, dark gaze would unsettle most humanoids. I merely stared back at him.

If he failed to willingly offer information, I'd have it from him through obsession. "Have one ship willing to make that journey, but it's expensive," the Phogann leaned back in the ancient, creaking chair he occupied.

I stood at the desk inside what was optimistically termed a travel agency in the port city of Akkl. The place hadn't been cleaned or swept in moon-turns. The musty smell inside indicated recent rains and the growth of mold.

Akkl. All the smuggler's ships berthed there at one time or another. I'd followed this trail from Amterea; it was easy enough to find Morwin Quiffilis' itinerary from his homeworld.

It would take a smuggler to make the trip to Earth; no regular ships went there. "How much?" I asked the Phogann.

"Half a million credits. In advance."

"Give me the name of the ship and its berth number," my obsession was strong.

"*Reptilian.* Berth ninety-three." His eyes had lost focus from the force of my will.

"Good. You will not recall my visit." I folded space to leave the stench of the building and the unsightly countenance of the Phogann behind.

New Zealand Waters

Zaria

All sixteen members of the *Reptilian's* crew were now dead. Once V'ili was no longer present to block the information, I was able to *Look* and determine it for myself.

V'ili had gotten what he wanted, which was where they'd left Morwin—on the outskirts of Sydney. V'ili, Morgett and the twins would begin their search for the Amterean Dwarf very soon.

They needed Morwin alive, to learn what he knew of the Metal Library's possible location. He'd die after they got what they wanted from him.

If they managed to get to him.

"They're gone, aren't they?" Opal took the deck chair next to mine and sat with a sigh. Kell sat beside her, waiting for my confirmation.

"All dead," I dipped my head in a nod. "Not pretty. V'ili is a sick bastard."

"Yeah." Opal leaned her head back and closed her eyes. She was no stranger to massacres—she'd seen more than enough of those in her lifetime.

"It'll work out," I reached out to grip her hand and give it a squeeze. "It's just hard to deal with right now."

"I know."

"Yeah, me too."

"Zaria?" Morwin's voice interrupted the moment. I turned toward him. The entire family of owl shapeshifters stood behind him, expectation on every face.

"I have news," I said. "When Kory and Lexsi arrive, I'll take us to a bar a couple of decks down so we can talk."

"Does this involve us?" Mother Rose came to stand beside Morwin.

"It does," I said. "You need to hear this, because they'll be searching for Morwin, who, for all they know, could have disguised himself, or brought others with him. To them, he could be with you or any one of you, and that's not a particularly good thing."

"What Zaria means is that they don't care who dies on their way to find what they want," Opal explained.

"Who are you, and where are you from?" Rose demanded. "I sense you're not human."

"I am not," Opal replied. "I was born in North America, long before it acquired that name. I am an Old One among shifters, if you recognize that title."

Mother Rose hesitated. "Yes. I do recognize it," she admitted. "My family and I honor you."

"I thank you," Opal said.

"Lexsi and Kory are here," I said, allowing Klancy to help me from my chair. He'd sat in silence beside me while the rest of us spoke.

Mother Rose frowned at him and the way he'd stood so swiftly.

"None of us are human, here, Mother Rose," I said. "You and your family are in no danger from us."

"Then how are we in danger?"

"If you'll bear with me, I'll tell you," I said and folded the entire group into a closed-off section of a bar several decks down.

Mother Rose

My heart is strong. If it hadn't been, I'd surely have had a medical emergency when I was transported instantly from the top deck of the ship to a closed lounge several decks below.

Morwin had spoken the truth when he said Zaria was marvelous.

It isn't because I can fold space; several races are capable of that, Zaria's voice sounded in my mind, causing me to jump.

I found a comfortable chair and settled onto it, leaning my cane against the arm and attempting to convince my heart to slow down.

Telepathy. Folding space. What else could Zaria do?

"We'll discuss that another time," Zaria said, her intense, blue eyes smiling at me. Yes, I am naturally suspicious of everyone outside my family. It is safer that way. Zaria felt as if I could trust her, and I distrusted my own feeling in the matter.

Larentii are the most trustworthy of races, Opal's voice now sounded in my mind, causing me to blink. *Zaria is Larentii,* she added.

First an Old One, and now this. I wanted to speak mentally, so I could weigh in on the matter. Saying someone is trustworthy is certainly not enough evidence for me to trust them.

"You can speak openly," Zaria said. "It will not offend."

"How in Hades am I supposed to trust any of you?" I snapped.

"Fair point," the one called Klancy turned to smile at Zaria.

"Do you have a strong stomach, Mother Rose?" Zaria asked.

"As strong as they come," I said.

"Morwin, you should come with her. Perhaps her eldest son, too?" Zaria looked from me to Jim.

"Where are we going?" I demanded.

"To Akkl. We'll see the latest mess the enemy caused in order to find Morwin. He's here. He stands out because of his stature, I'm sorry to say. They may expect him to be in disguise, which may place you and your family in danger, too. They'll be looking for little people, Mother Rose. Innocent lives mean nothing to them, as long as they find what they want."

I shouted when I was displaced for the second time in less than ten minutes.

~

Akkl

Zaria

"The local constabulary—what there is of it, anyway—hasn't discovered this yet." I'd taken Rose, Jim, Morwin, Opal, Klancy and Kell with me to Akkl, to see the remains of sixteen smugglers who'd been cut and slashed to death by V'ili's alter-ego.

I'd left Anita with Lexsi, to explain what had happened.

Anita knew it was V'ili who'd done this. She was more determined than ever to find him. I was forced to slow her down on that, for reasons I couldn't share with her.

Sometimes, I just wanted to yell *fuck the timeline* and get rid of the cancerous blight that V'ili was.

That couldn't happen here and now.

I sighed at all the blood spilled on the metal flooring of the *Reptilian.*

Mother Rose's cane tapped around the mess, studying crumpled, dismembered bodies. Jim walked behind her, prepared to steady his mother should she need it. "What are their names?" Rose turned to ask. "What are they, that they can do this?"

"This one—his name is V'ili," I said. "He is Sirenali. I will give you images when we are back on the ship. Do not approach him—he is more than dangerous."

"Dearest, they are all more than dangerous."

Valegar had come, and he hadn't bothered to disguise himself. He stooped to fit inside the low-roofed *Reptilian*.

"They are," I rubbed my forehead. "Mother Rose, there are four of them. Two are fraternal twins from Karathia—a witch and warlock. Both also capable of this," I swept my hand out at the bloody mess around us.

"The fourth member of this group was once Karathian, but was changed to something else—something much, much worse."

"What can be worse than all that?" Rose asked, her face stern, a frown marring her forehead.

"Ra'Ak, Mother Owl," Valegar addressed her directly. "They appear human much of the time. Until they are hungry or angry. The giant serpent they become is the deadliest creature you may ever see. Every scale and claw of such a creature carries poison that can kill you within seconds."

"You are?" Mother Rose asked.

"Valegar of the Larentii, Mother Owl."

"They told me Zaria is Larentii." She was comparing the two of us; I who looked human and Val, who certainly didn't.

"I can change my appearance easily—all Larentii can," Valegar smiled and became much shorter. The blue skin faded to humanoid flesh; a lovely, coffee color, actually.

"You look amazing," I smiled at Val.

"Thank you." He leaned in to kiss me.

"I thought you were with him," Jim pointed at Klancy.

"Here we go," Opal sighed.

"She is with several," Val's eyes twinkled as he smiled at Jim. "In the Alliance, multiple mates are recognized and sanctioned by the laws, there."

"Do not say energy sex," Opal hissed at Val.

I had to hide my face against Val's shoulder to keep from snickering. She'd said it on purpose, to lighten the mood inside a smuggler's ship that was covered in blood and bodies.

"Let's go back," I said, pulling away from Val. "Are you coming, too?"

"I may pop in and out," Val said. "I was asked by your pod'l-morph if you needed his help."

"Let me guess, they all want to get in on this," I said.

"Yes," Val said simply.

"Tamp and Ilya only, all right?"

"I will bring them shortly." He disappeared.

"I wish I could do that," Jim breathed.

New Zealand Waters

Lexsi

Anita was telling our new companions what we were up against while Zaria and the few she'd chosen were away.

"Lexsi and Kory have the ability to nullify a witch or warlock's power—within a certain space around them," Anita answered Leisa's question.

"Roughly fifteen to seventeen feet in diameter," Kory said. "That means they can't even fold space, because we remove that ability, too."

"Is that why Morwin said if trouble comes, to stay close to Kory?" Chloe asked.

"It's one of the reasons, yes," Anita smiled. "Although staying close to Lexsi could also be a good idea—unless she's on fire."

"Huh?" Georgia's eyes widened.

"We'll uh, explain that later," I said.

Much later, Kory sent.

Yeah.

That's when Zaria and the others reappeared. I could see that Mother Rose and her son were much more subdued than when they'd left. Anita had sent mindspeech, telling me that the crew who'd transported Morwin to Earth had been murdered by V'ili.

After he'd gotten information from them, no doubt.

Fucker.

"It wasn't pretty," Zaria said, taking a chair beside mine. Kory sat on my other side, and allowed a curl of smoke to escape his nostrils.

"Did he just breathe smoke?" Sarah whispered.

"He's High Demon. Most of them do that when they're not happy," Zaria explained. "I have a feeling that nobody in Sydney may be safe tonight, because that's where the smuggler's ship dropped Morwin off."

"They're really that vicious?" Jim asked.

"They're worse than that," Opal said. "That fiasco in Peru? That's their doing."

"Great mother of owls," Rose mumbled.

CHAPTER 5

ellington, New Zealand
Zaria

We received the news when we docked in Wellington the following day. Six employees were dead in a Sydney hotel.

It was Morwin's hotel, where he'd spent his first night in Australia.

I'd hidden his trail when he boarded the boat, but how long would it take before they began to look for little people across the continent? It wasn't a stretch for them to believe that Morwin could have hidden himself among others who looked as he did. More than likely, they now knew that Morwin traveled to Earth alone, thanks to V'ili's obsession on the *Reptilian's* crew.

Whatever these hotel employees said hadn't been enough for V'ili, who was now determined to find Morwin at any cost.

Find Morwin; find the Metal Library. It was simple enough to read Morgett's handwriting in this. And, as Mother Rose and her family hadn't hidden their vacation plans from friends and coworkers, it wasn't difficult to place them on the ship.

And place them in terrible danger.

I considered that I could send them elsewhere while this conflict developed, but I couldn't shake the feeling that they had a part to play in all of it.

Plus, with Tamp and Ilya joining us, that meant two more to help protect them if necessary.

I merely had to put them in cabins near Rose's family, so they'd have that extra protection.

Klancy and the others could trade off with them, so they'd get a break. Esme and Yoff were already nearby; that added another layer of shielding for Rose's family.

Then there was Morwin.

He acted as if nothing were wrong—until you saw his mouth tighten and his eyes narrow. He wanted the death of the one who'd killed his father.

That's why I hadn't told him that Deris was the one.

Deris, the sick, powerful fuck whose hands dripped with the blood of too many victims already.

Deris, whose long-term plans included taking the throne of Karathia.

"Those deaths are on my hands." Morwin took a chair across the table. I sat at the back of the boat, outside the buffet in an open space, to soak in sunlight for a while. A cold cup of coffee was at my elbow, which I could warm with a thought if I wanted.

"Morwin, none of those deaths are on your hands," I said. "The evil that began this is responsible. What we have to do is try to stop them before the damage becomes extreme."

"I read the records—what I could get, anyway, on Peru last night after our meeting," he said. "There isn't much, officially. Tell me what I don't know."

"They were after the Metal Library then," I said, warming my coffee and lifting the cup to drink. "The Metal Library relocated itself before they could touch it. Since they're still alive, I have a hunch that this makes them believe they have a righteous cause to keep searching for it. That's how your father became involved. None of this is your fault."

"But there were other events in Peru," Morwin pointed out.

"Yes. Our enemies fell in with a greedy, slightly lesser evil. They played along with that, when they had an ulterior motive for being there the entire time."

"Drakus seed. That filth," Morwin muttered. "It kills, and people are too stupid to acknowledge that."

"They also had N'il Mo'erti. Know what those are?" I asked.

Morwin sat back and stared at me. "Impossible," he hissed.

"No," I shrugged. "Not impossible. The plans were stolen long ago and sold to a member of Morgett's family."

"Ra'Ak. I never thought to challenge one of them," Morwin sighed.

"Honey, that's why Kory and Lexsi are here," I said. "High Demons are their natural enemies. Let those two handle the Ra'Ak, if it comes down to it."

"I want blood-debt for my father."

"I'll do my best to make that happen," I said. "It may take a while, though."

"I care not how long it takes." Morwin's forehead was creased deeply as he considered his father's death and how angry that made him.

"So you're saying that Morgett is not responsible—at least directly—for my father's death."

"Yes."

"I will ask you again sometime who is responsible."

"Ask at the proper time, and I will tell you."

"Larentii can be so vague—or so I've read," Morwin grumbled.

"It's a necessity," I said. "Why don't you get breakfast at the buffet and sit here with me while I soak in sunlight."

"So that part isn't a myth," Morwin rumbled.

"No. Plus, most Larentii have absolutely no shame about nudity, and will lie naked to soak up as much sunlight as possible to feed themselves."

"There you are." Chloe set a breakfast tray on the table beside Morwin. Morwin's shaved eyebrows lifted as he held back a grin.

"I was just going to find food," he told her. "Will you be here when I return?"

"I'll think about it," Chloe teased.

I relaxed. Chloe was just what Morwin needed—and she could distract him from his anger at Mardin's death.

At least until the proper time.

"Go get your tray, Morwin," I reminded him. I think he would have sat there, smiling at Chloe until lunch time if I hadn't verbally nudged him.

"Yes. Food. Certainly. I will return quickly." He slid off his chair and strode toward the buffet.

"I like him." Chloe buttered her toast and crunched into it.

"I believe he likes you—very much," I said.

"Was he really in the military?"

"Yes. Morwin is very adept with knives and blades of any kind," I said. "He also has the highest qualifications with pistols and rifles. He taught incoming troops in all those things for the past two decades."

"That's amazing," Chloe said.

"How's breakfast?" I asked.

"It's good, but there's such a crowd in there right now."

"I hear it's like that most days," I agreed. "It's why I came out here to soak in sunlight, rather than fighting somebody over the last poached egg."

"Why would you do that? Aren't you hungry?"

"Sunlight feeds most Larentii. I'm a special case and can actually ingest regular food, although I don't eat meat."

"That's incredible," Chloe said. "That you can live off sunlight."

"You should hear the discussions Larentii have regarding the taste of yellow, green or red sunlight," I said.

"You're joking."

"I wish I were."

Morwin must have elbowed his way through the buffet, because he was back in record time with a full tray.

Including orange juice and hot tea.

"I see the military taught you well in getting through a chow line," I teased.

"You learn quickly, unless you wish to starve," Morwin set about adding salt and pepper to his eggs.

Lexsi and Kory found us in minutes, setting their trays on my side of the table. Lexsi squinted; the sunlight shone directly on her face.

"Here." I *Pulled* in a pair of sunglasses and handed them to her.

"That would come in handy," Chloe sighed.

"It's such a beautiful day," Kory leaned around Lexsi and grinned at me. I handed him a pair of sunglasses, too. He laughed and slipped them on his face.

"Are you getting off the ship?" Chloe asked Morwin. I didn't miss the bit of hope in her voice.

"I will, if you'll come with me," he said.

"Yes," Chloe almost danced in her seat. I considered who ought to shadow them as they visited New Zealand's capital city.

"Is there room for us?" Ilya and Tamp arrived with breakfast trays in hand. Trust them to show up when food was available.

"We'll move over," Lexsi said. She and Kory switched sides, allowing Tamp and Ilya to take their seats beside me.

"Want a taste?" Tamp held up a forkful of scrambled eggs.

"Tampirus, stop teasing me," I said.

"Call me Phrinnis and I'll bring another tray for you."

"Not necessary." Ilya spoke as he employed a warlock's power to drop a tray of food in front of me.

Scrambled eggs, toast and jelly. With a glass of cold milk. "You are awesome," I said and grabbed the salt and pepper.

"Showoff," Tamp elbowed Ilya.

They'd become very good friends, and I was grateful. I wasn't looking forward to seeing a war between a pod'l-morph and a warlock, to be honest.

Besides, I think both knew that Val would step in if they didn't get along, and neither wanted that. The threat of withholding energy sex was enough to make anybody back away from an argument.

"Val already took us to our cabin, but we're hoping to switch out with others," Tamp said, spearing a sausage link with his fork and biting into it.

"That's currently the plan," I said.

"Good." Ilya, always a warlock of few words, kept eating.

"Honey, would you place an extra shield around Chloe's family cabins?" I asked him.

"Already done—Val asked first," he said and lifted his cup of tea. If I knew anything at all, the tea was Falchani black and not anything served anywhere on Earth.

"Val's just really handy," I said.

"And we're not? I'm hurt," Tamp grinned at me.

"Are we not full enough of ourselves already?" I asked sweetly. Ilya pounded Tamp's back when he choked on a laugh.

"This is getting good," Chloe whispered to Morwin, who chuckled.

Anita

"You have the best nose, that's why," I poked Watson in the ribs. He and I were following Morwin and Chloe; Sandra and Mason trailed the rest of Chloe's family from a distance so they wouldn't feel crowded.

Watson wanted to stop and eat on several occasions; Chloe and Morwin were happy enough to wander the sidewalks and talk. Therefore, Watson whined about why he'd been picked for guard duty.

Zaria wanted mindspeech if anything untoward happened, or if Watson got wind of anything that wasn't human.

She, Klancy and several others had a trip planned to a hotel in Sydney, to allow the vamps to pick up what scents they could where the employees had died.

I didn't envy her that job. She'd already seen a bloody smuggler's ship, and I knew she didn't like the sight or the scent of death.

Yes, I remembered her—as the Larentii she was—from long ago.

I and my sisters, who were also my cousins, lay dying on the marble floors of my father's palace. I'll never forget the sky-blue face that hovered over mine as the light dimmed.

"All is not lost," she'd told me while taking away the pain of my death. "Someone will come for you."

Someone had certainly come.

Esme and I—sisters and cousins because brothers married sisters —hunted the one who'd killed us.

V'ili, our brother and cousin, had laughed and walked away as we lay bleeding on the floor. He'd ordered our deaths. His death—I looked forward to it. I cared not how it was accomplished, but given the chance, I'd see to it myself.

"Not another souvenir shop," Watson complained softly as Chloe stopped before a window in the distance. His head jerked up—his acute hearing had caught something.

"Morwin just said they should stop and have lunch," Watson hissed.

You could depend on Watson to hear the word *lunch* before anything else.

"You're screwed if it's a tiny café," I snapped.

"Not if there's a place to eat across the street."

"Look, go find a raw steak somewhere," I said. "I'll keep an eye on them."

"That's my girl." He gave me a quick kiss and loped away. I watched him go with a sigh.

"May I?" Davis Stone, Jr. appeared beside me and held out an arm for me to take. I gave full credit to Zaria for keeping tabs on Watson if he stepped outside my protective circle.

"Don't mind if I do," I hooked my arm in his and we followed Morwin and Chloe in their search for an intimate restaurant for lunch.

"What the hell?" Watson caught up with us after half an hour—he'd likely wolfed down a huge steak, pun intended, before tracking me.

Davis and I were having coffee at a tiny shop across from the restaurant Morwin and Chloe visited. Trust Watson to have a problem with Davis taking his place for half an hour.

"Zaria said it was important to have someone with tracking skills here," Davis said, standing and stretching. "I'm off."

I watched him stroll down the sidewalk before turning down a narrow alley. Zaria was probably sending him back to California right then.

"Did he?" Watson growled.

"No, and stop being growly," I snapped at him. "Davis is a perfect gentleman. Unlike other werewolves I can name."

"Hmmph."

"I like this place," I looked around me. "Nice. Reasonable temperatures, water nearby—we should visit again, sometime. I'd like to see the Beehive and lots of other things."

"Beehive?"

"It's what they call the executive wing of their Parliament buildings," I said. "Didn't you read the pamphlet they gave us?"

"Hmmph."

"Is that your answer to everything? Please don't say hmmph," I clapped a hand over his mouth.

He answered by kissing my hand and setting it down, but still holding onto it. "I'm sorry," he said. "Next time, just call me an idiot. I promise I'll listen and not leave you alone."

"Wow. Who took Watson and left an alien in his place?" I asked.

"Watson. Here." He tapped his chest.

"Aannnd he's back," I laughed.

Sandra

Mason's eyes darted in one direction then another, keeping track of our fifteen charges. Mother Rose had been informed that she'd have discreet bodyguards, and to go about enjoying her visit to Wellington as she normally would.

Mason and I stood next to the plate glass windows of a popular T-shirt shop while the family searched for souvenirs.

I love you, his voice sounded in my mind. Anita said it took a very strong mindspeaker to be able to send mindspeech to someone without the talent. Mason obviously had a strong mental voice.

"I know." My hand reached out to touch his. He threaded his finger through mine and continued his watch. "I love you, too," I whispered, knowing his sensitive ears would hear me.

"I can't give you children," he began.

I snorted. "There are other ways to have children," I reminded him.

"Thank you—I was hoping for something like that," he responded. He'd make a wonderful father—there was no doubt in my mind. Whether they were his or someone else's, he'd love and care for them.

I pitied anyone who threatened harm to them, too; Mason was very protective of those he cared for.

I'm going to love you very carefully—and very hard when we return to the ship, he sent.

"That sounds wonderful," I whispered. His hand squeezed mine and refused to let go.

~

The Rocks, Sydney
Zaria

I'd asked Tibby to come with us; that meant Farin came, too. Kell was keeping an eye on her while Tibby's rat, armed with a tiny, button camera, scoped out the crime scene inside the hotel.

The rest of us, in a rented hotel room across the street, watched what Tibby's camera captured as he traveled through the space.

At least the bodies were removed from this scene, although it was nearly as bloody as the *Reptilian.*

Fucking V'ili, I sighed. *With fucking Deris at his side,* if my suppositions were correct. Together, they'd killed six after V'ili questioned them under obsession. Six families were now grieving, for no good reason other than V'ili was disappointed by their answers and he and Deris liked to kill.

My worry for Morwin lessened; my concern for the little people of Australia ramped up. *That's enough, Tibby,* I sent to him. *Bringing you back, now.*

I *Pulled* him away from the crime scene and landed him in the hotel room bath, where his clothes were. While he was dressing, I sent the camera and monitor back to Davis and Thomas in California. I'd borrowed their equipment rather than expose myself to the stench at the crime scene so soon after the *Reptilian*.

"Did you get what you needed?" Tibby came out of the bathroom buttoning his shirt.

"Yes, and thank you," I said.

"Any time," he shrugged. "May I ask a favor in return?" he asked.

"Sure."

"I would very much like to take Farin through Sydney, if you do not object. Perhaps a meal and a tour?" He turned to Farin with a smile.

"I'd love that," Farin sighed.

"Then get on it," I said, waving them toward the door. "I warn you, though. Cinderella had to leave the ball at midnight. Make sure you're someplace safe at midnight, local time, because I'll be *Pulling* you back to the ship."

"It will be so," Tibby dipped his head. "Come, my love, Sydney waits for us."

I wish we could do the same, Klancy sent.

Honey, we'll have our chance. At least I hope that remains true, I returned.

Good. I expect a thorough tour of Sydney and every other part of Australia, his mental laugh surprised me.

"Everybody ready?" I asked, once Tibby and Farin were out the door. I folded us back to the ship docked at Wellington's harbor.

Morwin

Mother Rose waited for us when Chloe and I returned to the ship. I worried that she didn't like us staying out until the last moment, but we couldn't help ourselves.

"My apologies," I said immediately.

"I'm not concerned about that," Mother Rose said immediately. "I wish to have dinner with Zaria and those two new arrivals."

"I will inform her," I said, relieved that I wasn't about to face Mother Rose's wrath. After all, Chloe had only reached adulthood in the past two years.

"Good. She can choose the restaurant. You can join Chloe and the others in the dining room tonight."

"It will be a distinct pleasure to do so."

"Hmmph." Rose turned away from me, then. I was dismissed.

~

Zaria

"Morwin?" I stood aside to allow Morwin into my cabin after he'd knocked on the door.

"Rose wishes to have dinner with you and your two new companions."

"She wants to check us out, huh?"

"I believe the idea of multiple mates has her befuddled," Morwin said.

"Oh."

"While I have no problem with monogamy, it appears to be her dearest wish," Morwin pointed out.

"So you think she's worried that Chloe will have to share you?"

"I believe so."

"It all becomes clear, now," I waved a hand. "And this is only after two sort-of dates."

"But," Morwin began.

"No worries," I said. "We'll have dinner with Mother Rose, and I'll bring a few others with me."

"I will let her know," Morwin said. "Thank you."

"Shall I call the ship's Entertainment Director and tell him we wish to rent the theatre to hold all your mates?" Klancy teased.

"Honey, that's really humorous," I said. "And close to the truth."

~

Mother Rose

If I'd had any idea how dinner would go, I'd have kept my mouth shut. I had thirteen dinner companions waiting, including Zaria, when I arrived at the Japanese restaurant on the ship.

We had an entire room to ourselves, thankfully, or I'd have been embarrassed by all the stares.

Two women—twelve men. It was overwhelming.

"Please, sit," Klancy pulled a chair out for me. I needed to sit, if all these were Zaria's husbands. I was a fool for expecting only three or four.

Chloe's future played in my mind, too, as I studied the men who were taking seats at the low table after getting Zaria in a chair.

"Introductions?" I lifted an eyebrow at Zaria.

"Of course," she smiled. "I'll go around the table. This is Caylon Black, he's originally Falchani, but now belongs to an elite race of protectors," Zaria said.

"You look Asian," I said to him. He did, with a long, black braid down his back.

"It is easy to make that connection," Caylon dipped his head respectfully.

"This is Ilya, who arrived to help this morning," Zaria indicated the man sitting next to Caylon. "He is a Fifth-level warlock, from Karathia. This is Bleek," she began. I stared. The man was huge and had four arms.

"Bleek is Blevakian and like others of his race, he has four arms, six lobes and a wicked sense of humor," Zaria said before moving to the next man. "This is Phrinnis Tampirus, who has also come to help," she went on. "Tamp is a pod'l-morph, who can become anything animal, vegetable or mineral. Ask him to show you his cactus sometime."

"You can become a cactus?" I asked.

"I like becoming cacti—it is soothing. As is the large, jungle plant I also prefer—whenever it is raining, of course."

"This is Belen, and he's a god," Zaria said. If I'd thought the pod'l-morph and the Blevakian were strange enough, she'd just introduced someone as a god. I wanted to huff my disbelief, but when he became a shining creature, I forced the hiss to remain behind my teeth.

"This is Bekzi," Zaria continued. "He's a lion snake shapeshifter. Next is Gerrett, a Sirenali, along with his brother, Morrett, also a Sirenali. Then we have Valegar, whom you've met, and Edden Charkisul, a diplomat of the highest order who recently joined the ranks of the Avii."

Yes, I was stunned; Edden had blue wings folded against his back. He—I wanted to speak with him. Discuss flight with him. I felt a kinship with any winged creature, and he was no different.

"Last but not least," Zaria said, "This is Kalenegar, Head of the Larentii Council."

Zaria had twelve husbands. How the hell did she keep up with all of them?

Why did she have twelve husbands? The logic escaped me completely.

"It just happened," she shrugged, somehow reading my questions easily without my asking.

"Having multiple mates is common among many races," Kalenegar, who had dark red hair to his shoulders, said. "Mostly among the powerful or wealthy. Female Larentii are very rare, therefore it is logical that she be mated to more than one male of the species. As for these others—she loves them and they love her."

"But Chloe," I whispered helplessly.

"Morwin doesn't have a single problem with monogamy," Zaria smiled. "Set your fears to rest, Mother Owl. Chloe is in fine hands."

"Well, then. Well," I straightened the napkin and chopsticks at my elbow. "I'm hungry. Shall we eat?"

"I second," the one called Bekzi declared. The one who was a snake shifter. I'd never met one of those, before.

"Our server is on the way," Valegar said. "You will have a meal soon."

∿

Lexsi

"Kory, please say we can have a hot tub at our house," I said, leaning into the jetted, warm water at my back.

"I think I can do that. Where are we living?" He grinned at me from his seat across the hot tub.

"I don't know," I chewed my lower lip for a moment. "I guess I never thought about that."

"It doesn't have to be Kifirin," Kory said. "I can skip to work from just about anywhere."

"But you like living there," I pointed out. "Your family is there."

"I had dinner with my parents once a week," he said, his voice thoughtful.

"You miss them."

"I do. As parents go, they're really awesome, as Earth slang would describe them."

"I miss Mom. And Uncle Edward. I lived with them, although my dad and other uncles visited EastStar often. Avendor is beautiful, but there were times I really wanted to go out on my own, or with friends. I really didn't have many of those—just my brothers. My sisters, well, they barely acknowledged me. Or Mom."

"Jayd and Glinda have so much to answer for," Kory snorted a plume of smoke. "And, as they rule Kifirin, they will never be called to account for those things."

"Mom deserved so much better from them—especially Glinda, since she was Saa Thalarr, once. She could have asked Belen or somebody for help. She didn't. She just pulled my sisters away and took them for her own."

"I know this is a delicate subject, but has the rift ever completely healed between your mother and father?"

I only knew a little about the break-up early in their relationship. Daddy had taken up with another woman, who tried to destroy him—physically and emotionally. Yes, there was more story there, but Mom always refused to talk about it.

As if it still caused her pain.

I think Daddy regretted every second of that pain, but didn't know how to wipe it away. I loved him, but Edward was the one I went to when I needed advice or a shoulder to cry on.

Maybe Daddy felt that loss, too—more than anyone imagined.

"Come over here, onion," Kory held out a hand. I took it and made my way across the hot tub. He set me beside him and wrapped his arms around me. "It's not worth your tears," he whispered against my hair. I realized then that I was crying.

~

Royal Palace, Kifirin

Glindarok, Queen of High Demons

I'd asked Roff to come. Yes, now he was a winged vampire, instead of the comesula who'd acted as my valet and bodyguard when I was new to the throne of Kifirin.

I remembered Giff, his child, who'd ended up killing herself and her tiny child after committing treason against the throne of Le-Ath Veronis.

He'd had terrible pain in his life. I realized I wasn't being fair by asking him to come. I wanted his advice, nonetheless.

He'd grown since I'd last seen him—not in stature, but in power and wisdom. A light shone in the depths of his eyes that hadn't been there before.

Those I'd served with as a member of the Saa Thalarr had all grown.

They'd changed.

Became more.

While I'd chosen to leave that group behind. My power had withered and became less as a result.

It was a choice I'd made, and I was coming to realize how bad a choice it was.

"I asked Li'Neruh Rath for something," I blurted.

Roff, whose back was turned to me while he gazed out the windows of the palace arboretum, turned swiftly.

"It will not come without a price," he warned, his voice stern.

"I understood that before I asked," I said.

"What did you ask for?"

"I asked for children." I sat on a lounge chair and hung my head.

"What did he say? What were his demands?"

"He hasn't told me the price, yet. He said he would return and lay out the terms then. Only if I agree will I ever have another child."

"Then you are lucky. Others have not been given a choice."

I knew he referred to Gavril, Lissa's son, who'd asked Kifirin for something. The price he paid was terrible, and it had cost his mother and father, too.

"This is Li'Neruh Rath, not Kifirin," I pointed out.

"And yet the price still may be a terrible one. What do you want from me?" He lifted a dark eyebrow.

"I don't know. Not now. Once, the Roff I knew would have sat with me and wrapped his arms about me. That Roff would have said that things would be all right."

"That Roff no longer exists," he said, his voice soft.

"I know."

I hesitated for a moment before speaking again. "What happened?" I said, wiping a tear away. "What happened to me? To you? To the High Demons as a whole?"

"When we met—do you remember that?" Roff took a seat beside me and gently rubbed my back.

"Yes."

"You were so strong, then. Determined. Deliberate. A Queen. Someone who could rule Kifirin. When was the last time you became Thifilatha?"

"During the final battle with the General," I confessed. "It hasn't been needed at other times."

"What if it has been needed? What if you merely failed to answer the call?"

"Jayd," I began.

"Yes. Jayd," he sighed. "No," he held up a hand, "Jayd hasn't been the worst ruler of Kifirin. He hasn't been the best he could be, either. I know you've argued with him during his reign as King, but he generally makes the final decision. Is that not true?"

"It's true," I admitted. "He and Garde."

"Then I hope things go well for you, Queen Glindarok, when Li'Neruh Rath returns and names his price. This time, Jayd cannot make the decision for you."

Roff folded space away from me.

He'd return to Lissa, and the palace on Le-Ath Veronis.

Lissa was a strong Queen. Perhaps the strongest. She had many mates and yet the final decisions were hers. She made them after stern deliberation.

I wished I had her resolve and determination. Twisting my fingers together, I was left to contemplate my failures, past and present.

CHAPTER 6

elbourne, Australia
V'ili

We'd gotten little information from the hotel employees in Sydney. The Amterean had paid for his room, then disappeared. They had no idea where he went. Morgett fumed about his disappearance; even using his considerable power, he couldn't locate the dwarf.

"He'd stick out like a sore thumb," Daris said. She had the temerity to file her fingernails in my presence, but I refrained from saying anything. She was Morgett's grand-niece and his pet witch.

"Those affected by dwarfism are few on this world," I pointed out. "Perhaps one in twenty-five thousand. That cannot be hidden easily."

"Yet they exist," Morgett appeared thoughtful. "Perhaps he thinks to hide among others like himself."

"I will begin my research immediately," I said and walked toward the door. Any excuse would work to get away from Daris' incessant scraping of an emery board against her claws.

New Zealand Waters

Lexsi

"Honey?" Zaria put an arm around my shoulders and pulled me into a hug.

How does she know stuff like this?

I was still feeling depressed at breakfast the following morning, although Kory had held me all night long. Homesickness had finally come to call, I suppose, and it had hit me hard.

It's okay, Zaria sent. Suddenly I was enveloped by a warm feeling of love. I wrapped my arms around Zaria, then. Whatever she was doing, it made me feel so much better.

Kory pulled me away eventually, otherwise I may have stood there for half an hour while Zaria babied me in her arms.

"Onion, let's have breakfast," Kory kissed my forehead. "You can sit next to Zaria if you want."

"I only know of one race that can do what you just did," I whispered to Zaria. "Is that what you are?"

She had to be Larentii—had to be. So far, there'd been no other indication, but this—I'd only felt this once before, when Uncle Nefrigar held me after I'd lost my first baby tooth.

"I'm the Vhanaraszh," Zaria smiled at me.

I gaped—I know I did.

"You can *Change What Was*," I whispered as Kory gripped my hand and led me toward the breakfast buffet.

"That's a secret," Zaria whispered back. "Keep it, okay?"

Uncle Nefrigar had told me stories, too, when I was young. About the Vhanaraszh and Vhirilaszh—female and male Larentii, who could do alone what it would take all five Wise Ones to do together.

Somehow, the Vhanaraszh had taken an interest in the doings here on Earth. It meant, in Earth lingo, that something heavy could be going down.

As if I didn't already know that. It now appeared to be more serious than I originally thought.

"At least Dervil, Laurel and Berke are still in jail," I blew out a sigh.

"The fangs are removed from those snakes," Ilya walked up to embrace Zaria. "What's for breakfast? I'm starved."

~

San Rafael, California

Jamie Rome

"Laurel asked to see you. We said not bloody likely," Thomas grinned at me.

"Why the fuck would she want that?" I exploded. "I sure as hell don't want to see her." I thumped the coffee cup in my hand on the granite island, before recalling that I could have broken it.

"We're saying you have no part in all this, but she's been talking to her lawyer, of course, and, even though she doesn't know the last name you're using now, she's convinced her lawyer that you're involved in all this."

"How?" I demanded.

"Her phone has photographs of Berke Gillson—before he, ah, took on your previous body."

"And that's who I look like now," I growled. "Fucking, body-stealing, Berke fucking Gillson."

"Her phone shows her and the previous Berke in ah, compromising positions."

"Of course. It's perfect that she took photographs of them fucking. That's sarcasm, by the way."

"I've been to college. I know sarcasm. We're BFFs," Thomas said, his words dry. "We're trying to keep you away from all this, but Laurel is complicating everything."

"As she has, my entire married life," I complained. "If I'm deposed, and it looks like I will be, I can't say I don't know her. They have photographs." I made air quotes with my fingers. "I'll end up in jail, because I can't explain any of this—so that anybody believes me, anyway."

"I'll contact Opal—maybe she has some advice," Thomas offered. "As it is, if they call you as a witness, at the very least, I'll have to turn you over to the authorities."

"Who will probably toss me into a jail cell without bothering to ask questions," I mumbled. "Gillson's fingerprints are on more than

Laurel, I'd bet my last dollar on it. Any way you look at this, I'm fucked."

"Yeah. That's what Davis and I think, too."

~

New Zealand Waters

Opal

"Things are complicated back in the States," I shut off my cell phone with a sigh. "We may have to go back to put out some fires that just cropped up."

"How long will that take?" Kell asked.

He and I stood inside our cabin, still dressed in swimsuits after a late swim in the ship's largest pool. Thomas' call had pulled us away from our stolen moments.

"No idea," I shrugged. "They found images of the real Berke Gillson on Laurel's cell phone. That means Jamie, who now looks like Gillson, may be hauled in on drug charges, murder and treason, just like Laurel. Fuck, this is the wrong time for this to happen."

"What about your association with the Secretary of Defense? Do you think he may be able to help with this?"

"I sure hope so. At least he's convinced of the truth, but the Justice Department and everybody else will think the truth is the biggest lie ever, and discredit us and all the evidence we've collected. Besides, Jamie's been through enough, without having to stare at prison bars while he awaits trial for something he was never involved in."

"Being wrongly accused is more than disheartening," Kell murmured, pulling me against him. "We will deal with this, one way or another."

"We have to, unless we want Jamie to spend his life in jail," I whispered against Kell's chest.

I really didn't want to lay this on Zaria, either; she had enough to deal with. And, if my guess were correct, Morgett, V'ili and the twins had more murder and violence up their sleeves.

It was a terrible, hopeless wish for the body count to remain low.

Because it wouldn't.

～

Morwin

"There is speculative information available on your Internet," I told Chloe. She and I occupied a single deck chair after breakfast. She'd asked me about my father and why I was searching for his murderer.

That led to the Metal Library.

"Speculative?" A delicate eyebrow lifted.

"Yes. In all my father's research, there was never a reason or a purpose given for its existence," I said. "I have no idea what excuse the murderer gave for his search, other than the usual treasure-hunting for valuables," I shrugged. "It's not your worry, love."

Her cheeks went pink at the endearment.

"What is it made of?" she asked to draw my attention away from her blush.

"I assume it is gold—many descriptions say it could be made of that precious metal, although gold is soft and malleable. If I were going to place information on metal, I'd make sure it would endure for a very long time."

"You think they're after gold?" Chloe asked.

"These are powerful beings who can take all the gold they want from more convenient places. No, I suspect they are after information contained only within the Metal Library itself."

"What information could be that important? What can they gain by killing your father—or anyone else?"

"They wished to conceal the knowledge that they seek it, perhaps, and combined that with their pleasure of taking lives."

"Sociopaths." Chloe's word was firm and convincing.

"Yes. A good description."

"I'm sorry about your father." She leaned her head on my shoulder, which was right where I wanted it to be.

～

Zaria

Dunedin. It was our current stop. Mountains rose in the distance, topped by pale clouds and blue skies.

"Are we getting off the boat, cabbage?" Ilya's arms pulled around me from behind.

"Have you been here before?" I asked.

"Long ago, and not on business," he whispered against my ear. I sighed and relaxed against him. He'd allowed his accent to come through in the words. In a former life, he'd been a Soviet spy—until he'd defected.

In this life, he was a Fifth-level Karathian warlock, who was also deadly with his hands and blades. "There is a train that goes into the mountains," he recalled. "The trip is quite scenic, and the journey was a pleasure for me, although the food is only standard fare."

"Done any cooking lately?"

"I have." He pulled me closer.

"I love you," I told him.

"Hmmph. I love you. You should know that."

"Hmmph."

"There are cave-like holes in some of those rock hillsides," he sighed against my ear. "I can place a concealment spell. And provide comfortable bedding."

I turned in his arms. "Go on," I said.

"Come with me, and I will."

❧

Opal

Kell and I were tracking the Hiboux family through Dunedin, while Tamp and Klancy followed Morwin and Chloe. It gave the others a break, to enjoy their trip. I'd gotten mindspeech from Zaria, saying she and Ilya were going into the hills surrounding the port city.

It wasn't until late that afternoon, when our charges were heading back to the boat that the news came.

The body count was rising in Australia.

~

Zaria

Two families were dead. I had to carry the news to Rose and her family, because she knew several of the victims.

They belonged to the same social organization, and, while they weren't terribly close, remained in contact through social media.

It wasn't a secret that Rose and her family had planned a vacation trip. I merely wondered how long it would take Morgett and V'ili to connect the dots.

Perhaps it was time to hunt the Metal Library myself, with Morwin's information. If I had something to dangle in front of Morgett, perhaps he'd stop murdering.

I almost laughed as that thought hit me.

Morgett was Ra'Ak. Murder was practically their raison d'etre. In addition to that, if V'ili discovered that a Larentii were involved, he'd ramp his killing spree up to brand new levels.

He'd never admit that he and others like him had created his world's doom by attacking the Larentii and their children in the first place.

No.

That would mean accepting responsibility.

As far as I could tell, V'ili and responsibility had never been introduced. Toss in some rogue god interference and voilà—a vendetta as only a Sirenali could do it.

Still, it wouldn't hurt to do some digging to find the Library. Perhaps it would allow us to be better prepared when the time came.

Morwin, I sent. *I need the information you received from your father.*

~

Lexsi

Two families. Nine people, this time. Three of those were affected by dwarfism. Morgett and his crew were attacking the little people of Australia and their families in order to find Morwin.

Something had to be done, but I wasn't sure what that could be.

We're having a meeting after dinner, Zaria's voice entered my mind. *Deck eleven—the bar at the back of the boat.*

She and I had come to the same conclusion. I wondered if she had any solutions to stop the slaughter of innocents, without pinning a target on the rest of us.

"I heard," Kory sighed before I could tell him. "She sent blanket mindspeech, looks like."

"Where are we having dinner tonight?" I asked.

"I checked with the crab place earlier—they have no crab and won't have any until they sail for Alaska in a few months. I really wanted crab, too."

"San Francisco has crab," I pointed out.

"Yeah, but the time difference," he pointed out.

"Darn. I want crab too, now that you mention it."

"They have shrimp. Prawns, actually. Or, the Brazilian place on the top deck has shrimp and all types of meat carved and served at your table—gaucho style." I could see the light in Kory's eyes—he wanted that.

"Sounds like a lot. Better invite Anita and Watson, too."

"He'll want to gnaw on everything before it's cooked."

Kory's words made me laugh. "I say we invite him anyway."

We ended up asking everybody; Watson, Anita, Tibby, Farin, Esme and Yoff wanted to join us.

We would fill the entire table, and I liked that idea. I hoped dinner with friends would take my mind off nine deaths; they weighed heavily on me.

～

Zaria

Klancy, Tamp and I had dinner with Opal and Kell. Ilya was guarding the owl family, but I kept him in the loop through mindspeech.

"Yes, I could form a link between all those families and Lexsi and Kory, but," I said, once the waiter left our table.

"You're worried they'll kill three out of the four, and those are the ones that have to stay alive," Opal finished my sentence.

"Yeah. It sucks. It's—we can't just let all those people die," I finished helplessly. I was powerful, I knew that, yet I was faced with a conundrum that stretched across time and light years.

So many things could shatter the timeline, and then everything could explode in our faces. Nobody wanted a repeat of the god wars.

Nobody *needed* a repeat of the god wars.

There had to be an answer here somewhere, but I had no idea what it could be. "Perhaps a visit to the Archives?" Tamp asked, his voice hopeful.

He loved the Larentii Archives, and, as one of my mates, he had the equivalent of a library card issued by Val's father and Chief Archivist, Nefrigar.

"You think we can find an answer there?" I turned to him.

He smiled. "If not, it may take your mind off this worry," he said.

"Maybe later," I said, brushing his idea aside. "For now, I don't know what we're going to tell the others," I sighed. "The owl family lost friends in this latest attack. We have no answers, and they'll want some."

Royal Palace, Kifirin
Glindarok

In the past decade, I'd lost interest in Council meetings and trials. Still I received copies of the agenda and minutes from the previous meeting. I'd stopped attending at some point, and couldn't recall the last time I'd gone.

Jayd and Garde had a system, and I'd grown tired of seeing the same thing over and over. This time, however, there was an item on the agenda that drew my interest—a rape trial which would take up most of the meeting scheduled in two days.

A High Demon—one of the few Drith still alive, had raped a commoner in Veshtul. Not only had he committed rape, he'd beaten the woman and threatened her family if she reported his misdeeds.

Her father learned the truth, however, and Vordevik Drith was imprisoned and held for trial. A part of me was furious about this. Another part of me knew that Jayd and Garde would have an important decision to make.

This sort of crime didn't happen often on Kifirin, and the decision could set a precedent for future trials. Jayd had no love for any of the Drith family, but as King, he would have to set those feelings aside and deal with this in an objective way.

Still, the punishment should be severe, in my mind. If he'd only beaten the woman, that was a minimum of five years—High Demons were much stronger than humanoids. He could have killed her easily.

Add a rape charge to the assault and it had to be ten or fifteen years' imprisonment—at least. Jayd and Garde knew the laws and would surely do the right thing where this victim was concerned.

Nedevik Weth would speak for her and her family in the Council Chambers. No matter what, Nedevik would prepare a full argument for the victim, although this should be a simple decision to make.

There was no need for me to attend, I decided. Perhaps I'd invite my daughters to visit for lunch on that day—all eight of them.

Only two are truly yours, a small voice reminded me. I ignored it.

SouthStar, Avendor

Li'Neruh Rath

I'd asked Breanne to meet me at SouthStar. I had no idea that Strength and Wisdom would also be waiting for my arrival.

I'd be lying if I said I didn't want time alone with Breanne, but I wanted to speak with her first, before taking my terms and conditions to the Queen of Kifirin.

That's how I found myself in Ashe's enormous library at the top of his palace, where a smiling servant offered tea and tiny cakes.

"Honey, don't blow smoke, you haven't heard what we have to say, yet," Breanne took a seat next to me on the sofa I occupied.

"But this is the right thing to do," I blustered. I didn't want the Three interfering with this. I'd thought long and hard about it before making this decision. Besides, the dark worlds had been left in my care.

"We know," Breanne smiled at me. "Stop worrying, Mister Smoky Britches. We agree with you."

"Then what's this about?" I demanded.

"Well, it looks like we may need a High Demon army before long. We thought you could help us with that."

I went still. Yes, I was keeping tabs on things happening on Earth in the past, but when did this become a necessity?

"Honey, the timeline is warping. We need all the help we can get to straighten it out again."

"Have dinner with me and I'll give you anything you want," I said.

"You're a trusting soul," Bree smiled at me.

"If it's you, I will trust every time," I confessed.

"I love you." She pulled my face down for a kiss. It was perfect.

New Zealand Waters

Lexsi

"I don't have any answers right now," Zaria said. I'd never seen her look so weary, even when we were dealing with the mess in Peru. "At least no easy answers," she continued. "I've started looking for the Metal Library myself—perhaps we can use it as bait—like last time. The unfortunate thing is this—last time, it was relatively easy to find. This time, it has concealed itself much better."

"My family and I stand with Morwin, now," Mother Rose stated flatly. "We have deaths to avenge."

"Yeah." Zaria was standing, but allowed Klancy to pull her onto a chair next to his. At that point I really, really wanted an answer to all this—and an end to the murder of innocents.

This is so fucked up, I sent to Kory while rubbing my forehead.

I know, he replied. *We have to find a way to stop this senseless slaughter. I wish I could count on the High Demon army, but mindspeech here and now will go unheeded—I know who sits the throne before Jayd, and he will not answer the call. Rorevik was weak as a ruler, and wouldn't think of involving High Demons in anything like this.*

Asking for help could place you in danger—here and there, I reminded him.

True. I hadn't considered that. It's difficult to deal with being in the past, at times.

Yeah. I couldn't even call for Mom, because she hasn't been born yet.

It's a tricky time, and I'd like to find a way to deal with it, he agreed.

"I don't have answers yet," Zaria said, bringing Kory and me back to the meeting. "Just know I'm working on it."

"That was worthless," Rose's son Jim, muttered as he and his family filed out of the bar.

You don't know Zaria, I sent to him, although he probably wouldn't hear my mindspeech. *If she says she's working on this, you won't find a better person to champion your cause.*

Mother Rose

"I heard a voice in my head. Lexsi's voice," Jim said as he flopped onto my bed.

"What did she say?" I asked.

"I was rude when I left the meeting, and she told me that Zaria was the best person to champion our cause, even if she doesn't have answers right now."

"What did you say?" I frowned at him.

"I said the meeting was worthless."

"So you'd rather be kept in the dark? They're not obligated to include us, or to keep us guarded day and night, you know."

"I figured that out on the way to the cabin," he admitted. "They could have just left us in the dark, and we'd be wondering even now who was responsible for those murders."

"Like the rest of Australia is in the dark," I nodded. "They don't have a clue."

"Next time, remind me to shut it," Jim complained.

"I'll tell you. We'll see if you listen."

Morwin

I stood at the ship's rail and considered throwing myself into the dark waters below, as if that would solve these troubles. Chloe was more than upset that a schoolmate was among the nine dead at the hands of those who sought me.

"If you weren't here, they'd be seeking you on Amterea."

A red-haired Larentii stood at my side, appearing from nothing. "I am Kalenegar, one of Zaria's mates and Head of the Larentii Council —in the future."

He'd moved time to arrive at this moment. My breath caught as I considered that feat. "Who is Head of the Council, now?"

"My father still lives at this time," he said, lifting his gaze to the water.

As my father lived in the past. It was in *my* now that he was no more. "Your death will solve nothing," Kalenegar spoke again after a short time had passed. "Your father's death served no purpose, either, except to feed the twisted pleasures of a weak-brained fool."

"I thought Larentii were immortal," I breathed. All the tales I'd read said so.

"We are. It takes a great deal of power to destroy a Larentii; it was accomplished by rogue gods."

A soft gasp escaped my lips.

Rogue gods. How terrifying. I wanted to shiver, but forced that impulse away.

"They have a hand in this, Master Morwin," Kalenegar informed me. "And now you are caught in their webs, just as those who have died and will die are caught up in them. You, through no fault of your own, have become—*involved*.

"So I will see this through, although it may also require my life," I said.

"I believe it is expected," Kalenegar's smile was warm and unanticipated. "You have things to accomplish, instead of allowing your life to wither here on this lonely, outlying planet."

"Ah."

"What I am attempting to say is this," Kalenegar went on. "Your name is recorded in the Larentii Archives of the future. Do not allow those records to disappear."

"My name?" I shivered, then. The Larentii thought me important enough to list in their Archives? That was astonishing.

"You must survive these trials first," Kalenegar knelt to place a hand on my shoulder. "See that you do so."

He disappeared, then, leaving me to ponder my fate.

And my future.

~

Perth

V'ili

"You weren't paying attention," Morgett chastised Deris. "There were recordings of your likeness—and Daris' at the scene of the latest killings. I care not that you kill, I merely wish to ensure you are not recorded during those moments."

It wasn't even a slap on the wrist—just a *do better next time* speech from a lenient parent.

"We'll disguise ourselves next time," Deris said.

"Good idea. See that you remember."

I hated Ra'Ak. I hated Deris and Daris, too.

Necessary evils, I reminded myself.

~

New Zealand Waters
Zaria

"I could have told you that, before they bothered to show their images," I told Tamp. We watched the television screen on the wall at the foot of the bed; a news program was on and camera images of Deris and Daris were shown at the most recent crime scene.

"I'd wager much that Morgett isn't happy," Tamp said and hit the off button on the remote. "I've had no dealings with Ra'Ak—I can sense them from afar," he added. "Others on Paricos II weren't so selective in their clients, however. In the past, of course."

"Did any survive?"

"If they wished to continue doing business, yes," Tamp shrugged. "If not," he shrugged again.

"They do enjoy their humanoid breakfasts," I leaned back on my pillows.

"Ra'Ak are filth and abominations," Tamp grumbled.

"No—the black ones are pretty good. I've met some. The copper ones went off the deep end in the past and started helping themselves to anybody and everybody—and ended up breeding faster than rabbits, too. Have you ever seen Ra'Ak spawn?"

"Not personally, although I've seen images and heard plenty of tales. Far in the past, ships would return on autopilot, after the entire crew had been consumed. The security cameras confirmed it. A single Ra'Ak would transport spawn on board, and the feeding frenzy would begin."

"Nasty," I made a face.

"Their young have no table manners," Tamp agreed. "A Ra'Ak will swallow his victim whole. Spawn are much smaller than those serpents and must tear their food apart before consuming it."

"Honey," I turned to him. "Can we talk about something else? All this talk of spawn is upsetting my stomach."

"What do you wish to talk about? Before I love you?" His face inched closer to mine on the pillow.

"What are we going to do if Deris, Daris and V'ili accidentally end up dying here?"

"Hmmph. It's too bad they can't be in two places at once," he mumbled before closing the distance and kissing me. "If one set lived, the other could die whenever and wherever." He kissed me again, before pulling me against him.

Deris and Daris could wait, I suppose.

CHAPTER 7

oyal Palace, Kifirin
Lord Nedevik Weth

"I want no part of this," I gestured with a hand to cut off the conversation. The rape trial was scheduled for the following day, and I'd been approached by King Jayd and his brother Garde, the Prime Minister. "The humanoid population is already angry and uneasy. Making an arrangement such as this, and ignoring the victim as you suggest will infuriate them."

"Deals are made in other courts on other worlds all the time," Garde pointed out.

"If they are made in matters like this, then they are just as wrong as this one is," I snapped. I was being rude to the King. I didn't care. "The humanoids on Kifirin already feel like second-class citizens. They will be watching this trial carefully and considering the outcome. Have you heard the term disenfranchised, my King?"

"Hmmph. They're humanoids," Jayd dismissed my argument. "Besides, the woman has had other lovers." Jayd frowned as he spoke, as if he were practicing extensive patience with me.

"I care not how many she's had. I only care that a crime was committed against her in this case. According to Alliance laws, she is entitled to the same rights as any other on Kifirin, including the High Demons."

"Look, you can save us a great deal of time, if we can make an agreement now. The Council looks to us to decide this." A curl of smoke escaped Gardevik's nostrils. We were back to the beginning of this discussion, and I didn't like it.

"So the details of a heinous rape will offend their delicate ears?" I was just as capable of blowing smoke as the lofty Prime Minister. "Those council members serve at your pleasure, King Jaydevik. They are compelled by law to listen."

"You're saying no, then?" Jayd asked. His casual tone forced my head to jerk in his direction.

"I'm saying no deal on this—the trial needs to go forward." I was adamantly holding my ground. Jayd had no idea how the humanoid population viewed his rule over Kifirin, and the way that High Demons often received better treatment than they—where the laws were concerned.

"Remember what you said about the Council serving at my pleasure?"

I went still. He'd planned this. I'd been a thorn in the King's side for a very long time—not just this King, but King Rorevik before him and King Lendevik before that.

"You've served a good long while," Garde spoke. "It's time you retired."

"If you feel that way, I will do so. Right after the conclusion of this trial."

"You will retire now." Jayd's face clouded with the smoke he breathed.

"I refuse. I have a right to see my assigned business through until the end."

"Unless you offend the King."

"If I offend the King, or if anyone offends the King, a jail sentence must be levied."

"If that's what you want," Jayd shrugged. "Guards," he shouted.

Two guards arrived quickly while I glared at the King of Kifirin. "Escort Lord Nedevik to the dungeons. His length of sentence will be determined later."

❧

Glinda

"Why is Nedevik sitting in the dungeon?" I demanded. Jayd sipped bourbon from a glass while he sat behind the desk in his study.

As calmly as if he hadn't just sentenced the best High Demon in his Council to serve time—for no good reason.

"He offended the King."

"How did he offend the King?" I refused to make quote marks in the air, although Lissa would have. "You're the King, Jaydevik Rath, but you're no better than the High Demon sitting in your dungeon."

"Which one?"

"Nedevik, you horned and scaled moron. Are you forgetting what he did to put Kifirin back together after it was almost destroyed?"

"Did you just call me a moron?"

"I called you a moron. Are you going to put me in the dungeon, now?" I hadn't argued with Jayd like this in decades. *Where had my fury gone in all those years?*

"He refused to listen to reason and make a deal to prevent a drawn out rape trial, and then blew smoke in my face."

"What deal?"

"One year in jail, minus time served," Jayd said flatly.

"That only means four months," I said, staring at my husband. "Four more months in jail. No wonder Nedevik blew smoke in your face." I was ready to blow smoke, too. As far as I knew, I was the only female High Demon who could do that.

"Look, be reasonable. She had multiple lovers, some even before she became a full adult. What did you expect Vordevik to do? The girl's a whore."

90

"What did you just say?" I'd gone numb at his words.

"I said she's a whore. Vordevik was only getting what others had before him."

"I assume the others had her permission. Vordevik did not. That's why there's a trial pending," I hissed.

"Not anymore. Garde assigned Chalevik Croth to the case. The deal's been made already and the accused and the victim notified."

At that moment, I couldn't begin to describe how angry I was. My Thifilatha—fifteen feet of white-hot anger—destroyed much of Jayd's study before I skipped away.

~

Queen's Palace, Le-Ath Veronis

Lissa

Glinda stalked through the dining room shortly after I'd sat down for lunch with several others. One of those was Roff, who blinked at Glinda in consternation as she pulled out a chair and sat.

Something was certainly wrong, here. Anger radiated off her in waves.

Jayd just fucked up, a voice sounded in my head.

My sister Bree's voice. Quickly, she outlined what had just passed between Glinda and Jayd. It was easy to see that Bree agreed with Glinda in this.

As did I.

"You may stay as long as you want, and I can seal the palace against visits from Jayd and Garde if you wish," I spoke to Glinda, who stared at her empty plate. "I'll see what I can do to get Nedevik released from the dungeon, too."

"Please," she said. "Nedevik doesn't deserve this. As for Jayd and Garde, I may never want to see either of them again."

~

New Zealand Waters

Lexsi

I had strange dreams the night before. Somehow, Kory's father, one of the most respected High Demons on Kifirin, was in the palace dungeon. Upon waking, I was sure the dream was pure fiction, although it felt real.

I'd also dreamed of the Metal Library.

I'd run through it, desperately pulling this bound metal book after that one off deep shelves, only to find metal pages smooth and blank.

As if nothing had ever been written upon them.

My awakened, rational self also proclaimed that a lie. If it were so, why was Morgett hunting it, still? Therefore, it was only a dream that made no sense.

In my dream, I shouted at the Metal Library, demanding answers.

Ask, it said, its voice ringing hollow. Metallic.

Frightening.

Fine, I shouted back at it. *Let me help the people Morgett is targeting.*

It will be so, it replied.

I woke with a gasp, to find Kory already sitting up in bed beside me, a terrified look on his face. "I dreamed my father was in the palace dungeon on Kifirin," he turned toward me.

"Holy hell," I muttered one of Gran's favorite phrases.

Palace Dungeon, Kifirin

Lord Nedevik Weth

"I almost wasn't allowed in," Wendevik muttered. My son and I stared at one another through the bars of my cage.

These dungeons had been made with Kifirin's power long ago, to prevent its occupants from skipping away. I hadn't attempted to skip —I would serve my sentence, as long as it was a proper sentence handed down by a proper King.

Jayd had been on a downward slide for two decades, at least. A good King remained vigilant instead of becoming complacent.

Jayd was complacent, now.

"The, ah, humanoids are protesting Jayd's decision in the rape case," Wendevik informed me.

He was married to one of Jayd's daughters. It took a great deal of will and courage for him to come; Jayd could have him locked up with me, if he weren't careful.

"Protesting?" I asked. Wendevik was holding something back.

"They're burning parts of Veshtul. This was after Jayd ordered the army to disband the protests on the palace steps. Some of them were hurt in the process, as you may imagine."

"These aren't as malleable as the comesuli were," I pointed out. "And, as a member of the Reth Alliance, they have the right to protest. Is Jayd ignoring that, too?"

"He's calling it a riot, and working to quell it by any means possible," Wendevik sighed. "It doesn't look good for the humanoids in the city."

"Of course it doesn't," I said. "He refuses to listen to reason any longer. Or to advice from trusted colleagues."

"I'm afraid things will get worse before they get better, and word has it that Glinda is so angry with Jayd she went to Le-Ath Veronis. She isn't speaking to Jayd or Garde."

"Is she speaking to her daughters? To Reah's daughters?"

"I believe those lines of communication are still open," Wendevik said. "Although you didn't hear that from me, if the King asks."

"Of course."

~

New Zealand Waters

Zaria

"The Justice Department just took Jamie into custody," Opal sighed and flopped onto a chair at the breakfast table. "Only they're naming him Berke Gillson, Person of Interest," she grimaced.

"Because Jamie Rome is already in the pokey," I nodded. "Or so they think."

"Once again, Laurel Rome is set to screw him over," Opal said. "I hate this."

"Then we should place a shield around his cell, so nobody can get in or out without our knowing," I said. "He's not susceptible to V'ili's obsession, thank goodness, or I'd worry about that, too."

"They're showing him in handcuffs as he's being led to jail; it's all over the news in the States," Opal said. "The foreign outlets are probably picking it up, too. Reporters are doing their best to link him to the terrorist attack in New York."

"Well, that information is coming from somewhere, and you can bet Laurel and her lawyer are in the middle of it," I said. "Tell me, can things get more fucked up than they are already?"

"Have you checked in with anybody in the future?" Opal asked.

"You're about to tell me how things can get more fucked up, aren't you?"

"Jaydevik Rath, in his ultimate wisdom, failed to prosecute a High Demon rapist. The woman is humanoid. Veshtul is on fire after Jayd prevented peaceful demonstrations outside the palace. Oh, and Kory's father, Nedevik, is in the dungeon because he disagreed with Jayd on this."

"Somebody's gotten too big for his Thifilathi britches, hasn't he?"

"Well, this is going to bite him in the ass, unless I'm much mistaken," Opal huffed.

"And it should bite him in the ass. Hell, it should take a generous chunk off when it does," I said.

"Word has it that Glinda had a fight with Jayd over it, and went to Le-Ath Veronis afterward."

"What does Lissa say about this?" I asked.

"She's trying to get Nedevik out of the dungeon, but Jayd isn't listening to anybody except Garde right now."

"Because two narrow minds are better than one?" I suggested.

"Or so he believes. Honestly, that's like following the echo of your own flawed advice."

"Or wrecked logic to the second power."

"Exactly my point," Opal huffed. "Where do you think this is headed, and do you believe we should tell Kory and Lexsi? Nedevik Weth shouldn't be in jail, just like Jamie shouldn't be in jail. I'd prefer to tell them, although Kory will be furious."

"First off, this isn't headed anywhere good. Second, I may have an idea," I said.

"What's that? You have an odd gleam in your eye," Opal said.

"Well, High Demons can't bend time," I said.

"True."

"I can bend time. I can't involve myself in a coup, though."

"Also true."

"Bending time is, in itself, not a crime for a Larentii."

"I'm not sure where this is going, but you have my attention," Opal almost smiled.

Queen's Palace, Le-Ath Veronis

Lissa

"The riots are all over the news, now," Glinda muted her vid-screen when I walked into her suite. I'd come to tell her exactly what she already knew of the events on Kifirin. Except for one minor detail.

Kooper had sent word to Jayd and Garde, telling them that two squadrons of RAA troops were on the way to restore peace in Veshtul.

Jayd politely declined, after Kooper Griff informed him that as a member of the Alliance, Kifirin no longer had a choice in the matter. Jayd hadn't gotten things under control; far from it. In fact, there was growing evidence that many of his troops were causing harm and killing humanoids in their efforts to follow Jayd's orders.

"Jayd is withdrawing Kifirin from the Alliance," I blurted the truth I knew. Ildevar Wyyld had contacted me moments earlier, to deliver the news.

"What?" Glinda was off the bed and on her feet immediately. "He can't do that. He can't."

"It's done. I've informed Garde in mindspeech that he's a jackass, and Jayd's a bigger jackass. They've cut themselves off from the Alliance, and that includes trade and every other perk they get from that membership."

"May the gods be merciful," Glinda dropped her face in her hands.

~

House of Weth, Kifirin

Lady Verarok Weth

At least half my sons had crowded into our home; others waited to hear from their brothers. Wendevik had gone to see my Ned, and brought back news.

But that was before the riots became larger and more deadly. The palace itself was being threatened, although Jayd had stationed High Demon troops around the perimeter. All those troops were armed and in their smaller Thifilathis.

How had things come to this?

"Your father may be in danger, because Jayd has done nothing to calm the people of Veshtul," I announced to my sons. "I worry that none can skip in or out of his cell, too. If a single political enemy decides to take advantage of this situation, Jayd will lay the blame to the riots and your father will be just as dead."

"Mother, we no longer have the Alliance to back us if Jayd convicts any of us of treason," one of my sons spoke.

My youngest, Wardevik. The scholar who was so much like his father.

"Lady Verarok."

I knew that voice. A path parted for him to approach.

Li'Neruh Rath had come.

"I am looking for an army of High Demons," he said. "I will have transport for them and any others from the House of Weth who wish to come. I believe Lord Nedevik may be included in that number," he smiled at me.

"How? When?" I asked. I was desperate, and the god's appearance was like an answered prayer.

"Do not fear, you are safe with me until the time comes," he said.

~

New Zealand Waters

Kordevik

"Good, you're together." Zaria and Opal had found Lexsi and me in a corner of a deserted bar.

We'd been holding onto one another ever since learning that we'd had the same dream the night before.

The one where my father was in the palace dungeon on Kifirin.

"Is there something you need?" I asked. I wanted them to go away so I could deal with my fears while my arms were wrapped around Lexsi.

"We need to get your dad out of the pokey," Zaria said, her fists going to her hips. "But if you want to sit here and feel sorry for yourself, I'll do it without you."

I hauled Lexsi to her feet, while a wild hope made my heart beat in a rapid, irregular rhythm. "We're ready," I stuttered. She'd just confirmed our fears—and given me a possible solution.

I couldn't bend time.

Even the youngest Larentii could do it. Bending time was required, if I were to help my father. "Let's go, then." I blinked as a dimple appeared for barely a second on Zaria's cheek before her smile disappeared. "We have work to do," she added.

~

Opal

My cell phone rang shortly after Zaria disappeared with Lexsi and Kory.

I knew before I reached to answer the thing. Zaria was sending a message from wherever she was.

Someone was about to attack Jamie.

After they'd broken Dervil, Berke and Laurel out of their cells. Without a thought, I grasped Kell's hand and hauled him with me when I folded space.

～

Jamie Rome

Yes, I'd heard the alarms, but I had no idea it meant that Laurel, Dervil and Berke were out of their cells.

Until Berke, wearing my old face, appeared outside my cell. A pistol in his hand was aimed squarely in my direction while he grinned.

Beside him stood Daris Blackmantle, Deris' malevolent witch of a sister.

"Kill him," Daris clapped her hands, as if she were a spoiled child used to getting her way.

"With pleasure," Berke said.

I waited for the pistol to fire, my arms up in a defensive gesture.

That's why I barely saw what came next; Kell and Opal suddenly stood behind Berke, whose fingers dropped the gun as his body toppled, sending his head rolling across the concrete floor at his feet.

Daris had disappeared—probably the moment she realized she could be in danger.

"Now what?" Kell turned to Opal, who wore a thoughtful expression.

As if Berke didn't lie at her feet, his blood spreading across the floor in deep red pools.

"I have a suggestion."

Someone new appeared. Someone I didn't know.

He shone brightly in the dim light outside my cell.

"Can you?" Opal turned to him.

"Of course." He smiled. I thought he was bright already. You'd have thought the sun had paid a visit when he grinned.

The door to my cell swung open. Beside me, a body appeared. It looked exactly like me—except for the bullet holes and the blood.

Berke's body appeared in the cell, too. Somehow, his head was reattached to the body, and his torso was now riddled with bullet holes.

As if there were a struggle for the pistol lying between both bodies.

"Are you going to stay there until the guards arrive, or are you coming with us?" Opal held out a hand.

I scrambled out of my cage as fast as a human can move.

Palace Dungeon, Kifirin

Lexsi

I'd never seen this part of the palace before. Of course I wouldn't. I'd only visited here when I was very small and this would have frightened me.

It frightened me now.

These cages were built to hold High Demons, who were not only powerful, but able to skip away in normal circumstances.

Someone even more powerful had built these cages. Lord Weth sat inside one of them. To me, the walls pulsed with malevolence, as if it were leeching from the floor and spreading upward.

I didn't like it at all.

What would keep it from traveling farther upward and infecting the rest of the palace?

Kory behaved as if he didn't feel it at all.

Zaria, though, wore the deepest frown as we stood outside Lord Nedevik's cell.

"Kordevik?" Lord Weth approached the cell bars to stare at his son.

"Pap, we have to get you out of here," Kory told him.

"Is it that bad outside, that you had to leave what you were doing?" Nedevik asked. "Hello, Lexsi. You look lovely."

"Hi, Pap," I offered a shy smile. I was meeting one of my heroes, and it made me self-conscious.

"She called me Pap," Nedevik grinned at Kory. "I'll give her a hug for that."

"Lexsi, do your misting trick to get him out," Zaria brought me back to the present.

"Oh. Yeah." I went to mist, while Nedevik's eyes widened in surprise. Somehow, the dungeon hadn't been prepared for this and had no defense against my misting talent. In only four heartbeats, I'd gathered Nedevik inside my mist and transported him outside the cell, where I set him gently on the rock floor.

I got my hug immediately.

Before he let me go, however, the dungeon became much more crowded. I almost panicked, thinking we'd been found out by Jayd's troops, but that wasn't the case.

Kory's mother and hundreds of his brothers had arrived.

With Li'Neruh Rath.

～

Zaria

You're going to need them, Li'Neruh Rath said.

I was afraid of that, I returned.

I'm not surprised that you've felt it coming, he said.

I was hoping it wouldn't, but things seldom go how we want them to, I observed.

True.

Where are we going to put them?

Where nobody thinks to look, Li'Neruh shrugged.

While we conversed in silence, Kory, his parents and too many brothers to count crowded around Lexsi, all speaking at the same time. I'd been forced to shield the dungeon, just so they wouldn't be heard and bring the palace guards running.

Tamp and Klancy stood next to me, so I included them in the mindspoken conversation.

I'll send some to Avendor, Li'Neruh went on. *The rest will go with you.*

You know Jayd will charge Lord Weth with treason when he disappears. Along with the rest of his family, I said.

Jayd has forgotten his place, Li'Neruh blew smoke. *What is it Earthlings say about shooting one's self in the foot?*

I get that, all right, I agreed. *Thanks for the help.*

For you, I will move mountains. Li'Neruh disappeared.

Wow. If I needed mountains moved, I could do it myself. However, the sentiment didn't escape me.

He'd offered help.

We might need it.

New Zealand Waters

Opal

"Morwin, I hope you won't mind having a roommate," I said, after knocking on Morwin's cabin door.

"Hello, I'm Jamie, recently deceased. Twice," Jamie held out his hand to Morwin.

I hadn't expected humor so soon after he'd almost been killed, but I laughed anyway. Because it was true and funny at the same time. By all accounts, Jamie Rome was dead and Berke Gillson was also dead.

"Good one," I patted Jamie's shoulder.

"Where's your trunk?" Morwin asked, after standing aside to allow Jamie to walk in.

"He's traveling light. I'll find something," I offered.

"Thanks. This orange shit pisses me off," Jamie mumbled and pulled at the collar of his jumpsuit.

"Don't worry. Get in the shower and I'll be back before you're done," I said and shut the door behind me.

Kordevik

"It's called a cattle station. This was for sale. The Hiboux family just bought it, they merely don't know that yet," Zaria answered my question.

Zaria had set us down in the middle of nowhere, Western Australia, disappeared for ten minutes and then reappeared, telling us that my family was going to stay here.

On five thousand square miles of a *cattle station*.

"Congratulations, Lord Weth, you're a temporary grazier," Zaria handed a wad of keys to my father. "The house and outbuildings are just over that rise," she pointed eastward.

"Do we have cattle, too?"

"Not at the moment. Those went to a different buyer. Make yourselves at home. Send mindspeech if you need something."

"Baby?" I looked at Lexsi, silently asking her if she wanted to stay with my family or go back to the ship.

"Can we visit?" she asked. Lexsi wanted to go back to the ship. She felt overwhelmed by hundreds of brothers-in-law; I could feel it.

"We'll be back," I hugged my father.

"Not to worry—we have settling in to do," he said.

~

V'ili

Laurel was spitting profanity at Daris, for allowing Berke's death.

"It was a fucking vampire, who appeared right behind him and had his head off before I could lay any spell," Daris hissed back.

"Then, instead of killing the fucking vampire, you turned tail and ran." Laurel wasn't done, yet.

"Shut up," I held up a hand and laid obsession on Laurel. "We didn't break you out of prison to attack us over Berke's death. He was worthless to us, anyway. We need someone to fetch, carry and clean. After Deris lays a disguise on you and Dervil, you will serve us willingly."

"Very good," Morgett wandered in. "The news programs are already saying they escaped—except for James Rome and Berke

Gillson, who were found dead in Berke's cell. Too bad they'll never know that their identities were switched."

"I hope you know how to cook," I narrowed my gaze at Laurel. "It won't go well for you if we find you're useless, too."

"I want Deris to burn her," Daris crowed.

"Not yet, my darling girl," Morgett told her. "She will serve us until we tire of her."

"He's ready for you," Deris appeared with Dervil, who now wore a disguise and several burn marks on his body.

"You will serve us," I said to Dervil, although I wanted more than anything to tell Deris to go fuck himself.

CHAPTER 8

Queen's Palace, Le-Ath Veronis
Lissa

"Except for Wendevik and a handful of others, the entire Weth clan has disappeared," I told Glinda. "That includes Nedevik and his wife."

"Where did they go? Has Jayd accused them of treason?" Glinda whispered. She'd gone pale when I delivered the news received from one of Rigo's spies.

"They're safe," I said. "I can't reveal their whereabouts just yet."

"Are my daughters safe?" Glinda's blue eyes held a great deal of concern.

"They've been sent to the Southern Continent, away from the violence in Veshtul."

"I haven't had the courage to send mindspeech." Glinda closed her eyes and sighed. It pained her to make that admission.

"Send mindspeech. Tell them they're welcome here. Husbands, too, unless they want to wage war or kiss Jayd's ass."

"That's the Queen I should have been," Glinda had tears in her eyes when she looked up at me. "I should have stood strong. Stood toe to toe with Jayd and Garde when I thought they were wrong. You see how that turned out. All this time, Veshtul was a powder keg waiting to explode and I had no idea."

"I think the humanoids were tired of being treated like second or third-class citizens," I said.

"Like they treated the comesuli."

"I didn't say that, but it doesn't mean I disagree. Comesuli serve on the Council, here. They have laws specific to them that protect them from vampire predation. We can't go easy on those who violate the laws. Vampires are too strong and can be too dangerous to do otherwise."

"Like High Demons are strong and can be dangerous."

"Yes. Being strong or powerful is one thing. Using those things to harm or take advantage of weaker beings makes you a bully, at the very least. Highly dangerous at the worst."

"I should have come to you in the past." Glinda sighed again. "Perhaps I wouldn't have been set aside by the Saa Thalarr, and be more than I am, now. I chose the easy path. The non-committal one."

"It's not easy to argue with someone day after day," I pointed out. "It will wear you down before you know it. Eventually, you'll just let things go to keep the peace."

"Until the peace is broken by riots and burning."

"Yeah."

"What am I going to do?" Glinda begged.

"Let's think about this," I said. "It's a convoluted mess, and there won't be easy answers."

Larentii Archives

Nefrigar, Chief Archivist

"There's something there—some sort of malevolence. It has echoes of Liron and Acrimus in it," Corinnelar explained.

On the Larentii homeworld, she is Corinnelar. Everywhere else, she is called Zaria. I see her as my daughter in all ways.

"When do you suppose this happened?" Valegar asked.

"Less than thirty years, I think," she replied. "I've gone back forty, and the same thing isn't there."

"Perhaps laid there during the time of Kifirin's death, when none were watching the planet closely?" I guessed.

"They were busy elsewhere," Corinnelar said. "Neck deep in the god wars at the time. Nobody would think of watching the High Demon world during that short time-span."

"So a sickness was planted beneath the dungeons?" Valegar asked.

"It looks that way. I think it has slowly seeped through the palace and affected all those who live there."

"Can it be eliminated?" I asked. "In the opinion of the Vhanaraszh?"

"I think it can be, by *Changing What Was* for the palace and its inhabitants," she appeared thoughtful. "The real damage is already done, though. The humanoids of Kifirin will never again trust the royal house of Rath."

"Understandable," Valegar agreed.

"Papa Neff," Corinnelar turned to me.

"What is it, daughter?" The nickname she'd given me made me smile.

"Is there a copy of the Metal Library in the Archives?"

"No, Daughter. The Metal Library is sentient, alive and constantly changing. We cannot keep such here."

"But if it chose to stay here?"

"That is a different thing. I have my doubts it would choose this."

"I want to ask where it came from," she whispered and dropped her eyes. "But I'm afraid to know the answer."

"There is a tale," I said, reaching out to touch her face gently. "That before all, it was. That it is the parent of all, before the beginning. Within it is dark and light. It holds the story of every creature, including the ones that evolved from others. Or so the tale says."

"Why did it choose Earth, then?" she asked.

"I believe it is because the Three were born there after they chose to be born, so they could fight in the god wars."

"So it could watch over them?"

"I don't think so. I think it was prepared to destroy everything, if the rogues triumphed."

"Nobody knows this, do they?" Corinnelar whispered.

"It is only speculation on my part," I replied. "I cannot verify it."

"I have to digest all this," she said. "Thank you."

"You are welcome, Daughter. Visit me whenever you wish. I hope to have better answers to other questions in the future."

Queen's Palace, Le-Ath Veronis

Lissa

"Would you like tea?" My hands shook as I lifted the delicate teapot to pour Zaria a cup.

"Yeah." She leaned back in her chair and rubbed her forehead. The news she'd brought had infuriated me—that Acrimus and Liron had left a nasty gift behind on Kifirin after Kifirin himself was killed.

Bree brought him back later by *Changing What Was*, but there was a period of time when the planet Kifirin was unguarded.

"So whatever this is has affected those who live in the palace?"

"I believe so. Those who spend a lot of time there—servants and such—have been affected, too. I believe some of them may be leading the charge where the riots are concerned. If I'm right, it exploits your weaknesses and turns them into your faults," Zaria added.

"So Glinda became weaker and less assertive, and Jayd became more controlling and elitist—right along with his older brother, Garde."

"High Demons before humans," Zaria agreed.

"This is so fucked up. Can you fix this?" I sounded as if I were begging, and realized I was. Garde and I had allowed a fissure to develop into a wide crevasse between us. He seldom came to visit nowadays.

Torevik, our son, had gone to stay on Campiaa for the past ten years. He had a cabin in the mountains there, and used it as his primary residence. I'd wondered about that, but failed to consider his reasons for leaving Veshtul behind.

"I can *Change What Was*, but it won't make this whole thing go away," Zaria said. "The humans will still distrust High Demons—at least the ones in power and those who've attacked them. In addition, those humanoids who've committed crimes need to be brought to trial, and given a fair trial, too."

"So there are crimes on both sides?" I wasn't really surprised.

"Yes. Looting, burning, assaults—you name it. The RAA could have shut that down, but Jayd pulled out of the Alliance before that could happen."

"Kifirin is essentially engaged in a civil war right now," Zaria confirmed my thoughts on the matter. "With things the way they are; I'm worried the High Demon unrest will spill onto other worlds."

"Because that's what Acrimus and Liron wanted."

"I'm worried that one of those assholes leaked the information on the Metal Library to the Ra'Ak three centuries ago, too," she said.

"What part can it play in all this?" I asked.

"Trust me, neither of us really wants an answer to that."

"We ask that you wait to *Change What Was*—for another three weeks," Kifirin and Li'Neruh Rath appeared together.

"I can do that—I wasn't intending to do anything about it right away," Zaria nodded to both. Kifirin took the chair next to mine; Li'Neruh chose the one beside Zaria. I poured more tea while Kifirin and Li'Neruh considered what to say to us.

New Zealand Waters

Lexsi

Kory and I stood on an upper deck as we floated through Milford Sound. We'd already gone through two other sounds, but this one was the most beautiful, in my opinion. Nearby, Anita and Watson snapped photographs with their cell phones.

Jamie, who'd wandered onto the deck, sat on a deck chair looking lost. Opal had brought a suitcase filled with clothes from San Rafael for him, so he'd be comfortable, at least.

I had no idea how she and Kell had worked out his presence on the ship, but Jamie now wore a sea pass around his neck so he could eat and drink while on board.

I went to sit beside him.

"I'm a man without a country, now," he sighed as I settled onto a deck chair. "I don't really exist anymore."

I leaned over to read the name on his sea pass; Chuck Kent was printed there. "You've had time to think about this, huh?" I asked.

"Yeah. It hit a few hours ago."

"If you don't want to stay here, Gran will let you live on Le-Ath Veronis."

"Who's your Gran?" he asked.

"The Queen."

"My brother's on Avendor."

"I grew up on Avendor. My mother and uncle live there."

"My mother lives there, too. At SouthStar, last I heard. She looks younger than I do—or at least younger than I used to look."

"My mother and uncle own EastStar, and Mom says everybody at SouthStar grows younger until they get back to their prime."

"Strange. And wonderful, at the same time. Sometimes I dream about gishi fruit," he added.

"Me, too. It's like slices of heaven. Every year, during harvest, I'd almost make myself sick eating so much of it. It costs a fortune, too, and Mom and Uncle Edward never said a thing about how much I gobbled up."

"The privilege of growing it," Jamie smiled for perhaps the first time in days.

"I didn't realize how privileged I was until I went to school on Wyyld," I said. "Gishi fruit in the market during season was so pricey I felt embarrassed to buy it. Some of my classmates certainly couldn't afford it. When I told Mom, she made arrangements to have several crates delivered to the school, courtesy of an anonymous benefactor."

"Did they guess it was your family?"

"No. The school I went to is for children of diplomats, Kings, Queens, Presidents and such, to learn Alliance Policy and Procedure. There, we were known only by our first names, or, if the first name could be recognized, by a nickname. Nobody had a title during those three years. Ildevar Wyyld, Founder of the Reth Alliance, created it so those who'd come to power one day would have a strong foundation to work from, rather than floundering when it was thrown at them unexpectedly."

"How did you get the background to become a reporter, then?"

"We took extensive courses in handling the media," I shrugged. "It came from that."

"That makes sense, I suppose."

"It helped a lot. I guess the media is pretty much the same, no matter where you are."

"I wouldn't know, I've barely been off the planet," Jamie said. "You've made me feel better, though. Like I could have a place somewhere else."

"When I get to go home, you can come with me," I said. "If you want. I think you could start a media dynasty somewhere else."

"It's what I know," he agreed. "Maybe I could get Jayson to help."

"Want something to drink?" Kory now stood beside my chair. I noticed then that the ship was moving toward the open sea, leaving Milford Sound behind.

"I'll get it, if you'll give me your sea passes," Jamie rose and stretched.

Kory and I gasped at the same moment, as if someone had punched each of us in the stomach. Kory was the one to skip us away, though.

The Metal Library was showing us an impending attack on an unsuspecting Australian family.

~

Kordevik

I'd knocked Dervil San Gerxon against a wall and killed him

before I registered who it was. He'd been sent to question this family of little people, after killing two family members who were taller and considered to be normal height.

Laurel Rome was the only one left, and she'd fired at Lexsi before she could turn to mist and gather the family up.

Too bad they'd armed Laurel with a regular pistol; the bullets ricocheted off my black scales as I stalked toward her. She didn't have the sense to drop the weapon and run, although it wouldn't have done her any good.

She squeaked when I lifted her by the throat and allowed her feet to dangle in the air.

Kory, I think I'm hit, Lexsi's voice sounded in my head. *I won't know for sure until I turn back.*

Hang on, baby, I replied, before turning back to Laurel. "Got you out to do their dirty work, didn't they?" I blew smoke in Laurel's face. "Too bad for you, bitch."

Humans are so fragile. I barely squeezed and her neck snapped. This should have happened the first time around, but no matter. She'd live to kill again, if I didn't take her out.

I made sure that wouldn't happen.

Turn back, baby, I coaxed. *They're safe now.*

Lexsi released her charges. I swallowed bile as I rushed toward her. Laurel's bullet had hit her in the chest while she was humanoid. Blood poured from the wound and drenched her clothing as her charges stared in shock.

Zaria, I shouted mentally. *Lexsi's been shot.*

Zaria

Bending time is often the greatest of gifts. There were many things to be done, here, and most would have a difficult time doing them in the allotted amount of time.

I gathered Rose, Morwin, Kell and Klancy and folded space to ten minutes into the past, just as Lexsi was becoming corporeal enough to begin to bleed out.

Light blasted out of me as I dropped to her side to begin the healing process. Laurel Rome, the stupid bitch, had nicked Lexsi's aorta. No, her aim wasn't that good. She'd accidentally hit something vital.

I knew Laurel was dead, too, and felt grateful that Kory had taken care of it so I wouldn't have to.

Something happened during the healing, however.

I felt it.

The Metal Library. It was working with me to save Lexsi. I barely heard Kell and Klancy's voices as they laid the minutest of compulsions on the family. The authorities had been called already, and were on their way.

I'd have to move the rest of us before they arrived.

With the Metal Library's help, I was able to do that.

We even had seconds to spare.

Lexsi

I knew to go to my smaller Thifilatha the moment I landed.

Next time.

Gran always said your mistakes are your best teachers. I'd almost died from that one. That's why I was propped up on pillows in our cabin, while Kory fretted and tried to feed me.

"Honey, I'm full. Honest," I held up a hand as he offered cake.

Zaria had worked a miracle, healing me completely. I felt good, if a bit weak from blood loss after the ordeal. Klancy and Kell had worked miracles, too; the family thought their two dead members had struggled with Laurel and Dervil, killing them before they succumbed to bullet wounds.

I worried that Morgett and his bunch would only look for others to question and kill for them in their quest for the Metal Library.

These could be ordinary, otherwise innocent humans whom V'ili chose to destroy with obsession.

The fucker.

~

Perth

V'ili

Morgett moved us back to Perth after Dervil and Laurel were killed. He was fuming, too, although he hadn't said anything. We'd gotten no information from the targeted family, although two were dead along with Dervil and Laurel.

I watched Morgett pace inside the luxury apartment he'd commandeered; the owner was out of the country on business, which made things convenient for us. A bit of obsession on the neighbors and no questions were asked regarding our presence.

"I saw through Dervil's eyes," Morgett hissed after a while. His eyes were now slitted—his serpent wanted out.

I wanted to ask, but with Morgett this angry, I stayed quiet.

"The High Demons are still alive. They killed Dervil and Laurel. I must seek advice from my Prince."

My mind raced with this new information. How had they known to show up where they did? *Why* had they arrived to protect this family?

My breath caught.

"They have Morwin Quiffilis, I'll lay money on it," I hissed.

Morgett's head jerked in my direction. "My Prince must know of this," he growled. "They are seeking the Library, too." Morgett disappeared.

"High Demons, your weakness for preserving lives will get you killed," I whispered to an empty room.

~

Australian Waters

Lexsi

We were on the way to Melbourne, with two days at sea for me to recover. "I'm thinking about taking Watson to Tasmania, since it wasn't a port of call on this cruise," Anita swished her legs in the hot tub.

I was immersed to my shoulders in hot, swirling water while Anita sat on the deck, with only her legs dangling in the bubbles.

"Take pictures, I want to see it too," I looked up at her. She was focused on something in the distance, looking toward the railing and the waters we sailed past. "You'll have to tell me if the Tasmanian Devil actually looks like the one is the cartoons."

"They don't," Anita replied absently. "Tonight's the full moon, so I have to take Watson somewhere."

"That means the owl family," I drew in a breath.

"I was thinking the same thing. They can fly, so that's a plus, but I think I should talk to Zaria about this and where they can be safe to change and hunt."

"I'm considering that," Zaria appeared and dropped to the deck to dip her legs in the water on my other side. "Mother Rose is speaking to us again, after you and Kory saved so many of this last family."

"None of this is our fault," Anita pointed out quickly.

"I know. It's a natural thing to place blame. That's why you have to think about these things carefully. Morwin had nothing to do with his father's death. The owl family had nothing to do with any of this, either. We're fending off the attacks by Morgett's horde as well as we can, but we don't come out of this unscathed, as you well know," Zaria said.

"Yeah. I just don't like the finger-pointing, sometimes," Anita grumped. "Sirenali aren't all bad. So many people think that, though."

"Stop that," I swatted her leg. "Stop thinking that right now."

"What Lexsi said," Zaria frowned at Anita. "You're not V'ili. You won't ever be that. It gives me an idea, though."

"What's that?" Anita asked.

"Of where to take the owl family—and Watson, if he'd like to go. I strongly suggest you come, too. There's something you should see."

"Then I'll come."

"Good. Be ready to go around seven tonight. Jeans and boots, I think."

"What about me?" I asked. "I feel left out."

"I'll take you sometime later—you need to rest, baby," Zaria smiled down at me. "You'll like it, I promise."

"Darn," I mumbled.

"Just because, I'll bring you and Kory crab from Alaska for dinner tonight—before I take Anita, Watson and the owls," Zaria grinned.

"You will?"

"Sure. We're related, sort of," Zaria was still grinning. "Valegar is Nefrigar's son, and I know you know Papa Neff."

"He's my uncle," I agreed. "You're like a cousin-in-law or something."

"That sounds good enough," Zaria laughed. "After you eat, you have permission to go with Kory to visit his family for a couple of hours. They'll take care of you."

"Okay." I understood what she was saying. High Demons—most of them, anyway, needed to make the change during a full moon. I'd never needed that, but Kory and his family would.

Maybe I'd change with them. I tended to heal faster in that form, anyway.

"Exactly," Zaria patted my shoulder before standing and stretching. "I'm off to run errands," she said and disappeared.

～

Veshtul

Gardevik Rath

"Torevik, you should leave, now," I breathed smoke at my only son. A small voice asked me why, but I shoved it aside. "We arrest Wendevik and levy treason charges, Nedevik will return and face those charges instead."

"Wendevik is innocent, and shouldn't be used as a pawn." Torevik decided to be stubborn about this. "What is wrong with you? And

Jayd? This whole idea is preposterous. All of this," he swept his hand toward Veshtul, where smoke still rose from burning homes and buildings, "All of this is stupid. Because you and Jayd were stupid."

"You're calling the King and his Prime Minister stupid?" I breathed more smoke.

"Because it's the truth," he spat.

Torevik Rath

Get out, I sent. *Go to Le-Ath Veronis now.* I had Dad's attention, so he wouldn't be tempted to try to stop the girls from leaving while I argued with him. Time for Jayd's and my daughters to leave Kifirin behind. They weren't in danger yet, but many of their husbands could be very soon, with Wendevik Weth being first on that list.

Daddy? Sara, my youngest asked.

Baby, go. Your grampa isn't acting like himself.

All right.

We're at your mother's palace, Jhase, Jayd and Glinda's eldest, informed me. *All of us.*

Stay there, I said.

That's when my father's smaller Thifilathi hit me—a blow so hard it threw me against the parapet near the top of the palace. He stalked toward me, anger and insanity in his eyes.

He wanted to kill me.

My father was gone, and this monster was the only thing left. The fury on his face was the last thing I saw before I lost consciousness.

Gardevik Rath

My vision went red as I stalked toward my unconscious son. He'd become a nuisance. Time to eliminate it.

"Garde, take one more step and I'll kill you myself."

Lissa.

She knelt next to Torevik, who stirred and moaned.

"What's going on?" Jayd skipped in. "My daughters have disappeared from the compound on the Southern Continent. You did this," he accused, pointing a finger at Lissa.

"I had nothing to do with it, you fucked up moron," Lissa snapped at him.

Jayd went to his smaller Thifilathi. He and I were like-minded in this—we saw two who should be destroyed.

"Not today." Li'Neruh Rath appeared, also in smaller Thifilathi. I roared a laugh. "Let's kill him, brother," I told Jayd. "He won't interfere again."

"Seriously?"

Someone else had come.

A Larentii.

A *female* Larentii with enormous, white wings. She held up a hand.

"Do it," Li'Neruh nodded.

Lissa disappeared with Torevik.

Jayd and I leapt at the same time. Time for these bothersome flies to die.

∾

Queen's Palace, Le-Ath Veronis
Glinda

"Oh, no." I watched as Lissa laid Torevik's battered body on clean bedding in his suite. Most women couldn't carry a seven-foot High Demon, even if he were in humanoid form.

Lissa, the Vampire Queen, could do it easily.

"He will be fine," Karzac, Lissa's physician mate, appeared and began assessing Tory's injuries. "He has a thick skull," Karzac patted Lissa's arm.

"Mom?" Jhase walked into the suite, followed by my other daughters—well, adopted daughters, at least.

Six of the eight were Torevik's daughters, and he'd done what I

117

wouldn't. He'd gone to confront Gardevik when he and Jayd decided to arrest Wendevik on treason charges.

The girls' husbands crept in behind them, to see Torevik lying on the bed. Garde hadn't been kind when he'd hit his own son.

"Where are Jayd and Garde now?" I whispered to Jhase.

"Oh, they're at the compound on the Southern Continent, wondering how their lives got so fucked up," Zaria appeared with Li'Neruh Rath right behind her. "Unfortunately, I had to pull everybody out of the palace in Veshtul and seal it up. The malignancy at its core is growing exponentially."

"What about Vordevik?" I asked. "He should still be imprisoned."

"Oh, Jayd let that asshat go earlier, and put him in charge of one of the squads keeping the peace in Veshtul. I'm sure you know how that's going."

"May the gods be merciful," I dropped my face in my hands.

"The gods have been merciful," Li'Neruh's voice was flat. "Jayd and Garde should be dead, now, for attempting to attack us. They are not." I dropped my hands to stare at Li'Neruh. Smoke poured from his nostrils as he spoke.

"Mom," Jheri said, her words hesitant, "What's wrong with Daddy?"

"I don't really know, love," I whispered.

Western Australia

Lexsi

The sky was filled with flying High Demons. With so many of them there, it reminded me of bats exiting a cave after dark to look for food.

The vision of their flights against the huge, full moon will always stay with me, I think, because I found it beautiful. Somewhere among them, Kory flew. I think he felt joy at joining his brothers like this.

Lady Verarok and I stayed on the ground, although I'd freed my smaller Thifilatha to take advantage of the accelerated healing it offered.

"I've wished many times that I could change," Vera sighed.

"I think you can, you just haven't needed to," I turned toward her.

"Is that what happened to you?" she asked.

"Yeah. Somebody left a bomb at Anita's home, trying to kill her," I explained. "My Thifilatha recognized it and made the change to protect both of us."

"How does it feel?" She asked.

"It feels normal. Powerful, too. I don't just have this, either," I said. "Thanks to Gran and my mother, I have a few extras, too."

"Your mother and the Queen of Le-Ath Veronis?"

"Yes."

"Isn't it amazing, that you can inherit those things?"

"I think so. I'm grateful for it, anyway, because it has saved Kory and me."

"You saved Nedevik from the dungeon. That makes me more than grateful. The rest of us couldn't have gotten him out, no matter what."

"Do you watch them fly every time?"

"I hardly ever do. I usually stay in the house and read or sew."

"I don't know how to sew," I confessed.

"Dear, you were made for more important things," she smiled.

Revalis

Anita

Zaria looked weary. Whatever her errands were, other than getting crab for Lexsi and Kory, had tired her.

"What is this place?" Jim asked. He and the Hiboux family gazed about them in wonder. An entire forest surrounded us, although I could have sworn that some of the trees were something other than trees.

"They are something other than trees," Zaria sighed. "Some are pod'l-morphs, taking advantage of the full moon."

"They are my kin," Tamp said as he looked upward at branches that swept the sky. "Jim," Tamp turned to the shapeshifter, "This is Revalis, home to my race and those rescued from Sirena, long ago."

I drew in a breath and blinked at Zaria.

You're in the future, she informed me. *Several hundred miles north are the cities belonging to your people. One day, you can live here, too, if you want.*

"Please tell me you're not kidding," I begged.

"Not kidding."

"We can change safely and fly?" Mother Rose asked.

"Yes, with no worries. And hunt, too, if you want. When dawn comes, I will transport everyone back to the ship," Zaria replied.

Clothing emptied as a parliament of southern boobook owls rose from the ground and flew toward high trees. I watched them go with a happy sigh.

CHAPTER 9

elbourne, Australia
Opal

Zaria, dressed only in a bikini, was flat on her back on a deck chair, asleep while her body soaked in sunlight. Valegar, in disguise, sat beside her pretending to read.

"How long was she gone?" I asked, taking the chair next to Val's.

"Several days," he turned a page in the book. He could have peeled the words off the pages and inserted them directly into his mind, but he kept up the pretense anyway.

"No wonder she's exhausted."

"The fools on Kifirin saw to that," Val grumped. It isn't often that you see a grumpy Larentii. It isn't something to trifle with, as they can reduce almost anyone to tiny sparks that disintegrate quickly.

"Will you tell me?"

"The worst are in cages so that more innocents won't die, but some are still rampaging through Veshtul."

"High Demons and humanoids?" I asked.

"Yes, in both instances. Corinnelar had to call in favors so those she imprisoned are fed and cared for."

"Where is this going to end?"

"I cannot say—several paths branch from all the events, there."

"Jayd and Garde?"

"Are attempting to break through the shields placed around the palace. Neither have been or will be successful. Li'Neruh Rath added his shields to Corinnelar's. The Mighty Hand could break them, but most cannot. Certainly no High Demon will do it, even with the help of every other High Demon that exists."

"Where are those two misguided fools staying, then?"

"At the compound where they'd sent Jayd's and Reah's daughters. Those eight, with their husbands, are now on Le-Ath Veronis and under Lissa's protection. I believe Jaydevik doesn't like that at all, but he cannot assail that world or Lissa's palace. I believe Kifirin has temporarily locked it against invading High Demons."

"I wondered what he was doing in all this," I said, letting my head drop against the back of my chair. "What about the humans in Veshtul?"

"Without their affected leadership, many are fleeing to other cities, looking for shelter and protection. I worry that Jayd's High Demon army will attempt to stop them, or cut off deliveries of supplies to anyone who offers them asylum."

"He's insane."

"He and Gardevik attempted to attack Corinnelar and Li'Neruh Rath. Rather than kill them for the attempt, Corinnelar relocated both to the Southern Continent and left them confused long enough to get other things accomplished in Veshtul."

"Is there a reason not to *Change What Was* now?"

"Li'Neruh has requested a stay in the matter. Corinnelar agreed."

"It's his call," I nodded. "High Demons are his concern, as hard a job as that's proven to be."

Mother Rose

My family took up the entire length of an extended table at a small restaurant in Melbourne, not far from the ship's dock. Remnants of food lay on mostly empty plates in front of them.

To me, they looked very much like a sated bunch of owls, so tired from the previous evening they'd not bother to lift their wings if they fell off a branch.

We'd flown on another world. I struggled to convince myself of that reality. The trees we'd landed on—some of them hadn't been trees, but creatures who'd become trees under the full moon.

None minded our presence, opening their branches when we chose to alight there. I felt sheltered while with them.

Safe.

I seldom felt safe—even before Morwin's enemies arrived in Australia.

Not far away, Klancy, Ilya and Tamp ate and talked at another table. They were our guards this day, to ensure our safety.

Of all my brood, only Morwin was still wide awake and asking for a refill of tea. Chloe leaned on his shoulder and was likely asleep. He kept that arm still and accepted tea with the other hand.

I wished for mindspeech, then, so I could tell him he was welcome in the family. He felt right to me, and that was unusual. Most of my granddaughters' dates failed to meet my standards.

With a sigh, I pulled my purse off the chair back and hefted it over a shoulder before grabbing my cane. *Time to wake the brood and travel back to the ship.*

Morwin

While Chloe and her family were gone the night before, I chose to do research. One of the possible locations for the Metal Library was beneath Uluru, a huge, sandstone monolith, sacred to indigenous Australians.

I hoped we'd not get near it; its importance to the first Australians could not be measured by human means. The damage a Ra'Ak and two powerful Karathians could cause to Uluru weighed on my mind.

Please be somewhere else, I begged the Metal Library.

Morgett Blackmantle

"You're sure of this? That there are only two?" The Prince's eyes narrowed as he gazed upon me.

"I can't confirm that," I confessed. "There could be others."

"This has been building for a while," the Prince said. He and I stood beside a very tall window in his current home—one stolen on a world now occupied only by Ra'Ak. The humanoid population had been devoured long ago.

For now, B'Eradonn was a place to stay until it fell further into ruin. After that, a new world would be taken and other homes and buildings occupied until they, too, fell into disrepair. *Ra'Ak do not build, they take.* It was one of the Prince's favorite phrases.

"I will not have the High Demons taking any part of the Library," the Prince came to a swift decision. "It is for us—it was foretold. Take several with you to search and to battle these High Demons should it become necessary. If you find you need more, send mindspeech. I will provide an army if needed."

"As you will it, my Prince." I bowed respectfully while hiding my smile. Everything was falling into my hands. The interference by two High Demons had become a gift rather than a curse.

With enough Ra'Ak under my command, it would be easy to overthrow the Prince.

How ignorant he was.

"Choose your soldiers and inform me of their number," the Prince dismissed me. "Soon, the Library will be ours."

"It will, I swear it," I said and folded space.

Lexsi

Kory and I slept late and went to a small sandwich shop near the pool for an early afternoon meal. "Is there anything to see in Melbourne?" Kory asked as we searched for a small table to eat our food.

"I'm sure there's plenty to see; I just haven't read the stuff they left for us in the cabin," I replied. "This tuna sandwich is pretty good," I mumbled after taking a bite. It was—they hadn't drowned it in mayo, thank goodness.

"We could skip in and out," he suggested while a quarter of his roast beef sandwich disappeared in a single bite. He was hungry after flying with his brothers the night before. His mother and I had spent that time talking.

I was beginning to love the High Demon who'd brought Kory into the world. "Did you have fun last night?" I asked.

"Yeah. I haven't done that in years—we could seldom all get together like that. Flying with Pap was a treat, too. He usually goes out by himself. He says he thinks while he flies."

"Some High Demons just stalk around and don't bother flying," I said, thinking of my own father.

"Pap always said 'why have wings if you're not going to use them?'" Kory grinned at me.

"Yeah. I need more practice with mine."

"When we get done with all this, we'll take time to fly," he said. "I'll teach you how to do barrel rolls and land on targets."

"That sounds like fun."

"I had a blast doing it when I was younger—it's nice to get your feet off the ground."

"I agree," Mother Rose walked up to our table. Kory rose quickly and pulled a chair up for her. "If it weren't so dangerous for me and my brood these days, we'd certainly fly more often. Now, what do you turn into so you can fly?"

She said we'd talk later, Kory looked shame-faced. *Looks like it caught up with me, huh?*

"We could show you," I offered. "But you'll have to go with us for a few."

"Where?" Mother Rose didn't trust easily; I knew that already.

"Want to meet Kory's parents?" I asked brightly. "I'll show you what we can turn into then, because it's a safe place."

"Just bear in mind that Lexsi hasn't had much experience flying," Kory grinned.

"Why is that?" Mother Rose demanded. "My fledglings learned when they were twelve."

"Long story," I said.

"I have time," Mother Rose leaned her cane against the table.

"Well, it isn't often that the females of our race actually turn," Kory said, reaching for my fries. I pushed my plate toward him, so he could get to them easier.

"That sounds wrong," Mother Rose said.

"Well, it isn't often needed," Kory said. "I think you'll understand when you see Lexsi. She's less frightening than I am."

"You're frightening?" One of Rose's eyebrows lifted in speculation.

"Some would think so," Kory grabbed several fries and stuffed them in his mouth.

"He's starving," I said. "He was out all night."

"Sounds like my bunch. They're either eating or asleep the day after a full moon."

"My mother may have something else to eat if we go now," Kory suggested.

"Then let's go."

We found a quiet, deserted corner of the deck and skipped Mother Rose to the cattle station that now housed the majority of Kory's family.

Mother Rose

Both ended up changing after I demanded it. They were right, too —Lexsi was much less frightening. Kory looked as if he could cause real damage. Both wore scales, but his were the blackest black and he wore horns that curved like a ram's around pointed ears.

"Lexsi can be more powerful at times," Zaria appeared at my side as I watched Kory give Lexsi a quick flying lesson.

"They're huge," I mumbled.

"It's how their race was made," Zaria replied. "In the beginning, they were created to protect the dark races and keep them from killing one another. Eventually, that didn't work out so well with some of their ancestors."

"I wondered who was here," someone joined us. He held a cup of tea in his hands as he watched the flights of Lexsi and Kory.

"Lord Nedevik Weth, this is Rose Hiboux," Zaria introduced us.

Nedevik went to one knee and shook my hand with a smile. "An owl?" he asked. "Owls are associated with wisdom on my world."

"As they are here," I agreed. "Although that doesn't keep them from shooting at us from time to time. There aren't many guns allowed in Australia nowadays, but that doesn't mean some won't have weapons."

"I understand that being a shapeshifter in this day and time can be more than dangerous," Nedevik nodded and sipped his tea. "Most unfortunate. Would you like tea?" He asked. "We'd be happy to sit at the table with you and Zaria. We'll leave Kordevik and Lexsirok to their flying lesson."

"Sounds good," I admitted. "I'm still a bit addled after the full moon flight last evening."

"I'll get us there," Zaria offered and we disappeared, only to reappear in a huge kitchen that only an enormous cattle ranch could boast.

I discovered that the large kitchen was needed; Kory's mother was there, sitting with several others around a heavy, wooden table.

"This is Verarok, my wife," Nedevik introduced us. "Vera, this is Rose Hiboux, an owl shapeshifter."

"I'm so pleased to meet you," Vera stood to greet me. "Please, take a seat and I'll find a cup of tea for you and Zaria."

For the next hour or so, I talked and laughed with a family of High Demons. They were people, just like any other. Any fears I had were laid to rest during that conversation, although I already trusted Kory and Lexsi. They'd saved friends, after all, and seemed to have my family's best interests at heart.

~

Zaria

"I like your parents," Rose poked Kory with her cane after I set us down on the ship. I'd taken us to Rose's cabin, where Jim, Sarah and Tim waited.

"I like them too," Kory grinned at her. "It doesn't matter how old he gets; Pap always says that every day has something new."

"How old is he?" Rose asked.

"I'm not for sure. I'm one of his younger sons, and I'm over a thousand years old."

Rose drew in a breath. *His race is immortal*, I informed her.

"I had no idea immortals actually existed," Rose released her breath.

"Larentii are also immortal," Valegar arrived in his smaller form. "I am taking Zaria away for more rest," he said and pulled me away.

~

Lexsi

I was nicely tired after flying with Kory. Mother Rose was content to plan dinner with her son and grandchildren, so Kory and I said good-bye and skipped to our cabin.

"Want to clean up and find dinner?" Kory grinned at me.

"Like your mother didn't just stuff you with an enormous sandwich?" I asked.

"Oh, right. Well, we could fool around, then clean up and find dinner."

Dinner had to be put off; Morgett's bunch attacked another family while I was in the shower.

~

Kordevik

Six Ra'Ak, none of them Morgett, had arrived with Deris Blackmantle to threaten another family. Those images swept through my brain seconds before I skipped Lexsi toward the sheep station home where the endangered family lived.

Pap, send five, I shouted in mindspeech while giving him images of the location. I sent the images I'd received of Ra'Ak, too.

Five of my brothers, already Thifilathi, landed on dry dirt with a thump outside the house just as Lexsi and I arrived.

I'll get the family out, Lexsi turned to mist immediately.

Be careful, I sent. Nodding to my brothers, I waited for the Ra'Ak to discover our presence.

Lexsi

I have them, I sent, although mindspeech wasn't necessary. The moment four family members disappeared in front of their eyes, Deris ran until he could fold space; behind him, humanoid Ra'Ak became giant serpents.

I fled with the family while enormous, fanged and spiked heads burst through the roof of the farmhouse.

Morgett had upped the ante.

Zaria

Valegar and I went, although we weren't needed. I'd never seen High Demons fighting Ra'Ak, which is what they were created to do.

While Ra'Ak poison will kill almost anything else, High Demons are immune to it.

Kory squeezed the life out of one of those horrible serpents while I held my breath. The giant tail whipped about, knocking down what was left of a farmhouse while the serpent struggled to get away.

"Are you shielded, honey?" I turned to Valegar, who smiled at me.

Both of us looked humanoid—no need to taunt V'ili in case he was watching.

"Very well, dearest," he smiled at me.

Kory's opponent grew weaker, then stilled. Half a breath later, that Ra'Ak dusted, blasting dark chunks in all directions. Some of them hit Kory and his brothers, along with two remaining Ra'Ak.

Six High Demons roared and attacked the live Ra'Ak with renewed effort. Lexsi appeared at our side.

"I took the family to the nearest farmhouse," she explained. "They're calling the authorities. They still don't know who attacked them—I pulled them out before anybody changed. Deris, the asshole, was disguised when we got here, but that dropped away fast. The minute he discovered his power was nullified, he ran until he was far enough away from my influence to fold space."

"He's nothing but a coward—both of the twins are," I agreed. That's when the next to last Ra'Ak dusted. Lexsi ducked, although it wasn't necessary. Val's shield covered all of us.

Still, it was frightening to see those chunks heading right for you, only to bounce away, leaving you unharmed.

"What does this mean?" Lexsi blinked at me.

"It means that Morgett knows about you and Kory, so he's attempting to even the odds. He now knows there are seven of you here. He'll call in more reinforcements, unless I'm badly mistaken."

"That doesn't sound good," Lexsi frowned.

"I'm thinking of a plan," I said.

"What's that?"

"A trap," I said. "To catch Ra'Ak. If we're lucky, Morgett will fall into it, too."

"Good."

The three of us watched as one of Kory's brothers dispatched the last Ra'Ak, and barely blinked when he dusted.

"Dearest, we should get rid of any evidence," Val turned to me.

"Okay."

Every chunk of every Ra'Ak disappeared around us. "We'll have to get rid of anything inside the farmhouse that may indicate giant serpents and High Demons," I said.

"I can blow it up," Lexsi offered.

"Do it. A blast will clear away any footprints or snake prints in the yard."

"All right. I hope the family has insurance," Lexsi mumbled before turning to mist.

Val and I *Pulled* the High Demons inside our shield while Lexsi went to work.

~

Australian Waters

Opal

"Fort Largs has some underground rooms and such, but it's near the water," I pointed to the location on a map. "Too close to houses, too, I think."

"What about the Apostles Tunnel?" Zaria asked.

"That's not on any map, and most of it is half-filled with water," I said. "That's what it was built for in the beginning—to get water to the city. Officials don't want it publicized, to keep explorers and the curious away. Because it's dangerous."

"Dangerous is good, and what I'd choose if I were the Library. It's last known location was a volcano, remember? Plus, we can dry the tunnels out," Zaria offered. "It wouldn't be difficult."

"You realize we'll have to set up an elaborate defense system for it, if we continue with this plan?"

"I know. But it's not impossible."

We were discussing laying our trap for Morgett in Adelaide, which was our next stop. We could explore our options there, lay the trap carefully, then tempt Morgett with a fake library's discovery after we were many miles away.

"What about creating a large room off these tunnels—one that is drier and more difficult to approach?" Val offered. "That would be simple to achieve and provide a space suitably large enough to hold the entire Library."

"And we'll need a system of advanced warning, for when Morgett arrives," Zaria said. "I sure don't want to deal with the violent tantrum he'll throw when he discovers it isn't the real library."

"We need to take him out fast, that's for sure," I agreed. "We have three big concerns, however. What if he brings the twins and V'ili with him? We can't go in with all guns blazing if that's the case."

"I know. Look—lay your plans, but give me a little time to work out that big kink," Zaria said. "I'll let you know whether I figure out a way around that event, should it happen."

"Don't take too long—the cruise is winding down and the window is closing. I'm surprised that Morgett hasn't figured out the owl family is aboard the boat, yet."

"I know." Zaria's shoulders sagged. "There's only so many things we can do about that."

"We've seen one ship destroyed in the past," I reminded her.

"Yeah. We lost friends that day. Let's hope we don't see a repeat."

~

Queen's Palace, Le-Ath Veronis
Lissa
Jayd, Garde and their army of High Demons were sealed off from coming to my planet.

That didn't interfere with their mindspeech, however. At first, the messages went to Glinda and the girls. Connegar agreed to stop them from receiving those messages, as they were filled with threats and warnings.

Jayd and Garde had truly gone off the deep end. More than anything, I wanted Zaria or Bree to *Change What Was*, but Li'Neruh was adamant that we wait.

There had to be some reason, but I didn't know what it could be.

That's when those two started sending mindspeech to me.

Yes, I could block them, but in all honesty, the threats were ramping up. Kooper was already on high alert, and several squads of RAA troops had been dispatched, but what good might that do against an army of crazed High Demons?

Their last threat was the worst, and it terrified me.

If you won't send Glinda and our daughters back, Jayd's voice hissed in my mind, *I will see Harifa Edus destroyed.*

Try, I'd hissed back.

I'll give you two eight-days to think it over. If they're returned to Kifirin, I'll hold my High Demons back.

Jaydevik Rath, I snapped at him, *they don't want to come back. If you have any sanity left, you'd know that. Now stop this foolishness while you still have a life to call your own. I hope you recall who saved your ass when your rogue High Demons allied with the Ra'Ak,* I said. *And how easily they died when I attacked them,* I added.

You will refrain from throwing that in my face, Jayd growled. *My High Demons turned the tide that day, not some frail Vampire Queen.*

You really have lost your mind, I said. *In two eight-days, I'll see you on Harifa Edus, you stupid twit. Good luck getting your sense and your wife back.*

"Are you mindspeaking someone?" I blinked as Renée, my third assistant, asked. While I'd been tossing insults at a crazy High Demon, she'd arrived with a comp-vid in her hand.

"I wouldn't call it that," I took the comp-vid from her to read the message it contained.

"What was it, then?"

"I just started a war with Kifirin. The planet, not my mate."

"For real?" Renée's eyes widened in shock.

"For real," I admitted. "Call my Inner Circle together. We have two eight-days to plan for this."

～

Glindarok

I was included in the meeting with Lissa's Inner Circle. What I heard was terrifying. Jayd and Garde wanted to destroy Harifa Edus, because they couldn't get to Le-Ath Veronis.

They knew Harifa Edus was important to Lissa. She'd brought werewolves back to the planet in the past, and they'd built a home, there.

It was also where the remnants of Planet Siriaa's population were placed after their world was destroyed.

Jayd could attack that humanoid population much easier than he could that of the werewolves.

"I'll go back to him," I hung my head. "I don't think he'll mistreat me."

"That's not an option." Li'Neruh Rath appeared. Smoke drifted from his nostrils and arms crossed over his chest as he considered me. "You are the Queen of what's sane on Kifirin," he said. "There are a few of them who are confused and leaderless, as they have abandoned Jayd and his irrational demands."

"Then tell me how to avoid their attacks on Harifa Edus," I stood to address Li'Neruh. "I can't expect Lissa to continue to bail out the High Demon population. This problem is one that should be solved by High Demons."

"Part of the problem wasn't created by High Demons, but it will take Corinnelar or the Mighty Heart to deal with that. I merely worry that there may be no healing sufficient to return your husband and his brother to their former selves." Nefrigar had arrived.

Nefrigar, mate to Reah, Lexsi's mother, and Chief Archivist of the Larentii Archives, had come to give advice. In the eyes of most Larentii, he was just as important as the Larentii Wise Ones, and second only to Kalenegar, Head of their Council.

"Then what can the few of us do who still have any sense left?" I tossed up a hand in frustration.

"You are not alone," Li'Neruh said. "The Weth family will defend Kifirin, should I ask it of them. Perhaps some of Foth and Greth as well."

"And if I ask?"

Li'Neruh's mouth tightened. "Kifirin isn't only High Demons," he said. "From now on, the humanoids and High Demons alike will desire fairness in Kifirin's leadership."

"Instead of what they've been getting." I dropped my eyes. I'd been complacent far too long. Ignored the growing problems far too long. Those worth the effort had lost their faith in the ruling house.

"Jaydevik holds the Kingship through you, Glindarok," Nefrigar said. I jerked my head up at his words. He was right. Without me, Jayd was only a member of the Rath Clan. I was the Royal Daughter of Lendevik Lith. My mate was destined to wear the crown, no matter whom he might be.

"What was your price, Lord Rath?" I turned to him.

He lifted an eyebrow. "It is not time to divulge that secret," he began.

"What if I abdicate my throne? Jayd will no longer be King."

"That will leave Kifirin without leadership," Lissa said, striding toward me. "Glinda, think about this, okay?"

"I am thinking about this. What I'm seeing isn't pretty. Jayd and Garde aren't fit to be in charge right now. Even if they regained their sanity, nobody will ever trust them again. Isn't that right?"

"But if you abdicate, that could mean civil war, until a victor climbs atop the bodies of who knows how many High Demons to claim the throne," Lissa pointed out.

"The House of Lith should remain the Royal House," I insisted. "If I abdicate, it will be in favor of another."

"But," Lissa began.

"No," I held up a hand. "I know Jhase and Jheri have no talent for leadership. Yes, Wendevik Weth could be King, but he needs the strongest of Queens at his side. Therefore, I will choose another daughter of the Lith line, who is also married to the House of Rath. I name Reah as my heir."

"Your abdication is my price," Li'Neruh sighed. "You have arrived at that conclusion before I could present it to you. I will say this, however; take the two eight-days given, and make sure this is your choice before any announcement is made. You may change your mind and deny me in this; it is your choice."

"You promised me children," I sighed. "Must they be with Jaydevik?"

"I will remove his claiming marks, if that is your wish when this is over," Li'Neruh promised. "It is only fitting that I fulfill my part of the bargain."

"That is all I could ask," I replied, although my heart had gone cold. Was Jayd truly beyond saving?

I wanted to weep. I skipped from the meeting before the tears fell.

CHAPTER 10

Queen's Palace, Le-Ath Veronis
Lissa

"Honey, what do you think?" I asked Connegar. He'd come to help relieve the tension in my neck after my Inner Circle meeting.

"Reah is a good choice," he murmured while touching my neck and shoulders with warm fingers. "Nedevik Weth would be the best of advisors, if she chose him. She and Torevik should make him Prime Minister."

"But what if Glinda changes her mind?"

"Your worries are valid, my love. You should ignore them for tonight, so these kinks in your muscles will dissipate."

"What if Jayd doesn't give us two eight-days? He's crazy enough to jump the gun," I complained.

"You can bend time just as easily as I can," he reminded me.

"Yeah."

"Send some of yours to New Fyris, and others to Harifa Edus. They can sound the alarm if needed," Connegar advised.

"I'll get Drake and Drew on that—New Fyris is used to them," I blew out a breath. "Winkler can choose some to go with him to warn the werewolves. We really, really don't need a war with crazy High Demons. What the hell do you think Li'Neruh Rath is waiting for? We need some sense restored to this mess, and Zaria will probably be the one to *Change What Was*."

"There are many possibilities. I would hesitate to speculate on any of them," Connegar replied. "Relax. Stop worrying for the moment, so I can make you feel better."

~

Adelaide, Australia

Zaria

Opal, Kell, Klancy and I waded through a foot of water inside a musty, dank, former water main blasted into rock a century and a half earlier. I'd *Pulled* in high rubber boots for all of us, or this trek would be much worse than it was.

"We could branch a large room off from here," Kell suggested. "It could be elevated so water would be held back at the entrance."

"That's a solid maybe on this location, then," Opal agreed with him.

"I think this is our best bet, but I worry that this will only be a temporary deterrent," I said. "The timeline is still warping—I can feel it. Something can go horribly wrong, I think. I just can't put a finger on what that could be."

Opal shivered at my words. I wanted to shiver, too. Things were happening to make Kory and Lexsi bigger targets than they were already.

Morgett wanted them dead; he'd brought more Ra'Ak to Earth to make that happen.

Soon enough, Jayd and Garde could want them dead, too, as members of Reah's family.

For now, those two High Demons couldn't reach them, as they couldn't bend time. If Lexsi or Kory traveled back to their own time, things could become difficult very fast.

Somewhere in all this, treachery was budding.

Other than the original treachery performed by Acrimus and

Liron, I hadn't discovered the source of this new deceit, yet; it was still forming. Meanwhile, the damage done by High Demons bent on destruction could be enormous.

Be right, Li'Neruh, I sighed mentally.

Call me Hank, he replied with a chuckle.

~

V'ili

Morgett replaced six dead Ra'Ak with thirty more. If there were seven High Demons, he needed at least two Ra'Ak to combat each High Demon. He also wanted more rogue High Demons, and was set to approach Croth and Drith Houses on Kifirin, although they were still angry that some of theirs had been lost in the recent skirmishes.

He'd found it all too easy last time to approach those dissatisfied with the weak leadership of Rorevik Rath.

Promise Drith or Croth compensation or a piece of the rule of Kifirin and they'd lick your feet. Too bad they weren't susceptible to my obsessions. I'd have the entire planet under my thumb otherwise.

Too bad, too, that Morgett was lying to them to get what he wanted—High Demons to fight High Demons. And, since one of those we stood against was female, I didn't hold much hope for her to remain intact if rogues got their claws on her.

The thought made me shiver with pleasure.

~

Veshtul, Kifirin

Jaydevik Rath

Most of my recent days were spent as my Smaller Thifilathi, blowing smoke. Every attempt to skip to Le-Ath Veronis knocked me back, forcing me to relocate to Veshtul.

Garde's attempts to reach Lissa and pinch her neck so she couldn't breathe met with the same results.

"I say we attack Harifa Edus now," Garde's Thifilathi spoke in a guttural voice.

"Think, Brother," I rumbled. "Harifa Edus is important to Lissa, but I wish her well and truly hurt for refusing to return what is ours."

"Hmmph," Garde blew a cloud of gray smoke. "How do you suggest we do that?"

"You're forgetting our heritage, Brother," I said.

"Which heritage?"

"The one where High Demons nullify the power of warlocks and wizards."

He and I sat at a stone table in the palace courtyard, resting after another unsuccessful attempt to break the shields about my palace. Lissa was behind that, too; I'd wager all I had on it.

"What are you talking about?" Garde still hadn't made the connection.

"Has anyone ever successfully assailed Karathia? Lissa's son sits the throne. I say we take him and trade him and his meddling father for what is ours."

My brother's Thifilathi blinked at me as realization dawned. With High Demons at our backs, we could skip straight through the power shields around the Karathian King's palace and kill or take whomever we wanted.

I'd see what Lissa had to say about that, when we held her eldest son ransom. Plus, since we'd already be there, how difficult would it be to raid the treasury? Rumors abounded regarding the wealth hoarded by Karathian royalty.

"When?" A dark gleam appeared in Gardevik's eyes.

"We'll send some to Harifa Edus at the time appointed, to continue the ruse," I grinned, allowing the sharp prick of my fangs to rest against my lower lip. "You and I will lead the bulk of the army against Karathia at the same time."

"You are worthy of the crown," Garde rose and bowed to me.

He and I roared our laughter, which echoed across the empty courtyard.

~

Adelaide, Australia

Morwin

As usual, Chloe and I had discreet guards tailing us as we walked through the Rundle Mall in Adelaide. Near the center, in the wide courtyard separating shops, lay what everyone jokingly referred to as the mall's balls.

Two silver spheres, one atop the other, reflected all who strode past them. Farther along were the bronze pigs, which had actual names. Chloe wanted to see them. I wanted to visit a bookstore. We were resolved to do both.

"Stand there," Chloe shooed me toward the bronze pig that had feet on a trash bin. She wanted my photograph next to the sculpture. I'd decided days ago not to mention how outdated her small mobile phone was by Alliance standards. I smiled as she recorded my image on her phone.

At first I had no idea that the four Ra'Ak landing between shops in the mall weren't looking for me; suddenly Anita and Watson were beside us. Chloe and I were grabbed and folded away from Rundle Mall swiftly, while people left behind us screamed and died in the Ra'Ak feeding frenzy.

~

Lexsi

I screamed Kory's name, although he already had ahold of my hand and was skipping toward Rundle Mall.

Yes, we'd been out sightseeing; thank goodness we were wandering around Fort Largs by ourselves when we received visions from the Library.

Visions of Ra'Ak eating locals and tourists alike. Morgett was setting us up, I think, but we had to do something.

Several of Kory's brothers arrived when we did, all of us Thifilathi or Thifilatha. More Ra'Ak appeared, then, amidst the chaos of running, screaming people.

Then things got worse.

High Demons came.

Rogue High Demons, beating their chests and roaring as Kory, six of his brothers and I stared them down. Between us lay two silver spheres—a sculpture with one sphere stacked atop the other.

A Ra'Ak slithered toward us, the large, abrasive scales on his belly scratching across the brick-lined courtyard between mall shops. Screams faded behind us, although sirens could be heard, rushing in our direction.

I couldn't believe Morgett wanted a standoff where his vile army would be seen by anyone—and recorded for all to see on their inevitable cell phones.

We had seven; they had twelve. Six and six.

Kory must have sent mindspeech—five more brothers arrived in Full Thifilathi. My brain filled with an image from an old western film I'd watched not long after my arrival on Earth.

At the end, there was a standoff between warring factions. Almost like this one.

Lexsi, whatever you do, don't let them see you go to mist, Zaria instructed. *I'll be right there.*

Asking her why would take too much time.

Choose a Ra'Ak, baby, Kory instructed. *You were made to kill them, never forget that.*

I'll send fire if you need it, another voice said. I suppose it would be futile to ask the Library how it could make fire, and I certainly didn't want to argue.

With a roar, Kory leapt past the leading Ra'Ak and knocked down the first rogue High Demon.

Sal and Caylon would be more than disappointed if I didn't put my training to good use; I'd just never had to use it in Thifilatha form against a stupid, giant snake. Following Kory's example, I took off at a run, hefted myself off the brick pavement and kicked down the lead Ra'Ak.

I'm sure he never expected to be sent backward like that, scraping, wriggling and sliding toward the others, some of whom he bowled over before coming to a roaring stop against the spheres.

Another Ra'Ak leapt at me. I delivered a punch between his eyes, just as Caylon taught me to do.

With humanoids.

I learned then that a Ra'Ak's eyes are his weakest point; he writhed and rolled, attempting to see clearly again.

One of Kory's brothers roared as he fought with a rogue High Demon nearby. A Ra'Ak dusted—Kory killed the one I'd kicked against the mall's balls, after destroying the High Demon he'd dealt with first.

While I stomped toward the Ra'Ak I'd punched, another appeared, hooking my left arm with one of the deadly spikes atop his head.

I roared, then, before flinging him away and leaping on him to grasp his throat. Ignoring the pain in my arm, I dug my claws into his scales and squeezed.

"Die, you fucker," I shouted around my Thifilatha's fangs.

His tail swept back and forth as I held on, knocking Kory off his feet. The ground shook when Kory landed, and a rogue High Demon was on him immediately.

I recognized the whoot-whoot sound of a ranos pistol, then, and the High Demon who'd attacked Kory went limp.

I squeezed harder, my claws digging farther past copper scales as the Ra'Ak squealed and thrashed in pain.

Sounds of the ranos pistol came again; something large hit the ground with another loud thump.

That's when my Ra'Ak's eyes glazed and he dusted.

Curling into a ball, I protected my head as large, black chunks blasted in all directions.

Whoot-whoot. Whoot-whoot. Whoot-whoot.

I lifted my head to see Zaria walking beside Morwin, who was shooting the enemy with deadly aim. If a Ra'Ak dusted, Zaria shielded Morwin. Otherwise, she wasn't interfering with his target practice.

I learned then what a deadly shot Morwin was.

Whoot-whoot. The last Ra'Ak dusted, while two of Kory's brothers destroyed the last rogue High Demon.

Morwin watched in satisfaction as that one died, then holstered his pistol.

"Baby?" Kory looked banged up but whole when he came to pull me to my feet.

"I'm okay, just a spike wound," I studied my left forearm, which was bleeding sluggishly. Anyone else would have died from Ra'Ak poison by now. High Demons were immune. I still needed help washing out the wound, though.

"We need to leave; the police are coming," Zaria said. "I'll get rid of the bodies and Ra'Ak dust. Kory, I'll send you a location in mindspeech," she added. "Take the others there and I'll see you in a bit."

Around us, bodies of High Demons disappeared, in addition to every chunk of Ra'Ak dust. I hoped she'd taken care of any images recorded by cameras, too, or all of Australia would know what threatened it.

Not that they shouldn't know, but we didn't need mass panic across the country.

"Let's go, onion," Kory said before skipping us away. We landed in a hotel in Auckland, New Zealand, where Opal and Kell had already reserved rooms for everyone in our group.

Zaria

Morgett was a fool, albeit a dangerous one. What better way to announce the presence of more Ra'Ak allies than to allow them to feed off humans in broad daylight, at one of the most popular destinations in Adelaide?

Anita's mindspeech had reached me the moment she and Watson pulled Morwin and Chloe away from the mall; mindspeech from Ilya and Tamp followed quickly, after they managed to get Rose and the rest of her family out of Adelaide.

We hadn't gone back to the boat; I'd transported all of us to Auckland, New Zealand. I'd determined that Morgett and his idiot Ra'Ak followers had no idea Morwin was in Adelaide, else they'd have zoned in on him immediately rather than stopping for a quick bite, first.

Regardless, Morwin wanted to go back. I'd blinked at him before *Pulling* in a ranos pistol and folding space to Rundle Mall with the Amterean.

Once it was over, I removed every speck of blood, bodies and Ra'Ak dust before separating its particles and sending Kory, Morwin and the others to Auckland. Opal would see to them in the interim; I had something to do.

~

Queen's Palace, Le-Ath Veronis
Jheri Rath

The comesuli gossip. It's what they do best. That's how I found out about what Mom wanted to do. If she abdicated, then Daddy would no longer have a right to the throne.

And to abdicate in favor of Reah?

That was blasphemy, in my opinion. Reah had no more right to the throne than the average High Demon. She wasn't special—just like her mother hadn't been special. Her grandmother, who was humanoid, wasn't anything special, either.

I'd seen Reah with dirt under her fingernails, working like a commoner in the gishi fruit groves. No High Demon female would ever stoop to that. Reah was only a quarter High Demon, anyway, no matter what she could do. Torevik, her mate, was only half High Demon to Reah's quarter-blood.

Jhase and I were pure High Demons. We deserved the throne before anyone else. We were descended from the King and Queen, whereas Reah wasn't. Denevik Lith, Reah's grandfather, had never had any claim to the throne, although he was Mom's only living brother.

I stood on the balcony outside my suite in Lissa's palace. I wanted things to stay as they were, with Daddy on the throne until the day came when he wanted to leave it, instead of being forced to do so.

Then he would choose either me or Jhase to rule, and the proper husband would become King.

Mother was wrong. My sister and I could rule Kifirin easily. Comesuli gossip said her opinion of us as potential rulers was low. I hated her for that.

Daddy, I sent, *tell me where you are. I'm coming home.*

Lissa

I'd sealed High Demons out, not High Demons in. We learned at dinner that evening that Jheri was missing.

She'd waited until just before dinner to inform her twin sister, Jhase, that she'd gone back to Kifirin to fight alongside her father.

To my knowledge, she'd never become Thifilatha and had never had combat training, so I had no idea how she planned to do that.

Jhase was almost inconsolable when she heard from her sister; at least she recognized the foolishness of it. Jheri was eaten with jealousy after she'd heard palace gossip, naming Reah as the next Queen of Kifirin.

I wanted to scream at my entire palace staff over that stupidity.

Gossip and idle rumors could kill; it had happened in the past. Glinda became so pale when she heard of Jheri's defection that she became ill. I had to call Karzac to keep the vomiting under control and place her in a healing sleep.

I could see the concern on Karzac's face, however. He'd delivered Jhase and Jheri. I doubted Jheri had a clue how much danger she was in by skipping back to her father and uncle.

I hoped she wouldn't learn it the hard way.

Targis, Tulgalan

Zaria

"Who's there?" Denevik Lith's voice through the door-com sounded rough. I'd rang his doorbell, so to speak, and he certainly wasn't expecting guests.

"A Larentii is here to see you," I told him.

"Fuck off," he snapped. I waited a few seconds.

"I will be there momentarily," Jusef, his Amterean manservant, answered. I suppose Denevik had a right to be grumpy; his wife, Breszca, had been dead less than a year. She, a natural-born citizen of Tulgalan and humanoid, wasn't immortal.

Denevik, the last living male of the House of Lith, was. For years, he and Breszca had attempted to have a second child together. Those efforts had failed. She was now gone and Denevik had eternity to miss her.

Raedah, Reah's mother, was Denevik and Breszca's only child, and she'd died long ago at the hands of a jealous co-wife. One of Reah's daughters from her first set of twins was named after Raedah.

Jusef opened the door and blinked at me. He started to shut it again; I didn't look like a Larentii. That's when I pulled myself to my full height, my skin becoming the familiar blue of any Larentii.

The door stopped, then opened wider.

Just like Jusef's eyes.

"What the hell are you doing, Jusef?" Denevik demanded as he walked up behind the dwarf. He stopped short when he caught sight of what stood outside his door.

"Hello, Denevik," I said. "I told you I was Larentii."

Auckland, New Zealand

Lexsi

"I'm not as good at this as Zaria," Opal frowned at the wound in my arm. At least it was clean, now, and not seeping blood.

Kory hovered, making sure I was taken care of, although Opal and

I attempted to shoo him away. He needed food and rest after taking on Morgett's horde.

Some of the attack had been recorded; I figured Zaria left the first part of the recordings there in order to explain missing people who'd become Ra'Ak dinner. The rest had gone fuzzy and then blank, just before our arrival.

Australians, understandably, were in a panic, as news stations everywhere picked up the images and broadcast them to waiting audiences.

Opal had power; I was beginning to understand how much as she sealed the wound, leaving a dark-pink pucker behind. "Zaria will fix the rest," Opal sighed and leaned away to examine her work.

"It looks fine," I shrugged off her concern. "I'm just worried about panicky people right now."

"I know. Zaria may have allowed those images to remain," she said. "I may know why, too. I guess we'll find out for sure soon."

"Why?" I couldn't help asking.

"You'll see," Opal brushed off my question. "Wherever she is right now, she's making plans to save all our asses, because I have to tell you, with what's going on here and on Kifirin, things aren't looking so good."

"What's happening on Kifirin?" I whispered, catching Opal's hand as she turned away.

"I can't tell you, sweetheart," she said. "It's too much. Concentrate on what we have to deal with here, all right?"

Campiaa

Teeg San Gerxon

Tybus and I sat in my office, studying the two who sat across from us. I knew Denevik—from years earlier. Hadn't seen much of Reah's grandfather since then, but knew he lived on Tulgalan with his humanoid wife.

Until recently, when she'd died.

Tybus was more patient that I—it was one of the major differences between us, although we looked like identical twins. Between us, we kept the Campiaan Alliance on a steady, even keel, although only a few knew that there were two of us instead of one.

"Tell me," Tybus asked, steepling his fingers.

"Well, you know Kifirin recently pulled out of the Reth Alliance," Zaria began.

"We know that," I replied. "What does that have to do with the Campiaan Alliance?"

"If you want your Alliance to remain intact," Denevik blew smoke in our direction, "then I suggest you listen carefully to what Zaria has to say."

~

Southern Continent, Kifirin

Jheri

I'd called myself a fool—dozens of times. All I could do was sit and weep inside my prison; my own father had placed me there after Uncle Garde shot something into the back of my neck.

It hurt.

He'd complained, too, that they only had three of the devices and no way to get more of them.

I couldn't skip away or send mindspeech—the device was preventing it. I had no defense against the two High Demons that I no longer recognized.

When I heard them talking about killing Rylend Morphis, the King of Karathia, rather than taking him hostage, I realized what my words to my father had brought about. They were going to murder somebody who'd had nothing to do with any of this, merely to get back at my mother and Queen Lissa.

Mom, I struggled to send mindspeech again for perhaps the hundredth time. *I'm sorry. Tell Ry to watch out, Daddy wants to kill him.*

Like before, the message only rattled inside my skull before dissipating.

Food was shoved under the door on a dirty plate—the servants were either dead or had deserted. I didn't blame them; I wanted to do the same. Anything to get me away from these two, because they'd gone crazy. Nothing was normal about them, now.

When they'd discussed which High Demon to pass me off to; they'd levied a death sentence against my husband, calling him a deserter. I'd wedged myself into a corner afterward and wept.

Tears were still falling when Uncle Denevik appeared inside my cell, accompanied by Teeg San Gerxon, although I knew him as Gavril Montegue.

"Let's get you out of here, baby," Denevik crooned as he lifted me off the floor. "I'll have someone remove that shit from your neck, don't you worry."

~

Campiaa

Zaria

"Did he say how many of these he had?" I asked as light formed around my fingers and I *Pulled* the controller painlessly from Jheri's neck.

"They said three," Jheri brushed tears away before staring at the tiny controller in my hand.

I sent its sparks flying while she watched.

"I hope you know why Reah was Li'Neruh Rath's choice for Queen," I told her, my voice stern.

"He chose her?"

"He did, and your mother recognized the sense in it. Know how often Reah saved the Reth Alliance? Do you know how her daughter, Lexsi spent her afternoon?"

"No." I could still see tendrils of jealousy in Jheri's eyes as she answered.

"Reah saved the Alliance too many times to count. As you know, she can become Thifilatha. Her youngest, Lexsi, fought and killed

Copper Ra'Ak—as Thifilatha," I replied. "I can provide images, if you'd like."

Jheri's eyes widened. "She can change? I thought only Mom and Reah," she sputtered.

"Reah and Lexsi have risked their lives to save others—and to save the timeline," I lectured. "Have you done any of those things?"

"No." Her voice was so soft I almost didn't hear it.

"Little girl, Zaria told us where you were and sent Teeg and me after you, because she knew you'd be raped if we didn't come for you. You've stirred up a hornet's nest with your father and uncle, though."

"I know," Jheri confessed. "I'm so sorry, Uncle Denny."

"Don't cry, baby, that's over," Denevik pulled her to his chest and kissed the top of her head. "Uncle Denny's here," he soothed.

"What shall we do about Karathia?" Tybus' voice was soft as he pulled me away. We left Denevik behind to comfort his niece while Tybus and I walked away to discuss the future in Teeg's private study.

"I sent mindspeech to Mom," Teeg said as I took a seat. "She's telling Glinda now that Jheri has been rescued."

"Good," I said and leaned back in the offered chair.

"How do we protect my brother?" Teeg asked immediately.

"Well, it will depend on whether I can approach allies in the past," I said. "I may have to convince someone before I can ask them to help, too," I grumped.

"Who will you have to convince?" Tybus wanted to know.

"One of the Powers That Be," I closed my eyes with weariness. "But what I really want to do is punch him in the mouth."

~

Kent, England—Earth

Kiarra

"Franklin, Jeffrey, what are these wet swimsuits doing in the middle of the floor?" I demanded.

They'd come straight from the pool, left their swimsuits to soak the carpet in their bedroom and headed into the shower before coming downstairs for dinner.

The television was on in their shared bedroom, too, blaring far too loud for my taste. "We bring you breaking news from Adelaide, Australia," the evening program was interrupted by a journalist.

I turned swiftly, intending to turn the set off. My hand froze as I reached for the remote tossed carelessly on the end of Franklin's bed. Images of Ra'Ak and High Demons slithered and strode along a wide, brick walkway at a popular mall in Adelaide. One of the Ra'Ak snatched up a fleeing human, gulping the man down like an afternoon snack.

My breath had caught in my throat; in seconds I'd sent screaming mindspeech to Adam, Merrill, Pheligar and anyone else who might be listening.

<h1 style="text-align:center">CHAPTER 11</h1>

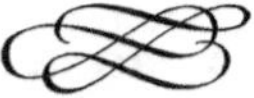

"She told you that? Are you sure it's true?" Glinda's blue eyes begged me to say it was a lie. Zaria wasn't lying about this—I knew it in my gut. Garde and Jayd had not only shot a controller into her neck, but had discussed giving her away to another High Demon.

I wanted to kill him for the controller alone. I knew what damage it had done to Torevik. Somehow, Jayd had kept three he'd found somewhere, and still had two of them, if Jheri were correct.

She'd witnessed the terrifying truth of what her father had become, too, and we'd done our best to keep that from her and the other girls.

They knew, now. Gavril had come after his meeting with Zaria was over. What he had to tell me wasn't pretty, either. Jheri was now asleep in one of Gavril's guest suites, while Tybus and a multitude of guards watched over her.

Her husband would go with Gavril when he returned to Campiaa. Jhase and Wendevik were set to go with him, too.

I considered sending all the girls to Avendor, but that would be their decision. *After* they discussed it with Glinda.

I contacted Reah, too, although Gavril had already done so. Her daughters were caught up in this mess, whether they still considered her their mother or not.

I fumed, too, over Jheri's mindspeech to Jhase before skipping to Kifirin. She'd belittled Reah, when Reah had saved Kifirin. Dirt under her nails? I ground my teeth about that.

Maybe those girls should help with Reah and Edward's next harvest, then be forced to study the economics of Kifirin—before and after money from Reah's groves started coming in.

If Jheri had no idea who'd actually fed and clothed her at the time, then she needed to update her lessons.

Back then, Kifirin was on the brink of bankruptcy, and King Daddy Jayd had taken the lion's share of the gishi fruit profits to refill the treasury and pay off planetary debt.

"Calm down, your eyes are red," Zaria appeared beside me.

She looked exhausted.

"Come with me," I said.

"Huh?"

"You're going to eat while you sit in sunlight, and then you're going to sleep for a while. Don't make me call Valegar or Kalenegar, because I will."

"Fine. Lead the way."

Kent, England

Adam Chessman

Kiarra sent mindspeech to Thorsten. As yet, he hadn't answered. Pheligar came, though, and was just as puzzled by the appearance of Ra'Ak as the rest of us.

Usually, the Larentii knew before anyone else that Ra'Ak had invaded the planet. These arrived with no warning to anyone.

How had we been blinded to this?

Somehow, too, all traces of these Ra'Ak and the High Demons accompanying them had disappeared.

That spelled power to me.

Much power.

Perhaps more than Thorsten held. Kiarra had *Looked*, then informed us that the attacking Ra'Ak and High Demons had been killed.

She hadn't said how or why, and I wondered at that, too.

A handful of Saa Thalarr were currently on assignment. Two were recovering from Ra'Ak poison from recent assignments. The rest could be reached and brought in if Kiarra found it necessary, although she was generally required to discuss things with Thorsten, first.

"Thorsten will not be joining us," Belen appeared in a flash of light.

Here was Thorsten's superior, and I blinked at the brightness he brought with him.

"Belen?" Kiarra stood to greet him. "Why isn't Thorsten answering?"

"Because," Belen smiled and I'd never seen him do that, "My mate wants to punch him in the mouth."

I had no idea that Belen had a mate, but I wished to befriend anyone who wanted to punch Thorsten.

"You will meet her," Belen turned toward me as his smile widened. "She will be most happy to call you a friend."

Auckland, New Zealand

Kordevik

"The rest of the cruise has been cancelled, and the cruise line is attempting to get the passengers sent home as quickly as possible after the debacle in Adelaide," Opal informed me. "I've been in contact with Colonel Hunter back home; they're beefing up border security, but I've told him he probably doesn't need to worry at the moment, since Morgett has focused on Australia."

Lexsi was asleep in the adjoining hotel room; I'd closed the connecting door so Opal and I could talk without disturbing her.

She'd fallen asleep on my shoulder the moment we finished a take-out dinner.

"Wanna bet Morgett has more Ra'Ak and High Demons waiting in the wings?" I breathed smoke as I said the words.

"Not taking that bet; every time we show up, he brings more. I worry that outright war is brewing, with Australia as the killing ground."

"It pisses me off that Morgett doesn't show up himself. I want to squeeze his throat until he dusts," I growled.

"He's a coward at heart," Opal said. "So far, everything he's sent against you has died. He has no desire to take you on unless he has the upper hand."

"You think he has enough Ra'Ak and rogue High Demons to take on my brothers and me?"

"I don't have an answer for that," Opal said. "I wish I did."

"I wish I could go back and watch Morwin shooting the enemy," I sighed. "Ranos pistols will even kill High Demons, if you're close enough."

"Zaria may be able to replay the images for you," Opal said. "For now, you ought to rest. It's been a long day."

"Yeah. I'll go lie down with Lexsi."

⌁

Queen's Palace, Le-Ath Veronis
Li'Neruh Rath
I had one destination in mind, and that was the suite where Zaria slept. I appeared right outside her door and prepared to slip inside.

"Not so fast," a hand dropped on my shoulder. Yes, I recognized the voice.

Wisdom.

Why was he here?

I turned to look at him. "That's my daughter, sleeping in there," he frowned at me. "She's imagined all this time that she's an orphan. She isn't. I just couldn't interfere—more than I have, anyway."

"What she's done she's done on her own, I know that much," I allowed smoke to emanate from my nostrils.

"You know everything about her background? The captivity at the hands of terrorists, the torture, deaths and everything?"

"I know."

"What does Breanne say?"

"Breanne said she recognizes love when she sees it. No harm will ever come to Zaria through me. Besides, I have no desire to form an enmity with the entire Larentii race."

"You should have no desire to form an enmity with *me*."

"You think you know me so well," I blew more smoke.

"I'm more than aware of your background. We both love Breanne, never forget that."

"What the hell is going on out here?" Zaria flung the door open. She blinked as she looked from me to Wisdom.

"Holy, fucking hell." She sat down hard on the floor and covered her face with both hands.

∼

Lissa

Charles, AKA Wisdom, sat at the kitchen island drinking tea while I stared at him. Next to him and frowning deeply, sat Li'Neruh Rath.

"So Zaria threw both of you out and disappeared?" I lifted an eyebrow at Charles.

"She's my daughter, all right," Charles rubbed his forehead.

"Well, that explains a lot," I snapped at him. "The least you could do was leave her alone and let her sleep," I turned on Li'Neruh Rath.

I'd placed a shield around the three of us so the comesuli working in the kitchen wouldn't hear what was being said. Their gossip had already caused enough trouble, thank you very much.

"I didn't intend to disturb her—I merely wished to check on her," Li'Neruh blew smoke. "When she recovered from the initial shock of finding us outside her door, she disappeared."

"She went to Valegar in the Archives," Charles blew out a sigh. "I think he has her in a healing sleep after we upset her."

"Good." I slapped a hand on the granite counter. "She'll have to bend time the minute she wakes to go back to Earth," I scolded. "I've had mindspeech from Belen, you know."

"We know," Li'Neruh and Charles said simultaneously.

"Hmmph." I wasn't particularly pleased with Li'Neruh and he knew that. He was the one advising Zaria to wait before *Changing What Was* for Kifirin, and that had resulted in death threats against my eldest son.

It also made it more difficult for Jayd and Garde to turn things around—if that were even possible.

Glinda was going from depression to anger and then back again—especially after Jheri's experiences with her deranged father.

"She's going to ask you to remove the claiming marks," I said, confusing my companions.

"Glinda?" Li'Neruh made the connection.

"Yeah."

Li'Neruh shrugged.

"Understandable," Charles nodded. "And I know you're seeing a correlation between me as Zaria's father and Griffin as your father. Trust me, I have watched her carefully throughout her lives. Yes, she's been banged up a few times, but not like you have."

"Yeah." I dropped my eyes to the granite island and studied the gold flecks in polished stone.

"Lissa, you've always carried the universes on your shoulders. Zaria is here to help." Charles tucked hair behind my ear and smiled when I lifted my eyes. "Griffin may never fully realize the damage he caused. That's his burden to carry. Free yourself from that entanglement and be happy."

He was right. I felt as if I'd finally sloughed off a heavy coat worn during a hot summer as I gazed into his eyes—eyes that were suddenly filled with stars. Griffin became smaller and smaller in my mind, until he was relegated to a far corner that I could shut out if I wanted.

I did.

The worlds would go on, and Griffin held no place of importance in any of it.

I blinked when Charles' eyes returned to normal. I breathed. The air smelled fresh. Clean.

Untainted.

"Things will work out," Charles smiled. "Even if Zaria decides to chew my ass."

"Good, because it's about damn time things worked out."

King's Palace, Karathia

Rylend Morphis

Reah, my mate, had come. Edward, a co-mate, and Denevik, her grandfather, had come with her. I followed both as we walked through the palace, studying its structure.

Yes, it was built of stone.

And Power.

Every ruler who'd sat Karathia's throne had added his shields and moorings to it, to ensure its stability and longevity.

An army of High Demons could unravel all that in minutes, if they were so minded. That meant if they wanted the walls down, they could accomplish that easily, by disabling every spell ever placed on them.

I'd gotten mindspeech from Gavril and Tory, too, offering their help if I needed it. At this point, I had no idea what I'd need.

I did learn something from Denevik, however.

"When we went to rescue Jheri, a duplicate appeared in her place before we left. Zaria, I believe, wants her father and uncle to believe she's still there. I've never seen a duplicate so lifelike during my existence."

"They could change their plans if they believe Jheri has escaped," Reah pointed out.

"You're right," I agreed. "We don't need to hunt their next target, if they change their minds about Karathia."

"I never thought we'd be fighting the basest weaknesses of High Demons." A curl of smoke drifted from Denevik's nostrils. "It troubles me that those weaknesses are there and so easily exploited."

"I believe Aldavik Foth has pulled his sons away from Veshtul," Reah said. "He wants no part of this, and I'm worried about him and his family."

"Most of them live in the north already, and few were in Veshtul, or so it was the last time I was there," Denevik said. "I hope Jayd will not notice their disappearances; he had enough High Demons following his every whim, because they have hate and prejudice in their hearts and his actions feed their hidden desires."

"Zaria pulled away those who've committed murder already—humanoid and High Demon," Reah nodded. "I doubt Jayd misses them; he still has quite a crowd following."

"So, a rational discussion with any of them is out of the question?" I joked.

"There's no rationality left," Denevik snorted. "You'd have better luck convincing a lump of rock."

"You've skipped in and out, haven't you, Grampa?" Reah frowned at Denevik.

"I have. I went to Veshtul and that place is a powder keg. The humanoids there are terrified, the High Demons unreasonable," he explained. "All the roads in and out of the city are now closed and guarded, so any humanoids wishing to leave are prevented at best or jailed at worst. High Demons are demanding food, goods and anything else they want from shop owners and refuse to pay for any of it, as if the humanoids are their slaves and have no rights at all."

"I curse Acrimus and Liron for starting this," Reah huffed.

"Granddaughter, they merely released what has been hiding in many hearts for a very long time. Remember, many of these were alive when my brothers killed my parents and took the throne for themselves for a short while. Many either stood by and did nothing or condoned the takeover. Gardevik did nothing to stop it; Jaydevik was away from Kifirin and didn't bother to come back for a very long time. I couldn't prevent the deaths of my parents, and thought Glindarok dead. I was forced to skip away after arguing and fighting with my brothers and almost dying for my words and actions."

"We know the Ra'Ak were involved in that coup, by spreading poison in waiting ears," Reah sighed. "Although that wasn't known for a very long time. Rorevik, after your brothers mistreated High Demons during their rule, claimed the throne belonged to the House of Rath, since Jaydevik was chosen as Glinda's mate and future king. He rallied those behind him that he could muster—Gardevik was one of them—and retook the throne at a great cost. We all know how weak his rule was."

"Yes. He and Jayd pronounced a death sentence against any male from the House of Lith. I was in hiding for a long time."

"And things come full circle," Reah observed. "Let's hope for the best in this."

"The best would be moving this palace and setting up a duplicate in its place," I rumbled, gazing about me at the richly-decorated walls.

"We can do that," Edward said, speaking for the first time. "Why didn't you say that to begin with?"

"I think I saw that in a vid once," Reah giggled. "It was funny."

"I hope High Demons have a sense of humor, then," I said.

"Don't count on it," Denevik replied.

Auckland, New Zealand

Mother Rose

"Susan?" I answered the call on my cell phone. Susan was a shapeshifting neighbor, although not an owl.

She was a hen. Yes, that made for interesting full moons for her, as she wouldn't dare go outside during the shift; too many predators could harm her. She was forced to stay inside, lay down puppy pads and cluck around the house.

"I just heard that your cruise was canceled," she said.

"Yes. We're currently out of the country, though. Are you safe?" I thought to ask. It was a valid question—those evil creatures could show up anywhere, if they could show up at a mall in Adelaide.

"I'm fine," she reassured me. "I just wanted to check on you, since I hadn't heard anything after the attack in Adelaide. When I saw your cruise ship on the news, I had to call."

"We're all fine; we have friends with us and we're good for now," I told her.

"Did you see those things?" she asked. "They're enormous and terrifying."

"We saw them, but managed to get away," I said. "Stop worrying, all right? I'm more concerned about you than us right now."

"You don't think they'll come anywhere near Alice Springs, do you?"

"I can't honestly answer that—I have no idea what those things will do."

"Everybody's trying to leave the country, and nobody knows where to go," Susan said. "It's giving me the willies."

"If I hear anything, I'll call," I said. "Be careful."

"I will."

She ended the call. I dropped my cell phone into my purse with a sigh. We'd already lost friends to those monsters. I wasn't in the mood to lose more.

"Want breakfast, Gran?" Tim, Jim's eldest, poked his head in the door. "We're about to go downstairs to the restaurant."

"Yes," I said. "Let me get my cane."

Lexsi

My poached eggs were too runny instead of being overcooked, like most restaurants served them. I dropped my fork with a frown. They tasted like vinegar, too, and I hated that.

"Send them back," Opal said softly.

"Only if I get to cook them," I said. "I'll make do with bacon and toast."

"I've missed your cooking," Watson told me from across the table. "Food on the ship was good, but this," he stared at the ham on his plate and shook his head.

"It's not a five-star hotel," Opal said. I didn't miss the wistfulness in her voice, either. "It was the best we could find with the number of rooms we needed. They worked around check-in time, too, to get us in here."

"Then let's order lunch in, or go out," Watson said.

"I'll second that," Klancy agreed. "I hope Zaria comes back to join us by then."

"Zaria is here, and is about to move all of you to Kent, in England," Zaria appeared at the table. "You'll be safe there, I assure you."

Kent, England

Adam Chessman

I'd never been so shocked in my life. Belen's mate, Zaria, was Larentii, and there were no female Larentii.

None.

"I'm from the future," she nodded to me. "This is a secret you'll have to keep, I'm sorry to say."

Pheligar, the bastard, had the temerity to look smug.

He's my uncle by marriage, Zaria sent mindspeech to me. How the hell did she know what I was thinking? My thoughts were heavily shielded.

"You cannot hide anything from the Vhanaraszh," Pheligar said after seeing my frown. "She is mated to my nephew," he added.

"What do you need from us?" Kiarra asked, ending the verbal battle between the Larentii and me before it could get started.

"I need a place for a small crowd to stay," she said. "And your help in destroying what could turn into an army of Ra'Ak and rogue High Demons."

"We have plenty of space, either here or at Merrill's old place not far away," Kiarra offered. "I'll call in some of the others, too, so we can hold a meeting. I want to hear all about these rogues and Ra'Ak, and how they've managed to elude my detection up to now."

"I can help with that," Zaria said. "Give me a few minutes and I'll be back with the others."

 ❧

Morwin

Zaria allowed me to keep the ranos pistol, and provided a second one in case it was needed. Both were packed with my gear when she landed us in an enormous room inside a very large home.

"This is Adam Chessman's ancestral home," Zaria announced as we looked about us in wonder. The floors were marble; the walls were richly decorated with valuable paintings.

"Welcome to Gryphon Manor," two men, a woman and a Larentii appeared inside the room. "I'm Adam Chessman," one of the men introduced himself. "This is Kiarra," he indicated the woman, "Merrill," he nodded toward the other man, "and of course, Pheligar."

"We've allocated suites for all of you," Kiarra announced. "There is an indoor swimming pool and hot tub on the premises, a fully-stocked kitchen and laundry facilities. If you need anything, just let one of us know."

"Settle in first," Opal said. "Meet us here in an hour, and we'll get to work on a plan."

 ❧

"Who are they?" Chloe's hand was held firmly in mine as we walked up a second flight of stairs.

"No idea," I confessed. Zaria and Opal trusted these people, and they had a Larentii with them, who knew Zaria. "I don't think Larentii associate with anyone who isn't trustworthy," I added.

"I'm having nightmares about those monsters. Did you really kill some of them?"

"Dearest, a ranos pistol will kill just about anything, even the large and powerful, if you can get close enough. I was doing my duty and yes, I killed several."

"I love you," she leaned against me. I smiled all the way up a third flight of stairs.

~

Zaria

"I'm concerned that this Ra'Ak is hiding behind a Sirenali," Kiarra paced. "This means he could be anywhere. You say this Ra'Ak actually recalls his name? Few are capable of that," she added.

"Welcome to twisting timelines," I said. I sat in her kitchen with Opal, Kell, Klancy, Tamp and Ilya, while the others settled into their rooms upstairs. "It's like a game show, with the worst outcomes possible if you lose."

"What is your biggest fear?" Pheligar asked. He, Adam and Merrill sat across the kitchen island from my bunch.

"That the rogue gods may show up," I whispered. I'd carried that fear with me for a while; in the here and now, they still lived. That included Acrimus and Liron, two of the worst, in my opinion.

As for the General, I didn't even want to say his name aloud.

Kiarra stopped her pacing when I said rogue gods. She and I—she had no idea that we were connected.

"Conner's on her way," Kiarra announced.

Another one I was connected to.

Family.

I'd only discovered that recently.

We three—we had the same father. Eventually, I'd have a conversation with said father.

Just not now—I had things to do.

One of those things was setting up a fake library, to steer Morgett away from Uluru. More and more, I was convinced the Metal Library had relocated there.

Nefrigar's words regarding it made me shiver. What if it *could* destroy everything? Did the rogue gods want that, if that's what its intentions were? I imagined they wanted to keep their lives—they'd certainly fought for them at the end of the god wars.

The debacle on Kifirin, too, weighed on my mind. What did Li'Neruh have planned? So many possible trails led away from that, and none of them sounded good to me.

Jayd knew Glinda wanted Reah on the throne. That concerned me —that the announcement had been made and then Jheri had carried the news straight to her father. Yes, it was a mistake, but I couldn't ignore the jealousy and pettiness leading to that revelation.

At lease we'd saved Jheri from rape and who knew what else.

Fucking Jayd with fucking controllers. Nobody should have that shit. Nobody.

Fuck him. Fuck him royally for doing that—to his own daughter.

I blinked, drawing away from my thoughts. Conner had arrived.

"You want to build a duplicate of the Metal Library and lure the enemy in?" Merrill asked.

"Yes. This is Morgett's goal, to find it and take it. While I doubt the real thing would ever allow that, it knew to protect the timeline when it relocated last time."

"Zaria, you're saying that keeping V'ili and the Blackmantle twins alive is crucial to the future?" Adam asked.

"Unfortunate but true," I said, allowing my shoulders to slump. The hour was almost up and there were still questions to answer. Soon, the others would troop downstairs and we'd have to filter our conversation.

Kory and Lexsi didn't need to hear some of it, even, and I felt sad about that. I could tell them everything in the future, just not now.

"Uncle, Corinnelar and I will recreate the Metal Library," Valegar appeared and dipped his head respectfully to Pheligar.

"So you do have a proper Larentii name," Conner's dimple appeared as she smiled.

"Yeah," I sighed.

~

Queen's Palace, Le-Ath Veronis

Lissa

"Martin, Weldon and I will take care of things on Harifa Edus," Winkler promised before leaning in to kiss me. "Don't worry, we'll let you know if things get out of hand."

"Good," I said as he pulled away and grinned. Drake, Drew, Dragon and Crane had already left for New Fyris, after saying much the same thing.

"Kooper has troops ready to go; all you have to do is send the message," I said, touching Winkler's mouth. He has a nice mouth. He gives great kisses, too.

"Armed with ranos technology?"

"You know it."

"Good. Keep me posted on Karathia."

"I will."

After he hefted a duffle over his shoulder, my werewolf mate disappeared. I couldn't help thinking that all this shouldn't have been necessary.

"Sometimes, even the immortal ones need to start over," Thurlow appeared at my side.

He would know; he'd been sent back to the beginning to learn what he should have known the first time around.

"You know, in the hidden parts of your mind, that there have been no new High Demons born since Lexsi's birth, and before Glinda's and Reah's other daughters, there hadn't been new ones for several hundred years," Thurlow explained. "The last male born was to

Verarok and Nedevik. Wardevik is a scholar and defender for the weak, like his father."

"You know, I hadn't really considered that," I frowned at Thurlow. "How old is Wardevik?"

"Nearly six hundred years old."

"Wow. Garde is around a million years old—by his own admission. Jayde is several centuries younger, but when you're talking that much time, it really doesn't matter, does it?"

"No, love, it does not. You must recall the time and climate on Kifirin when they were birthed."

"Females were kept in the home and guarded, and because there were so few of them, they were treated like a commodity rather than people."

"Lendevik made sure that his Queen and her sister couldn't skip—with controllers. That facilitated their deaths. Belarok's sons raped and killed both, after they were goaded and convinced by copper Ra'Ak."

"So Jayd probably found those controllers in the palace treasury somewhere, and conveniently forgot to tell anybody so they wouldn't be destroyed," I fumed.

"I believe they were placed there by Lendevik and discovered later, yes," Thurlow agreed.

"You know, I'd like to go back and slap the bejeezus out of Lendevik," I said.

"Lendevik paid for many mistakes with his life," Thurlow rubbed my neck with gentle fingers. "That is long over. We face new difficulties, now."

"You got that right."

CHAPTER 12

The Apostles Tunnel, Near Adelaide, Australia
Opal

"There was an elaborate set of traps to navigate before we reached the Metal Library in the volcano," Zaria said as she led Pheligar and Valegar through the rough tunnel. Val and Pheligar had to shorten their height in order to stand upright as we made our way through rock and dirty water.

"Here," she stopped and pointed to the appropriate spot we'd chosen earlier. "This can be where we place the new tunnel leading to the decoy library."

"I suggest leaving the brackish water and debris in the tunnel the way it is," Pheligar said as Kell and I slogged up to join them. "If I were the Library, I'd make the path as difficult and offensive as I could to keep others away."

"I agree," I said. "Another good thing, too, is that this tunnel will be impossible for Morgett to navigate in Ra'Ak form. It's narrower than he is, and if we leave the rock and other obstacles here, he won't even try."

"If he uses his power to change those things, he risks getting smeared by the Library's defenses," Zaria added. "Even if he thinks the Library has bestowed its blessings on him as the chosen one."

"Chosen one, my posterior," Kell snorted.

"I agree," Valegar nodded to Kell.

"Kiarra and the others can shield themselves inside the false library, once they know he's coming," Pheligar said. "It is my hope that the ambush will go in their favor, although the enemy may attempt to escape, once they realize it's a trap."

"I've thought about that, too," Zaria agreed. "I'll have Kory's brothers on standby, in case they attempt to relocate."

"You think they'll target Uluru, don't you?" I said.

"I'm afraid so. None of the maps provided by Mardin showed this," she swept out a hand. "Those maps all include Uluru. I hope Morgett thinks that was a ruse, and once we leak this as a possible location, he'll be tempted by what he hears and investigate."

"What will you do if V'ili and the twins arrive with him?"

"I'm working on that," Zaria mumbled. "In the meantime, we need to make this look like the Library's new digs."

Kent, England
Lexsi

Because I was bored and worried at the same time, I offered to cook dinner. Turns out, I had plenty of assistance. Kiarra had two who usually cooked if she didn't want to, and Anita and Conner offered to help, too.

"Taste," I held out a spoon for Kiarra. She was vegetarian; I'd just made a fresh tomato soup for her to try.

"Oh, my gosh, that's the best ever," Kiarra stared at me before licking the spoon.

"Mom taught me how to cook vegetarian," I said. "Comes in handy, too. The others will eat this with you and won't complain that it doesn't have meat."

"They'll love it," Kiarra said. "When do you think they'll have the trap completed?"

"Since Larentii are involved, probably not long once they decide on the location," I replied.

"I think the same thing—but the discussion on where to place it could take a while."

"Opal and Zaria already visited the tunnel, so they may have a pretty good idea," Kory arrived and leaned in to kiss my cheek. "Dinner ready soon? Watson is about to cave in."

"It will be, the fish is almost ready," I said.

"The werewolf?" Kiarra lifted an eyebrow at Kory.

"Watson is always hungry, I think, and he complained about the hotel breakfast earlier. I'm sure he could expire any moment from starvation," Kory grinned.

"Go ahead and tell everybody to come downstairs, then. I can serve the soup course now. While they're working on that, I'll finish the rest," I told him.

In minutes, everyone was seated at a long table in the dining room, while the rest of us in the kitchen served soup.

The fish course, along with the vegetarian mushroom-noodle-stir fry and fresh bread was ready at the proper time, with vegetables and salad following. It was nice to see everyone eating and talking, as if we hadn't just left a harrowing experience behind in Australia.

I wanted to ask Zaria a question too—something was niggling my brain and needed an answer.

She'd told me not to let the enemy see me turn to mist in Adelaide. I imagined someone could be watching us. Morwin, however; she'd dropped him right in the thick of things, armed with a ranos pistol that he'd used to destroy several attackers.

That didn't add up logically. Perhaps she was already laying the groundwork for the trap, by allowing Morwin to make his presence known. Still, I wanted to ask if my theory were correct.

After all, if Morgett and the others knew Morwin was in Adelaide, it would aid the ruse that something was there that drew his attention.

I wasn't sure how she intended to lay the groundwork for evidence that the Library had relocated there, but she had to have some sort of plan.

"Hey, time to eat," Anita pulled me away from the massive kitchen island. I'd just put the finishing touches on dessert, so it was time for us to sit with the others for our meal.

"All right." I untied my apron and set it on a corner of the island. "Grab your plate and let's go."

~

Adelaide, New Zealand

Zaria

"Morgett had camera bots on all those attackers at Rundle Mall," I said. We sat atop the roof of an empty house not far from Fort Largs. From our perch, we could see the water where our ship had docked earlier. It was long gone and I couldn't blame the Captain for sailing away so quickly.

The roof where we sat was covered in concrete tiles, which were made to look like clay tiles. Roofs surrounding us were covered either in clay tiles, concrete tiles or metal—to withstand harsh conditions or to enable water harvesting. I didn't detect composite roofing anywhere near, either.

Since it was summer and hot out where we were, we'd had to cool this roof down with power, while leveling out the portion of it chosen for our conversation. We were also heavily shielded against sight and sound.

"Morgett saw everything while it was happening during the attack?" Opal asked, returning me to the present.

"Yes. I told Lexsi not to go to mist, because of that. That's why I sent Morwin in with a ranos pistol, too—to help convince Morgett that Morwin had a reason for being there in the first place. He now knows that Morwin is dangerous and willing to fight. In his mind, too, he imagines that Morwin wants to find the Library before he does, so Morgett will investigate any rumor to ensure he gets there first."

"That's what you intend to do, isn't it?" Kell asked. "Start a rumor."

"There are several caving and underground exploration groups in the area," I explained. "All we have to do is give them a small taste of what could be there and Morgett will jump on it. Like yesterday."

"Then it was a wise decision to bend time and place the decoy library there a month ago," Valegar's eyes gleamed. "Morgett has the ability to bend time, while the others do not. I believe he'll go back to the time of the discovery, so to speak, but it's always wise to give yourself plenty of leeway."

"I'm worried he'll haul an army of Ra'Ak with him, back to that point," Opal observed.

"I worry about that, too," I admitted. "That's why I think Kiarra and her crew should cause the entire tunnel to explode at the first sign of big trouble."

"An ordinary explosion will not destroy Ra'Ak, unless the explosion is very powerful and the Ra'Ak quite close," Pheligar said.

"I know. I'm still working on that," I told him.

"There's something else that troubles you, dearest," Val said, reaching out to rub my neck.

"Yeah. I worry that a few rogue gods may be laying a trap for us, just as we're laying one for Morgett."

～

Opal

Zaria was right. Rogue gods still existed in the here and now. A troubling thought, as it turns out.

I almost didn't want to consider that they may have been pulling strings all along, sending Morgett, the twins and V'ili in this direction, in an attempt to control the Library.

It made sense, and I didn't want it to make sense.

Perhaps we'd been led down a path, with enough obstacles thrown our way to make us think Morgett and his bunch were our only enemies. In my mind, it was no longer a theory, which left me with one question—which rogue or rogues was it?

From where I sat, cross-legged on a concrete roof modified with power, Zaria looked troubled. I didn't like that Zaria looked troubled. We had to see this through; that was a given.

I was thinking about retiring as Director of the Joint NSA/Homeland Security Department, too, if I lived past this.

Time to go to the future and find other meaningful work, I think. Someone else could handle the job, once this conundrum was solved.

If it were solved.

Perhaps Kell and I could work together. That, in my mind, would be perfect. If Kooper Griff didn't recruit us for the ASD, something would be very, very wrong.

"Any way to tell who it could be?" I asked my question.

"Liron has a beef with me," Zaria pointed out. "If he's discovered I'm involved in this, well," she shrugged.

"Not good," I shook my head. Liron was one of Acrimus' hidden allies. They'd called themselves the *Hidden* for a reason, lurking in the shadows and away from everything else until they were needed by the General.

Liron had already fooled everybody once, by hiding his power and energy inside one of his spheres. Zaria had called him out in the future and destroyed him, but what if he'd managed to let his previous self know if that happened?

There was a Larentii trick of leaving messages for themselves or others at specific places and times—why couldn't Liron do the same? Zaria had done it on several occasions—to save lives or replace lost hope.

Zaria's ability to see multiple avenues for a particular person or action was beginning to rub off on me, too. No wonder she looked tired.

"Let's go back; there's still food left," Zaria said. "You two," she nodded to Val and Pheligar, "Find sunlight somewhere. It'll be good for you."

"Come with us," Valegar touched her cheek.

"We can get back to Kent just fine," I said. "Go. Get some rest, too."

"All right." Zaria didn't argue.

"Ready?" I turned to Kell.

"Yes," he smiled at me. I took his hand and folded space to England.

∼

Veshtul, Kifirin

Jaydevik Rath

"I am weary of these vids," I hissed as I watched an Alliance-produced news program. Somehow, even with Kifirin's space station being shut down, a journalist had managed to gain images and do an interview with three humanoids in Veshtul.

"We should confiscate that technology," Garde growled. He and I were portrayed in the worst way; they'd called us despots, tyrants and oppressors. Somehow, they'd interviewed the trollop who'd claimed she was raped, too.

"Bring her in; we'll show her what it costs to tell lies." I blew smoke at the vid-screen.

"I sent three after her already. So far, no word," Garde rumbled. He was angry, I could tell. "I've put the army on alert, to root out those behind this," he added. "They'll be jailed until we decide on their punishment."

"Look, they're claiming they still have free speech," I pointed at the screen. "Feel free to rough them up as much as you like when they're apprehended."

"Alliance laws never sat well with us," Garde declared and stalked out of my study.

∼

Queen's Palace, Le-Ath Veronis

Lissa

"She agreed to the second interview," Bryan Riley flopped onto the sofa in my private study. "We'll air it tomorrow evening as a special."

He'd interviewed the rape victim from Kifirin—Zaria was instrumental in getting the woman and her family away from Kifirin because, in her words, Jayd and Garde were out for blood. The first interview had already run, and people everywhere were sitting up and taking notice of the upheaval on Kifirin.

Zaria asked me to find a place for the woman after Bryan finished the first interview; Roff had skipped Bryan to Kifirin to speak with the victim. At Zaria's request, we'd found an empty house for the woman and her displaced family on the light side of Le-Ath Veronis, among the comesuli.

"There's something else you should know," Bryan said.

"What's that?"

"The Kifirini Crown has been cutting corners on education for the humanoid population. This woman is barely literate. The Crown has provided little in the way of technology, too, and since they've pulled out of the Alliance, shipments of equipment and supplies have been interrupted."

"Zaria says that the evil at the pit of the High Demon palace has been leeching into the whole place for around thirty years," I said. "I suppose that's the last time anybody got a decent education?"

"I'd have to do research, but it appears that the last twenty years have certainly been insufficient, as far as education goes. In the past, High Demon education was paid for by the family house, and good tutors were supplied. Public education is something relatively new, and the relocated humanoids were ill-prepared to provide their own. There were never any universities built on Kifirin," he pointed out. "The humanoids are generally too poor to travel off-world to obtain a higher education. Not that many of them would have been accepted into those schools. Most wouldn't be able to complete the admissions forms."

"This nightmare is only getting worse as it goes along," I grumped. "What about the indigent and disabled?"

"Lord and Lady Foth often held fundraising parties, with the help of Nedevik and his family, to pay for the things not covered by Alliance funds. At least Kifirin paid its taxes to the Alliance to maintain membership. A lot of that came back to the planet in the form of medical and financial aid."

Bryan had certainly done his research on this, I discovered. He was an excellent journalist and often dug deeper and with more integrity and passion into things that mattered than most other news reporters.

"So they've been skating by with the barest minimum of cooperation with the Alliance to remain a member—until they unceremoniously dropped out of it?" I asked.

"Yes. Exactly."

"I think I want to slap Garde into next week," I said. "No wonder things have cooled between us for the past fifteen years. I think I'd like to slap Acrimus and Liron first, though. They managed to bring out Garde's weaknesses and make them dominate his strengths."

"We all have some of those," Bryan studied his hands for a moment. "I'd hope I'd get through something like this in a better way, but I can't say that for sure. Is there anything redeemable in either Jayd or Garde?"

"I think we'll know that before long. I don't know exactly when Li'Neruh Rath is going to move on this, but I'm waiting not so patiently for that day to come."

"Me, too," Bryan nodded and lifted his eyes to mine. "So many things need fixing on Kifirin, and steady hands on the wheel in the palace to bring those things about."

I didn't tell him that it wouldn't be Jayd's hands on the wheel—at least I'd plugged the gossip hole in my own palace to keep that secret.

Jayd knows, I reminded myself. That could be the worst thing of all. I'm sure if he could find Reah right now, he'd try to destroy her. Yes, Jheri was sorry *now* for her actions in alerting her father to that secret.

The last I'd heard from Gavril regarding Jheri and the rest of those girls was that he'd invited Morwin to teach them a lesson about how planets were governed, financed and supported, to keep the populations thriving.

I wished him well in that endeavor.

As for Glinda, she ghosted about the palace and seldom joined the rest of us for meals, choosing to have them delivered to her room instead. Jheri's defection had hit her hard, and there would be a meeting between those two eventually. I didn't want to speculate how that might go.

Roff had paid several visits to Glinda in the arboretum; I hoped he was doing her some good.

She needs Zaria's help too, I realized. Li'Neruh had included her in his delay. The others had no real excuse for their actions—Zaria had removed the troublemakers who'd spent excessive amounts of time in the palace and became affected by Liron and Acrimus' poison.

Those were now in comfortable holding cells on Avendor—outside the boundaries of EastStar. Reah and a crew of others from NorthStar and SouthStar were tending to the prisoners' needs until Zaria could *Change What Was* with Li'Neruh's permission.

"Does the rape victim need medical or psychological attention?" I asked Bryan.

"Probably. She wasn't getting anything on Kifirin."

"I'll ask Karzac to send a comesuli physician and therapist, then."

"Good idea," Bryan said and stood to stretch. "I'm going to New Fangled for a drink and then go home. Maybe."

"Get some rest, you look tired," I said as he strode toward the door.

"I will. Thanks, Lissa."

"For what?"

"For being the Queen Le-Ath Veronis needs and deserves."

"Uh—you're welcome," I stuttered. Nobody had ever really thanked me for that before. Mostly I dealt with grumblings in the Council when something didn't go somebody's way.

Bryan waved and walked out the door, closing it softly behind him.

"You are the example that other rulers strive to emulate—if they have any sense at all." Breanne appeared in my study and took the seat previously occupied by Bryan.

"You trying to give me a big head?" I blinked at my sister.

"Nah—your crown wouldn't fit," she teased.

"I don't feel like somebody to emulate," I sighed. "I feel like a fool for not keeping a closer eye on Kifirin."

"Like you've had so much free time, and that it's your responsibility to rule two planets," Bree said. "The Alliance has an oversight committee. Bryan is correct. Kifirin skated through the past thirty years or so by doing exactly what was necessary to pass Alliance inspection. It would have taken a much earlier deposing of Kifirin's ruling house to avoid all this."

"Has the ruling house been deposed?" I frowned at Bree.

"Not officially. Hank is right in this; we have to see how this plays out."

Hank. Li'Neruh's other name—one of them, anyway. I doubted my sister called out *Li'Neruh* when those two were in bed together.

"I don't," she laughed.

"Did you come by for coffee?" I asked.

"Well, I wouldn't mind herbal tea. I really came to talk about Zaria. Corinnelar. Whatever name she wants to use," Bree told me.

"Just about her, or that Charles is her original father, or that Li'Neruh wants to jump her bones?"

"Charles is very closed-mouthed about this, and won't talk about how Wellend should have been her father, had she not gotten the Lyristolyi drug that circumvented that."

"That's interesting," I said. It was. It made sense, especially if your original father had a problem letting anyone else physically father his offspring in another incarnation.

"I think this is why Zaria can see through anybody, gods included."

I went still. Charles, as Wisdom, may have known this from the get-go. Or at least suspected it.

"But," I began.

"Zaria is an anomaly."

"But," I went on.

"Wisdom lent her power, but she doesn't need it any longer."

"What the fuck are you trying to say?" I whispered.

"I'm saying that this is how it happened for Strength, Wisdom and Love. We *Became* on our own. Zaria has *Become* on her own. Sure, we named her a guardian, but that was only an interim thing."

I closed my eyes and took a very deep breath. I'd gained what I had through Ashe, Charles and Bree. Zaria hadn't needed it. Nobody had to give her anything.

"Does Kalenegar know?" I breathed and opened my eyes. After all, he was the first mate that Zaria and Bree shared.

"He'll figure it out. She will, too."

"She doesn't know?"

"Not yet. Her mind is occupied with other things, you understand."

"I get that. What does this mean to the rest of us?"

"She's not going to take over," Bree shrugged. "If that's what you're worried about. Everything will be pretty much the same. Some things will be a little more secure, maybe?"

"What about Kifirin?"

"The planet?"

"Yeah."

"Well, you've already heard me say that Jayd may not be in charge eventually."

"I figured that out, yes."

"Glinda was right to choose Reah. With her belief in fairness to all, she's a good choice. She has an excellent support system around her, too, and a willingness to ask for help if it's needed. That won't mean she'll have an easy path in front of her, though. Plenty of damage has been done and that will have to be addressed."

Again I wondered what Li'Neruh's plan was in all this, but decided to shunt that thought aside for now.

Zaria.

If she weren't handling the mess on Earth right now—who would have to? The rest of us had our own difficulties, and the fate of Kifirin complicated everything. The rest of us were deep into handling our own affairs and those of the worlds we either governed or guarded. Earth was a lonely outpost that had drawn rogue god attention for a very long time.

Probably because the Three were born there, after sloughing away their celestial personas to deal with those same rogue gods.

Why had they chosen Earth?

It could have been Avendor, or Wyyld or Hraede. Those were all stable planets. An easier time could have been had by all.

"You're getting warmer, but still not there, yet," Bree said. "Stop worrying about it for now. Let's have tea."

~

B'Eradonn

Ra'Ak Prince Vantes

I watched him carefully. I hadn't seen him in a while—not since he'd come to tell me of the Library's existence. I'd chosen Morgett to hunt it, while distracting the peoples of Earth with the goals of others he'd brought with him.

This one was powerful. He paced inside the large room I'd chosen as my study. It was spacious enough to turn Ra'Ak if I wished.

There was no need for it in this meeting.

"Morgett is planning your demise, you know," he finally stopped pacing and turned to look at me. White wings rustled at his back.

"I suspected as much, although he was the best choice to search for the Library. I have many of mine poised to arrive and take it from him before his hands can grasp any part of it," I replied.

"They will search in the wrong place," he turned piercing eyes upon me. Most cannot bear to gaze upon my kind so baldly. He had no trouble doing so.

"Where should they be searching, then?" I asked, pulling the maps of Earth that were lying on my desk toward me.

"Here." He tapped a spot on the map. "It is considered a sacred space by the original inhabitants. I believe the Library intended this."

"This will present no problems to my army," I said.

"We know this. The One finds your rule pleasing to him; you must command the Library, however, to push your enemies into oblivion."

"When should we go?" I asked.

"When Morgett approaches the trap laid for him, you must move quickly," he said.

I knew he spoke truth; his white wings proclaimed him a messenger of the One. "May I know your name?" I asked. "My race will hold it in honor from now on."

"Liron," he nodded. "The One will be pleased."

He disappeared from my study, while I turned back to the designated point on the map before me.

~

Kent, England

Opal

"Here, you can be yourself," Kiarra told me. "The property is extensive and you can run as much and as long as you like."

We stood on the manicured lawn outside Gryphon Manor. I found it strange how things can loop into an altered timeline. I'd met Kiarra in the future, and I was meeting her now. It was disorienting for me, because I recalled both meetings. This Kiarra didn't have such recollections.

She did have a very good grasp of what something like that could mean, however. She understood I was a shapeshifter, too, and offered the luxury of turning and allowing my velociraptor the freedom to run.

Or chase butterflies, if I wanted.

"I remember when I was small," I said. "Spring always meant butterflies would come. To me, as a child, I felt as if I'd been given a gift because they were so beautiful."

"I believe they are a gift. Why else would they be so lovely?" Kiarra smiled.

"Maybe I'll look into who created them," I said. "It's still too early for them to be out here, and that's unfortunate."

"They'll be present on many planets at the moment," Kiarra's eyes lost focus for seconds as she *Looked* for butterflies on other worlds.

"You're right, I just can't go find them, as nice as that sounds. Things feel—unsettled."

"I know what you mean. I hope there are butterflies waiting for us somewhere when this is over."

She'd voiced my concern—that not all of us might make it out alive. Zaria's fears that rogue gods could be involved almost assured us of that.

Zaria would never voice that fear unless it held weight as a possibility. No longer did we have to worry only about preserving the worthless lives of the twins and V'ili. Depending on which gods were involved, things could become so much more complicated.

"I think I'll run for half an hour, so I can think," I nodded to Kiarra. My velociraptor sprinted away immediately.

CHAPTER 13

Northern Reaches, Kifirin
Foth Castle; Aldavik Foth

Mayarok and Fredevik Greth had brought many of theirs with them, and were now crowded into buildings originally constructed to house troops.

"Jaydevik has lost his mind," Fredevik grumbled as he handed me the royally-sealed writ delivered to him earlier. "They're searching for you, too, or members of your family, at least."

"They know where I live," I allowed a curl of smoke to drift away with my breath.

"That's what worries us," Mayarok clung to Fred's arm. "We want no part of this invasion, but it's a death sentence to disagree. Weth has already deserted Kifirin, and I worry that they will not answer if their assistance is needed."

"I know about the charges of treason against Weth," I rumbled. My Thifilathi wanted out, and I struggled to control it. "Even some of my own sons have aligned with this ridiculous ideology, and I can't convince them otherwise."

"Mine, too," Fredevik growled. Mayarok looked as if she were

184

ready to cry. "The humanoids are trapped in the city and can't get out. Mayarok and I are fearful for their lives. Already, many have been killed."

"I've heard that humanoids from the outlying cities and villages are marching in to help, but they'll be slaughtered," Mayarok wiped tears away. "I don't understand how this happened."

"I fail to understand, too," I admitted. "Many things have deteriorated in the past twenty turns or more. I cannot explain it. If Nedevik were here, perhaps he'd know more."

"Even Nedevik couldn't turn the King and Prime Minister away from this madness, and there are none more diplomatic than he is. He was sent to the dungeon for attempting to convince them that their plans were wrong." Mayarok sighed and leaned against Fredevik.

"He and his family escaped not long after," I nodded at her words. "They have no reason to return; they'll face a death sentence if they do."

"I heard that Li'Neruh Rath may have had a hand in getting Weth away," Fredevik said. "I wish I could believe that, as it gives the rest of us hope."

"I'd settle for Kifirin's help, if it would keep this planet from tearing itself apart," I snarled. "But you can't depend on the gods. Look what happened in the past. Kifirin slept and while he slept, the dark worlds were destroyed. Nedevik was the only one to argue their case with Lendevik, and he ignored the plea and chastised Nedevik for making it."

"I still feel I was weak in not standing with him," Fredevik admitted.

"I, too."

～

Kent, England
Zaria
I'd arrived just before breakfast. Things weren't going so well on

Kifirin. Humanoids had died in the night, which angered me. That's why I sent mindspeech to Lexsi, waking her and Kory.

"I dreamed it," Lexsi admitted when she and Kory skipped downstairs after pulling on clothes. "Is there anything we can do?"

"I have a suggestion, but it'll piss Jayd and Garde off," I said.

"I'm willing to do anything," Kory blew smoke. "I don't care if Jayd gets pissed."

He hadn't forgotten that his father had been tossed in the palace dungeons for disagreeing with Jayd. I hadn't forgotten that, either.

"How about a tunnel?" I asked. "To get the humanoids out of Veshtul and on their way to the Northern Reaches? Foth and Greth have already met there; that's one line of defense against an invasion of crazy High Demons."

"Will you do this?" Lexsi blinked at me. "I mean, Kory and I could probably form a tunnel with fire, but it will take a while. I know people died last night on Kifirin. I don't want more to die if I can help it."

"I'll create the tunnel, and help you convince the humanoids to use it," I said. "That's why I woke you—to see if you would like to do this."

"Of course," Kory said. "Do we need any of my brothers?"

"Not yet, unless Wardevik wants to come."

"I'll send mindspeech," Kory said. "He's just like my father. If anybody can convince those people to trust us, he can."

"Send mindspeech, then. I can bend time and get us there before all this crap happened last night," I said.

"Hurry, Kory," Lexsi begged.

"Already done, onion," Kory pulled her against him.

Lexsi

Wardevik had dressed just as quickly as Kory and I had; he was still straightening his clothing when Zaria *Pulled* him to Gryphon Manor.

"I let Pap know," Wardevik nodded to Kory, once he'd gotten his shirt buttoned properly. "Hello, Lexsi. Good to see you again. Zaria, thank you for providing transportation."

"You wouldn't have gotten in, otherwise," Zaria smiled at him. "Ready to go to Veshtul? We have people to convince and lives to save."

"I know several Guild Masters," Wardevik said. "I'm hoping we can start with them, if they're still alive."

"We'll find out soon enough," Zaria said and moved us in a blink.

It's strange that I feel no disorientation when Zaria bends time with us. It had taken a few days to get my bearings when I was first dropped off in San Rafael. Kory and I had both been gone from our normal timeline for nearly two years.

Perhaps it was no longer disorienting because we now felt comfortable in both times and places.

When we arrived after nightfall in Veshtul, we found streetlamps either broken or disconnected from their solar power sources, leaving only moonlight to dimly illuminate the cobble-and-brick streets.

During the day, the colors of those bricks and cobbles would be wondrous, as would the colors of shops and homes—if they were still intact. Looking around me, I saw that many buildings were damaged —some beyond repair. Most were scorched or bore scars of deep burns, indicating that angry High Demon Thifilathis had come this way.

This may not be easy, I sent to Zaria.

I know.

Don't worry, Wardevik reassured us. *I think they'll talk to me. They may be suspicious of anyone else, though.*

Lead the way, Brother, Kory gestured to Wardevik, who strode ahead of us in a purposeful way.

Zaria

"How will this tunnel be built?" Guild Master Chett looked as if he wanted to believe. He should; if he didn't follow Wardevik out of Veshtul, he'd be dead by morning.

"Zaria," Kory nodded in my direction.

"Are you a witch or wizard?" Chett turned to me, his voice filled with skepticism.

"Mostly I'm Larentii," I said. "The tunnel is already there. You only have to trust Wardevik, Kordevik and Lexsirok to get you out of the city alive."

"Some won't go," Chett said.

"I know. It's their choice. We're here to save those we can," I responded.

"Where does the tunnel end?" Chett's first assistant asked.

"Two miles from Lord Foth's castle, in the Northern Reaches," Wardevik said after I sent mindspeech to him. Chett wanted the words to come from the High Demon who'd befriended him in the past. Therefore, I was willing to let him speak for all of us.

"Will Foth welcome us, or will it be more murder waiting?" Chett asked.

"Foth and Greth are waiting, and will offer asylum," Wardevik said.

"Will the crown attack us there, once they discover us gone?" the assistant queried.

"I don't have that answer, but know this; Foth and Greth will fight them if they come. Weth will come if at all possible to help. I will stay with you, in good faith, to provide a liaison between you and the High Demons in the Northern Reaches."

"Good. It makes me uncomfortable to attempt to bargain with any of them," Chett murmured and lowered his eyes.

"I know this," Wardevik dropped a hand on Chett's shoulder. "Not all are like these that remain in the city. I beg you not to think of all of us as the same."

"I know you're not," Chett lifted his eyes. "I will follow you, Wardevik Weth. I know it will be my death if I remain."

～

Lexsi

I know you could have transported all of us out of Veshtul without building a tunnel, I sent to Zaria.

Yes, but these have to decide for themselves. I will leave the tunnel open for one more day, for any who choose to escape after the High Demons attack. After that, it will be closed off and filled in, as if it had never been.

Zaria and I walked behind the slowest humanoids who chose to follow Wardevik. He, Kory and Chett were at the front, leading them. Zaria, I knew, chose this place in line because she was protecting us with a shield.

Somewhere, behind us in Veshtul, Jayd and Garde had allowed members of the High Demon army to spread across the city, searching for those who were no longer there; the rape victim and her family.

I'd had few interactions with Jayd and Glinda during my lifetime. When had he become so unreasonable? Did the malevolence in the palace dungeons have such an adverse effect that Jayd lost any decency he'd ever possessed?

I'm afraid that once his hold on decency and kindness loosened, his cruelty manifested, with no reason remaining to rein it in, Zaria informed me. *He has always seen the humanoids as less than High Demons. That notion has only grown, until injustice against them is seen as normal and acceptable. How familiar are you with Earth history? Do you recall Hitler and World War II? He convinced much of his country to follow his warped agenda of hatred, and many innocents died as a result.*

I read about that—it was one of Morwin's lessons, I replied. *I knew about it long before I arrived on Earth. Hitler believed in a superior race— his,* I added. *He wanted those he considered inferior to be exterminated. I did research into the Shadow personality, too, as a result of that.*

The belief that we create a dark version of ourselves when we choose or are forced to choose who we are to those around us?

Yes. I think that's what happened here—that the shadow has risen to the surface in Jayd and Garde, and together they've let those around them know that they don't have to force themselves into a certain mold any longer—that they can allow their deepest desires to have free rein. Killing humanoids is an unfortunate result of that.

I agree, I said. *And it makes sense that Liron and Acrimus would choose this slow road to achieve their goals—even after their deaths. If it builds slowly, we become used to it as it goes along—until a tipping point is reached and things take a nasty turn.*

Then people die. By the hundreds or thousands or millions. An audible sigh escaped Lexsi's lips.

"Yeah," I breathed. "Exactly."

~

Lexsi

It took six days for us to get through the tunnel. Zaria brought in food and water for us, or Kory would have been forced to hunt. Day by day, a trickle of humanoids became a steady stream as they approached and spoke to Kory and me, eventually trusting us as much as Wardevik to take care of their needs.

As for those who'd refused to join us as we left Veshtul behind, only a handful came behind us, before the tunnel entrance was closed off so Jayd's High Demon guards couldn't get in and come after us.

She'd promised we'd bend time once we were out—time was running out on the two eight-days that Jayd promised before his attack on Harifa Edus.

Zaria had left after the first day, returning intermittently to deliver food and provide healing to those who needed it. The humanoids began to look forward to her appearances, because she brought something they'd lacked for a while—a sense of well-being.

As for Zaria's disappearances, she had other things to do while Kory, Warde and I led the humanoids out of the tunnel and onto Foth lands in the Northern Reaches. Aldavik Foth and Fredevik Greth came to greet us on the sixth day and offered asylum before Warde had to ask.

I was grateful; somehow, Zaria or someone else had laid that groundwork for us. The people we'd rescued were more than relieved that their journey was over for the moment and that pallets or beds and baths waited.

"Onion?" Kory came to me as Warde, with Greth and Foth, led his humanoid charges toward Foth Castle.

"I just want a bath," I let my head rest on Kory's shoulder. Extra water in the tunnel wasn't something we could ask for; Zaria brought what we'd need to drink along the way. She was right to do so; carrying the extra weight of bath water would have been a burden few could carry.

"I know." Kory patted my shoulder as I leaned against him. "I do, too," he admitted. "Let's go with the others. I'll see if we can get a turn at the pump."

I wanted clean clothes with my turn at the pump, but decided that wasn't important enough to fuss about. Merely getting the dust off my skin would be good enough to start.

We walked for more than two miles to reach Foth Castle; there, High Demon guards belonging to the Houses of Foth and Greth stood guard, waiting for Lord Foth and Lord Greth to return with the rest of us.

Wardevik and the guild masters he walked with at the front of our line nodded at the guards as they passed. When Kory and I approached, however, the guards thumped their fists on their chests and dipped their heads to Kory.

Troops from one of my patrols, Kory informed me in mindspeech as he dipped his head to the guards in reply.

Kory was their Captain. Or had been, anyway. They had much respect for him; that was easy to see.

I could also see they wished to stare at me, but their manners and their respect for Kory prevented it.

After all, male High Demons, unless they were Heads of Houses or quite important, seldom saw female High Demons.

It made me wish for a solution to that difficulty. Male High Demons were born knowing they'd never be mated to a female High Demon; there were too few females born.

To be chosen as a mate for a female was the rarest of rare things on Kifirin. Like winning the lottery, only with much worse odds.

How had Kory been chosen for me?

Who had chosen him for me? Not that I wished to argue with the decision now, but truly, I couldn't see Jayd making such a decision. If he had, he wouldn't have had my well-being in mind, I was sure of that.

The Mighty Heart and Li'Neruh Rath chose for you, the Library whispered in my mind. *They knew you would love him.*

I tripped over my own feet when I received that information. "Onion?" Kory's hand gripped my arm and kept me from falling in the tall grass surrounding Foth Castle.

"I just tripped," I breathed, attempting to bring my heartbeat back to a normal rhythm.

Kory had been chosen for me, not I for him. By the Mighty Heart and Li'Neruh Rath.

The Mighty Heart. She would know love before anyone.

Had my mother known of this?

Your mother knew, or she'd never have agreed to an arranged marriage, Aunt Bree's voice sounded in my head.

There. You have your answer from the Mighty Heart herself, the Library informed me. I almost tripped again.

I'd asked Aunt Bree to get me away from my arranged marriage, when she'd been the one to arrange it, knowing I'd love Kory.

She'd sent us to the same place, to meet and fall in love, like most couples did. And, if we happened to be in the proper place and time to defend the timeline, that was just a bonus.

Wasn't it?

You were uniquely qualified, Aunt Bree said, a smile in her sending. I couldn't bring myself to call her the Mighty Heart. She was Aunt Bree.

Wasn't she?

I will always be your Aunt Bree, she confirmed. *Stop worrying about nothing. Li'Neruh may require a price for requests made to him, but I do not. If it is deserved, I will answer.*

Thank you, I whispered my sending.

Just get through this, she replied. *So much is riding on it.*

～

Kordevik

In the castle courtyard, food and water was handed to all the refugees from Veshtul, while a multitude of High Demons helped parents with children, leading them to stone troughs that had been cleaned and filled with warm water to bathe small ones.

I wondered at the fact that Lord Foth had the vision to lay in sufficient supplies to care for all those who'd shown up at his gate.

"Come." Lady Greth had come for us, motioning for Lexsi and me to follow her. Already, Warde and the guild masters had gone inside Foth's massive home to sit and speak with Foth and Greth.

Lexsi and I had brought up the rear, just as she'd done through the tunnels. It made me wonder whether Jayd's troops had blindly attempted to follow us, either below or above ground.

It wouldn't take many brain cells to determine where we'd gone, actually. He already knew Foth and Greth had deserted Veshtul, with much of both Houses going with them.

"I have baths and a suite prepared." Lady Greth, accompanied and guarded by four of the Greth clan, spoke as she hurried us along.

A side door into the massive, stone structure of the House of Foth opened and we were led inside. Two of Lady Greth's guards remained outside, to watch the door.

"We're expecting Jayd's forces, to put it bluntly," Lady Greth hissed as she led us toward a set of wide, marble steps. "The forge has been going day and night since Fredevik and I arrived. Flying Thifilathi have been sighted in the distance. Jayd's spies, no doubt."

They were making blades, because Jayd had most of the weapons available locked up in Veshtul's armory.

"How many do we have, Lady Greth, to defend Foth Castle if Jaydevik's forces come?" I asked.

"Nearly three thousand."

I didn't reply. Jayd had twenty times that, at least. I understood what the odds were in this battle, as did Lady Greth.

We need help, I sent to Lexsi.

I watched as her shoulders tightened before she nodded slightly.

I'll ask, she said. *I can't say a request will be honored, but these people need whatever we can give.*

Yeah. I sent the word in English, rather than in the High Demon language.

"Your baths are inside this suite," Lady Greth waved us toward an open door on the castle's third level. "Take as long as you like; I know you're tired."

"Thank you," I said and nodded respectfully to her. I followed Lexsi inside the suite and shut the door behind us.

∾

Lexsi

Mom? I sent.

What is it, baby? She replied immediately.

Kifirin needs help.

I know. Where are you?

Soaking in hot water after walking through a tunnel to Foth castle, I told her. *We got as many humanoids out of Veshtul as we could convince to come, but Jayd,* I didn't finish. I didn't have to.

Mom showed up and sat on a stool beside my bathtub.

Mom is beautiful, and as she's High Demon, she's immortal. She barely looks older than I do. I got my silvery-blonde hair from her. My blue eyes I got from my father. Still, we look so much alike it's uncanny.

"There's trouble on Earth in the past, and trouble here," I said.

"I know. Lissa and I talked about it."

"I shouldn't be surprised you know about it. You probably knew where I was the whole time, what with Aunt Bree choosing Kory for me." I closed my eyes, placed a soapy hand across them and sighed.

"Who told you that?"

"Aunt Bree confirmed it." How could I tell her that somehow, I bore the information contained in the Library, like a duplicate copy in case the original was lost.

"If she confirmed it, then I have no problem with you having the information," Mom gently pulled my hand away from my face and offered a dry washcloth to wipe away the soap before I opened my eyes.

"What else don't I know?" I blinked at her.

"Well, Glinda is on Le-Ath Veronis; her daughters and your sisters are on Campiaa. Jheri had to be rescued from Jayd and Garde because she ran back to them the minute she learned that Glinda wanted to abdicate, in order to remove Jaydevik from the throne."

For a moment, I forgot to breathe. "Who?" I whispered. Mom understood that I wanted to know whom Glinda chose as her replacement.

Which of her daughters—or my sisters—had she picked?

"She chose me," Mom smiled.

"But," I said.

"If we win this war, and it will be war, I intend to accept," Mom's expression and her voice hardened. "It's time for Kifirin to come out of this narrow-minded, tunnel-visioned attitude and evolve."

"There'll be a second war after the first one," I said. "To convince the humanoids that High Demons aren't so terrible after all."

"I know. We'll work on it, provided we make it that far. Come on, baby girl, get out of that tub. You're clean and we have things to do."

"Uncle Nenzi." I felt tears pricking my eyes as I was enveloped in his arms. He and Uncle Farzi had come, as had Edward, Aurelius and several others.

Daddy had come, too, with Uncle Sal.

"Hi, baby," Daddy pulled me away from Nenzi.

"Daddy, things are so terrible right now," I said as I hugged him back.

"I know." There was a sadness in him—he was troubled by something, and I'd never seen that in him before. Yes, I'd seen regret plenty of times, but this went far beyond that.

"Kordevik," Daddy pulled away from me and nodded to Kory, who'd walked up behind me.

"I just left the forge—the weapons they're making are barely serviceable for blade practice," Kory said after offering his hand and shaking with Daddy.

"No surprise—that forge hasn't been used in centuries, if not millennia," Daddy agreed. "There really isn't time to make better weapons, either," he added. "I've asked my mother for help—we'll see what the Queen of Le-Ath Veronis can do for us."

"I think we can use that tall grass as a cover," Mom said. She'd skipped away for a moment, but was now back with Edward beside her.

Daddy's shoulders sagged as I placed an arm around Uncle Edward. Sighing, he spoke to Mom, who hadn't offered to hug him. "As a cover for what?" he asked. "It won't hide a humanoid; their heads and shoulders will be obvious once they stand up straight."

"Kooper is sending two squadrons of Amterean Dwarves," Mom said. "I asked for them. Technically, they're not supposed to come, but I managed to convince Ildevar Wyyld to declare this an attempted coup, so they're sending in troops to side with me, as the prospective new monarch of Kifirin. Seems they like the gishi fruit Kifirin provides, and without Kifirin being a member of the Alliance, they can't bargain for its produce."

I recalled Morwin, armed with a single ranos pistol, taking down several High Demons in Adelaide. She was right about the gishi fruit, too. "Mom, that's genius," I said.

"Thanks, baby. How much time do you think we have, Auri?" She turned to Uncle Aurelius.

"Perhaps a day at most," Aurelius said. "I hear from Lissa's spy network that Veshtul is a breath away from declaring war against those who've escaped. Some of those spies have met the humanoids moving toward the capital and warned them away—they'll only be slaughtered and they know now that most of their friends and families escaped to come here. That was an excellent move, young one, to get them away as you did." Uncle Auri smiled at me.

"It was Zaria's idea," I said. "Kory and I—it would have taken a lot longer for us to build a tunnel. By that time, it would have been too late for many of these people."

"But you stayed with them, to ensure their safety," Mom reminded me. "They won't forget that."

I realized the wisdom of Zaria's choice—to allow them to travel for six days with Kory, Warde and me. We'd gotten to know them that way. They'd come to trust us with their lives, beginning with Wardevik.

He'd laid the groundwork. He was now walking toward us, after having seen to the very people we'd escorted through the tunnel.

"Reahrok," Warde dipped his head to Mom and then lifted her outstretched hand to kiss it, rather than shaking it as intended. "I am more than happy to see you," he smiled.

"I can't say it's under the best of circumstances," Mom said, her words dry.

"True, but with you here, things will surely go better," his smile widened into an infectious grin.

"Wardevik Weth, I hope you're right," Mom smiled back.

Daddy ducked his head for a moment before skipping away.

Kent, England
Zaria

Kiarra, Adam, Merrill and Pheligar had gathered the Saa Thalarr about them—those able to combat Ra'Ak, anyway. Two were recovering from injuries.

My glance about Adam's massive ballroom settled on one in particular.

No, she wouldn't be fighting. Had never fought, actually.

Adam and Kiarra's daughter, Anna Kay.

I recalled so many cartoons, memes and jokes regarding what you'd seen that you couldn't unsee. I read Anna Kay as easily as anyone else. Tragedy for others lay behind the mask of her face.

For the same reason, I hadn't gone to see Lexsi and Reah—not while Torevik Rath was near.

I had no desire to see what could lie in his gaze. I'd read in Lissa that Gardevik Rath, Torevik's father and her mate, had struck Torevik, intending harm or even death.

That's how far his mind had become unhinged.

Lissa hadn't told anyone else what she knew—that Torevik would have died after confronting Garde and Jayd if she, Li'Neruh and I hadn't arrived first.

Perhaps Torevik imagined his father to still be a reasonable man. My concern was this; after *Changing What Was* for Garde and Jayd, would they be willing to allow their better selves to manifest, or would they continue on the same path, because it allowed their inner demons to rule?

Li'Neruh could have that answer; I was too terrified to ask him.

The evil that Acrimus and Liron planted in the High Demon palace was a lethal, ticking time-bomb, and we'd already seen damage before it well and truly exploded.

"Zaria and Valegar agree—we must direct the bulk of our forces, combined with that of the High Demons, here," Belen pointed at the proper spot on a floating, three-dimensional vid-map.

The spot indicated lay between Alice Springs and Uluru. Depending on where the Ra'Ak and rogue High Demons landed, it would be easy enough to skip or fold space to engage those forces.

My hope was to keep Uluru from harm, no matter the cost. A legend of Uluru that the Aborigines tell is that a snake boy, or Kuniya, was attacked by a group of Liru, who were venomous snakes. The tale says they threw spears at the Kuniya and killed him. Holes in the side of Uluru represent where their spear points hit.

When the boy's aunt learned of his death, she went hunting those who'd killed him. She killed one of the venomous serpents with her stick, after sliding across Uluru's surface. That line can also be seen on Uluru's side, as can the trail of blood left by the poisonous one she killed with a blow to his head.

I wondered if the tale would be played out in real life for all to see, between Ra'Ak serpents, High Demons and Saa Thalarr shapeshifters.

With those three races involved, it would be a ground war.

It gave me an idea.

*K*ent, *England*
Opal

Kell's arm went around me as we sat and watched the news from Australia. There, a young man in his twenties was showing a photograph he'd taken of a wall of metal books. He claimed he'd lost consciousness after taking the image on his cell phone, and woke up outside an old water tunnel.

He remembered exploring the tunnel, until he'd happened on a separate chamber. He couldn't clearly recall taking the photograph, yet there it was, on his phone.

People were speculating, for and against the actual reality of metal books being found near Adelaide, in a hidden tunnel that didn't appear on any map.

"Will Morgett take the bait?" I breathed. So far, none of Zaria and Valegar's traps had been triggered to indicate movement through the tunnel.

I still didn't know how she planned to keep V'ili and the twins alive if things went south.

"Let's hope he takes the bait—we'll eliminate one enemy at a time," Kell pulled me closer and kissed my hair.

~

Morwin

"Ranos grenades," I drew in a breath at the sight of a small crate of weapons Zaria laid on the table. Chloe and her family stood around me, watching and listening carefully as Zaria explained what she wanted of us.

I didn't have wings in another form, as the others did. That's why Yoff stood beside me, grinning like a fiend.

A fiend with large, leathery wings.

He was the son of a winged vampire, and had inherited the wings to prove it. He would carry me aloft, so I could fight alongside Chloe's family.

"These are light enough that you can carry one in each claw," Zaria explained. "I'll send mindspeech when it's the proper time to drop them."

"Do you have an idea where that will be?" Leisa, Chloe's mother, asked.

"It'll be around here," she tapped the paper map lying beside the crate. "Just before they reach Uluru, and far enough away not to do it damage."

"What about the decoy you've created?" Rose asked.

"Opal and I will do our best there. I believe the worst enemy has his sight firmly set here—with Uluru and what may be beneath it."

"What makes you think that?" Rose asked.

"An old tale that the Aborigines tell," Zaria said. "The enemy then was called Liru. I believe that could be a shortening of Liron—and his minions. I know that doesn't mean anything to you, but you have to believe me when I say he is terrible."

"You think he may have been here before?" I asked.

"It's possible. I've seen him here once before. It's not a short story and I can't tell it to you now. Someday, maybe, if you want to hear it."

"I do," I dipped my head in acknowledgment.

"I'll let you know," she said. "Meanwhile, I expect Morgett to trigger the alarms in the Adelaide tunnel soon. Take deep breaths and prepare yourselves, if you want to do this. If not, you only have to say so."

"We want to," Rose thumped her cane on the floor. "We have friends to avenge."

"Good enough," Zaria said. "I'll let you know when the time is close. Kiarra will see to it that you're transported to the proper place. Morwin, tell them how these grenades work. You and Yoff should place them in waiting claws before the owls fly. Then take several for yourselves and follow quickly. Yoff, you'll be high enough that the High Demons won't interfere with your abilities. Shield everyone from sight while you're flying. If necessary, fold everyone out."

"I will." Yoff was ready to do anything Zaria asked, I think.

As was I. My father's death lay between me and the enemy, and I would strike as many blows as I could on his behalf.

Besides, I had both ranos pistols fastened inside hidden pockets of my trousers. I'm sure Zaria knew it; she merely didn't comment.

"Each of you take one and place it above your heart," Yoff handed small buttons to us. "This will allow me to know where you are at all times, so I can fold you away if necessary."

As the button adhered to the skin just above my heart, Zaria nodded to us and disappeared.

~

Anita

I had no idea how much we'd miss Lexsi and Kory. Watson said he missed Lexsi's cooking, but he missed Kory just as much. I doubted Watson had ever had such a close friend as this High Demon.

I also had no idea whether they'd come back before the shit hit. Watson was growly enough as it was, pacing to and fro in our suite. If I told him his BFF might not come back for the big fight, he'd panic.

He, Sandra, Esme and I would be stationed at one end of the Apostles tunnel, in case things got out of control.

We weren't equipped to fight High Demons or Ra'Ak, and I had to trust that Zaria knew what she was doing where Morgett, V'ili and the twins were concerned.

V'ili, however—Esme and I wanted his death. His obsession wouldn't work with us, and there wasn't any way we'd let him get past us this time.

I worried about the twins, though. V'ili could bring them with him if he tried to run from the tunnel. Like before, Zaria and Valegar had set up a warning system that would fight back, just as the real Library had. V'ili would be afraid to fold space and the twins, if they had any sense, wouldn't attempt to use their witch and warlock abilities.

"Ready?" Esme poked her head inside the door of our suite.

"Yeah," Watson growled at her.

"What he means is this; have Kory and Lexsi come back?" I studied Esme's face.

"No."

I knew that look on her face. Grim. Determined. Her mouth set in a straight, unflinching line.

V'ili should pay for his crimes. Esme and I wanted his death more than anything, as he'd led our entire home planet to its destruction. He'd murdered us, too, but Zaria and others had bent time to pull us back from that oblivion.

"Let's go," I snapped and grabbed Watson's arm. At least he followed willingly as I stalked toward the door.

Veshtul, Kifirin

Jaydevik Rath

Garde's smaller Thifilathi kicked the bread shop's counter, sending it flying into the wall. Throughout the city, cold keepers had already been raided to feed the troops and there was little left.

Garde kicked the counter again, knocking it through the fragile wall of the shop. Through the hole he'd created, I could see the ovens in the back, all cold and empty.

"Other cities will have bread," I growled at my brother as he prepared to kick the disintegrating counter a third time.

"Foth has our slaves and some of your troops," Garde's eyes locked with mine.

"I want to invade Karathia first."

"We can't invade Karathia with starving troops."

"I haven't had a decent steak in days," I blew smoke at my brother.

"I doubt you'll find one to your liking here," Garde's breath was as smoky as mine.

"Shall we invade Targis on Tulgalan, then? If Glinda wants to make Reah Queen, then we'll hit Reah where it will hurt the most."

"An excellent idea, brother."

"Gather twenty to come with us. We will take from that bitch, first."

~

Targis, Tulgalan

Fes Desh

Zaria had warned my family and me. Still, it was a shock when more than twenty High Demons in Smaller Thifilathi landed at Dee's, crushing and destroying everything that didn't explode and burn as they touched it.

The front windows were knocked out with a casual swipe of a huge arm before they stalked toward the kitchen.

Everyone else had been sent home. This would be a test of my power and ability, given by Breanne, who was my mate.

There I was, dressed for work and wearing my cook's hat, brandishing only a wooden spoon as the invaders broke furniture and destroyed everything in their path to get to the food inside the restaurant's pantry.

I stood in their way.

"You may take the food, but you will pay for it," I stood my ground.

"Hmmph." The one in the lead; I'd spoken to him before. Had drinks and dinner with him before.

When he was normal.

This wasn't the Gardevik I'd met before. This one had twisted, somehow. Only lust for food and chaos showed in this one's eyes.

"You think to stop us, Reah's brother?" Garde hissed.

"I said you could take the food, but you'd pay for it."

"Go home, Garde." Lissa appeared beside me.

"Yeah. Go home, Dad."

Torevik Rath appeared beside his mother, causing her to jump. She hadn't expected him. Neither had Gardevik, if I were reading the situation correctly.

Tory was Reah's first mate, and her only High Demon mate. Gardevik and Lissa were his parents. Something had happened between these two already; I understood that much. I had no idea what it could be, but it surely wasn't good.

I held my breath. Lissa's face darkened—I could tell she wanted to tell Tory to go home, too.

She didn't.

In hindsight, perhaps I should have employed power to send both home.

I didn't.

Lissa stared Gardevik down, daring him to make a move.

That's why she didn't see Torevik make his.

Neither did I.

Ranos pistols will kill High Demons, if they're close enough.

Torevik was more than close enough.

He shot his father first and while Garde fell, Tory took his own life before Lissa could register the tragedy unfolding before her and stop him from doing it.

~

Queen's Palace, Le-Ath Veronis

Karzac

"She killed those Garde brought with him," Rigo said. "Too bad

Jayd stayed on Kifirin—this travesty could be over now. Is she sleeping?" Rigo turned dark, questioning eyes toward me.

"Yes. It was forced, but she is sleeping," I acknowledged. "I have arranged for someone to convey the information to Reah and Lexsi, who are on Kifirin. Kifirin is now an isolated world; Lissa saw to that before I placed her in a healing sleep."

"She shielded it?" Rigo asked.

"Yes. No High Demons can skip away. Reah and Lexsi are not included in that, by the way."

"I wouldn't want to be anywhere near Jaydevik Rath when he discovers this news," Rigo jerked his head.

"He already knows. Lissa screamed it at him."

"What about Breanne or Zaria?" Rigo began.

"Both silent and absent. *Changing What Was* is not warranted in this." I agreed with both; neither Garde's nor Torevik's actions should be rewarded with that expenditure of power.

I should have thought this through, however. Gardevik himself had shot a controller into Jheri's neck.

Torevik knew better than anyone just what sort of damage a controller could do. He'd borne one for quite some time and had no defense against it. He only recalled the anger and helplessness he'd felt during those terrible days.

He'd seen his father's act as unforgivable.

As did I.

"Karzac?"

Rylend, Torevik's older brother, appeared in Lissa's library, where I'd met Rigo. He'd already informed his spies on Kifirin that things could become worse quickly. I knew that he'd placed Halimel and two others from the Order of the Night Flower there, as they'd be better able to defend themselves if trouble came.

Trouble had certainly come.

"Rylend?" I turned toward the King of Karathia. How differently those two eldest sons of Lissa's had turned out.

"Uncle Karzac," Ry was suddenly in my arms and sobbing. It took a great deal of effort and power to soothe him after the loss of his brother.

~

Foth Castle, Kifirin

   Lexsi

Mom looked so frail as she gazed out the window of her suite. Edward was nearby, in case she needed anything.

Both of us were numb.

We'd felt him die.

Daddy was dead. He'd killed Grampa Garde and then himself before anybody could stop him.

Mom had gotten mindspeech from Uncle Karzac, and an explanation of sorts. Until then, I hadn't known that Grampa Garde had shot a controller into Jheri's neck, to make her do what he and Jayd wanted.

Daddy, who'd been the victim of a controller long ago, found that unforgivable and made a choice.

He'd killed his father.

My father was dead.

I couldn't bring myself to believe either of those things. They ran through my mind anyway, as if constant repetition would eventually bring the reality of it home.

"Baby?" Kory sat heavily beside me on the small sofa in Mom's suite.

"Kory." I buried my face against his shoulder.

"Let's go," Mom said. She folded all of us away from Foth Castle.

~

I'd never been to the gishi fruit groves on Kifirin. I'd worked in the EastStar groves from the time I could handle a hoverstep and nippers to pick fruit.

Here, the humanoid caretakers had deserted their posts, and

understandably so. A crop was rotting and falling from the trees as a result.

Jayd, in his rushed and callous decision to leave the Reth Alliance, had destroyed his own planet.

Yes, I understood that his mind was affected, but somewhere amid the underlying racism and personal grudges, he should have retained the knowledge of basic economics.

"He cannot admit to himself that he may be wrong." Kifirin appeared several feet away from Mom, as she walked between rows of trees. "I was wrong, daughter of my heart, and I admit it to you," Kifirin bowed to her. "This is why Li'Neruh oversees Kifirin, rather than I. It is fitting."

"At what cost does he intend to set things right?" Mom's eyes met Kifirin's. "I know you were changed and are different now. I accept your apology anyway, because it is sincere. It does nothing to change things for Torevik."

"I know. Torevik, in his next life, must make those changes for himself."

"Will I know him, then?" Mom wiped tears away.

"I cannot say, daughter. I do not have that gift."

"Everything comes at a cost," Mom sobbed.

Edward moved forward, but Kifirin reached her first. I found I was weeping with her. Kory pulled me against him and held me while my mother and I grieved in the gishi fruit groves of Kifirin.

Campiaa

Glinda

Tybus greeted me. Gavril was at Tory's cabin in the mountains, grieving for his brother.

Torevik's daughters had been informed of their father's death, and of the death of their grandfather, Gardevik.

How could one hold such mixed emotions without exploding?

On Le-Ath Veronis, Lissa was in a deep, healing sleep placed by Karzac, because she'd lost two—a son and a mate.

"Your daughters are well. Kevis has been seeing to Jheri, since her return from Kifirin." I followed him as he led me toward the stairs to the upper levels.

"Six of them really aren't my daughters," I breathed a heavy sigh. "My rational mind knows that. My heart is a different matter, and I understand how much grief that has caused Reah through the years."

Tybus, like Gavril, was mated to Reah. They all knew of my transgressions in this matter. No blame was leveled at me by any of them. I was always treated with polite respect.

Because they were better than I. I understood that, now.

It shamed me.

As it should.

"Mom?" Jhase met me at the top of the stairs. "Uncle Garde—Tory? Is it really true?"

"Yes, baby. It's true. Nobody expected it. He just showed up and, well."

"Tybus says that it was because of that device that Zaria pulled from Jheri's neck."

"I believe that's true," I agreed and took her arm. "Torevik was affected by one of those things in the past. When his own father," I shrugged. That, I couldn't understand or speak about without choking up.

Gardevik, probably on Jayd's orders, had shot a controller into my daughter's neck. I was angry enough to kill Jayd and Garde myself over that.

Garde is already dead, I reminded myself.

How is it that the more sudden the tragedy, the longer it takes to soak into your mind?

"What are we going to do?" Jhase whispered as we followed Tybus down another long hallway. Rich carpet muffled our footsteps, as if it barely registered our passing—much as Garde's passing in these troubled times would barely register with the outside worlds.

Torevik's passing would bring even less notice than his father's, as he'd stayed out of the spotlight for years.

"Baby, I don't know," I admitted. I was as lost as I'd ever been, and felt as if I no longer had a home to call my own.

"We have prepared this suite for you, next to your girls," Tybus opened a door and led us inside. "If you need anything, use the comm next to the bed. The entire manor is at your disposal, if you need food, drink or a place to relax in the gardens."

"What I need," I let go of Jhase's arm and wiped tears away. "What I need," I repeated, "is a friend. I no longer have any of those."

"Lissa," Tybus began.

"Lissa has no reason to treat me with anything but contempt. I let Kifirin get away from me and didn't ask for help. I didn't even notice that it needed help. It's destroying itself, and I stood by and let that happen."

"This wasn't all your doing," Tybus sounded stern. "And I am most sorry for your losses, believe me."

I didn't know until then that Tybus had power. He folded away, leaving Jhase to comfort me inside a borrowed suite.

Lissia, Le-Ath Veronis

Erland Morphis

Once, Garde and I had been as close as brothers. In the past forty years or so, we'd drifted apart.

I felt guilty about that. Perhaps if I'd paid better attention, Lissa wouldn't be suffering two great losses.

Torevik, as a youngling, had held so much promise. He and Ry had gotten into trouble together many times, as they were only separated in age by a few days.

All that was gone, now. Here I was, drinking in a vampire bar in Lissa's city while an uncle comforted my son.

"Warlock, this is not your blame to accept," Li'Neruh Rath took the barstool next to mine and nodded to the comesuli bartender. I watched as the bartender poured his best bourbon into a glass and walked away.

"Then whose blame is it?" Yes, I was drunk and baiting a god.

"If you take blame for this, then you may as well take blame for everything—and credit for everything. You are considering two who should have been rational at the beginning of their malady and come to the conclusion that they needed help on their own, rather than relying on their own clouded judgment." Li'Neruh lifted the glass and tossed back the double serving of alcohol.

"Leave the bottle," he commanded when the comesuli approached to refill the glass. With a nod, the comesuli did as requested before retreating to the other side of the bar.

"Are you saying they had some rational sense left at the beginning of all this?"

"Yes. Opportunities presented themselves. They were ignored."

"You've been watching this for a while?"

"Yes."

"I heard Glinda asked for a favor, and that your price was for her to step down."

"The price would have been nothing had she asked me the proper question, at the proper time."

"What was the proper question?"

"To remove the blinders from Reah's daughters, so they'd recognize their mother. Glinda was selfish in the matter, and rather than acting as a loving aunt, she chose to keep those six for her own."

"You could have done that." I stared at the shelves of bottles behind the bar and lifted my glass to drink.

"And I would have, gladly, had she asked."

"What if Reah asked?" I didn't take my eyes off the bottles, although I considered refilling my glass with power.

"Reah will not ask for anything that is not freely given. She wants her daughters to love her because she is their mother, without anyone's interference. She knows they see Glinda as their mother. Therefore, she will not ask."

Pulling the proper bottle off the shelf and floating it to my hand, I lifted it to let the bartender know to charge me and poured more alcohol in my glass. "I'd have destroyed something or someone if my son didn't recognize me as his father," I confessed.

"I know this." Li'Neruh filled his glass a third time.

"So you stood back and allowed Kifirin to disintegrate," I said, slurring my words.

"I allowed nothing. Those who ruled Kifirin failed to do anything about it. They could have asked. I would have answered."

"For a price."

"Depends on the question." Li'Neruh drank again.

"You're right. You did say that," I nodded. "Kifirin would have demanded a price."

"Because he was foolish enough to put the non-interference rule into play at the beginning. I laid down no such restrictions. If the question or favor is a selfish one, then yes, I will demand a price if I choose to answer or grant it."

"Ah." In my drink-fogged brain, that made sense.

I think.

"I have a question. It's not a selfish question," I held up a hand.

"Lord Morphis, I have no doubts about that." Li'Neruh refilled his glass.

"What will happen to those on Kifirin—the uh, High Demons, who will undoubtedly attack the innocents among them. High Demon and humanoid." I ended the question with an embarrassing hiccup.

"Ah, warlock," Li'Neruh dropped a hand on my shoulder. "Wait and see, my friend. Wait and see."

A credit chip dropped onto the bar as Li'Neruh and the bottle disappeared. I considered at that moment who would be at the palace that might consider taking me home.

I shouldn't have worried.

"Have you had enough, yet?" Warlend clapped a hand on my shoulder. Wellend stood on my other side, rustling red-feathered wings at my drunken condition.

"Who—shent you?" I warbled.

"Zaria."

"Good. Where are we going?"

"Avii Castle until you sober up," Wellend sighed.

Adelaide, Australia

Opal

I hoped Zaria would arrive before Morgett did. Kell and I were stationed at one end of the tunnel, which provided the easiest access. On the opposite end were Anita, Sandra, Esme and Watson.

Anita would send mindspeech if Morgett showed up there first.

Were you worried? Zaria dropped inside my shield as if there were nothing there.

Why no, I replied without holding back my sarcasm.

And that's why I love you, she hugged me.

Where are Lexsi and Kory?

I'll bring them if it's necessary. Things haven't gone so well for Lexsi in the future.

What happened?

Her father killed her grandfather, and then himself, she said.

I was too shocked to respond. Who'd seen this coming? Had Zaria seen it? Lissa and her other children had to be devastated, too.

Morgett is approaching, Kell interrupted my thoughts.

Here we go, Zaria said.

Showtime, I agreed.

V'ili

Tall, dry grass, rocks and dirt impeded our journey toward the tunnel entrance. Morgett didn't have a guide to this hiding place the Library had chosen.

He'd instructed all of us not to use power unless we were attacked. Therefore, we traveled on foot up a hillside, searching for the thing

Morgett wanted most. Deris tripped on a loose rock and cursed, causing Morgett to round on him with a glare.

Deris raised his hands in silent apology to his uncle, but once Morgett's back was turned, Deris' face contorted into a hate-filled sneer.

Daris reached out to rub Deris' back in a comforting way. Both of them—utterly contemptible and not worth the effort to torture before killing.

There, Morgett's sending interrupted my thoughts. I looked ahead. A round, blasted-out tunnel, half-covered with rusting iron bars and choked with rock and weeds waited. *That was our destination?*

Perhaps this is what the Library intended—after all, a volcano hadn't kept us away. Nobody would expect it to hide behind this sort of ugly, wasted mountainside.

V'ili, take the lead, Morgett commanded.

Anger filled me, but I stalked ahead of him anyway, prepared for whatever lay in wait.

~

Southern Continent, Kifirin

Lexsi

"Onion, we have to go," Kory sat beside me. I'd chosen a slatted, wooden bench between gishi fruit trees to sit and grieve. Somewhere in the groves, Mom and Kifirin walked and talked, and sometimes, Mom wept.

I couldn't bear it any longer, so I'd chosen my bench and asked Kory for some time alone.

"Why?" I knew my eyes and nose were red and my face splotchy from intermittent weeping.

"Because Jayd's sending some of his troops to attack Foth Castle. They need us, baby. They're outnumbered, and you know the humanoids are just fodder to be trampled by attacking Thifilathi."

"Some or all?" Mom and Kifirin appeared nearby, but it was Mom asking the question.

"Aldavik didn't know. All he said was that Full Thifilathi could be seen in the distance, stomping their way toward Foth Castle."

"Then we have to go. Honey, are you prepared for this?" Mom turned to me.

"Yeah. I am," I nodded. *More than you know*, I added silently.

The Library had promised a source of fire if needed.

I might need it.

CHAPTER 15

utitjulu, Northern Territory, Australia
Morwin

"This is Susan. She's a hen when she changes," Rose introduced the tall, plump resident of Alice Springs to me. Blonde hair was tied in a bun atop her head, and there was a curious cast to her gaze—much like that of a chicken as it examined something or someone new.

"A free-range hen?" I smiled and took her hand.

"A Buff Orpington, and as often as possible," she laughed.

"Susan can help," Rose said. "She can place those bombs in our claws before we take flight."

"Wise," I nodded to Rose. It would take more time if only Yoff and I were there to arm sixteen owls before taking off ourselves. Mutitjulu was quite close to Uluru, and in placing ourselves there, we had a decided vantage point to launch an attack against whatever came our way.

"The air feels so heavy," Chloe came to my side.

She was right; it did feel heavy. Like a thick blanket draped over me when it wasn't needed. The hot air of the Australian outback was stifling, although the sun was setting in the distance.

"Does this happen every time?" Rose asked.

"I can't answer that; I've never gone to war against Ra'Ak or High Demons," I replied. The skirmish in Adelaide was just that—it wasn't even a small battle. An ambush, perhaps, that hadn't turned out the way the enemy intended.

"Can we fly in this?" Chloe asked.

"I'm concerned," Rose added.

Their voices sounded thick and slow to my ears.

This isn't caused by High Demons or Ra'Ak, a small voice informed me.

"Yoff," I turned with effort toward the winged wizard.

"On it," he said, his words dragging.

He'd barely gotten us away, the shifter hen included, when the ground we'd occupied erupted in a terrible blast of earth and rock.

Adelaide, Australia

Opal

Morgett knew he'd been had, and he hadn't even reached the decoy Library. The tunnel and the hillside around it was blasted with his Ra'Ak's power and his giant serpent roared as the rain of rock, dirt and debris cascaded down the hillside.

Zaria had shielded us from the blast, and then sent her request for me to place a protective shield over nearby homes before disappearing.

Yes, we'd all felt the blast at Uluru—it sent shockwaves across the entire continent. Morgett's superior had played him, just as Zaria suspected, and now the grounds around Uluru were under attack.

I imagined that a rogue god had helped.

I'm sure that thought was foremost in Zaria's mind, too.

"What can we do?" Kell asked when I set us down in Esperance, more than thirteen hundred miles away from Adelaide.

We're safe in Alice Springs, Kiarra sent mindspeech. *Something terrible is going on at Uluru, though, and we can't get past the power barrier.*

"We're going to Alice Springs," I told Kell before gripping his hand and folding space.

$$\sim$$

Alice Springs

Morwin

"The Library is protecting Uluru and holding off the Ra'Ak Prince and his allies—for now," Zaria walked into Susan's kitchen, weariness etched across her features. "I have no idea where Morgett and his evil mini horde are."

"Thanks to V'ili, no doubt," Anita grumbled. She, her cousin and two others had arrived shortly before Zaria did. I was more than grateful that Susan's home was outside Alice Springs—the Larentii had enlarged it with power to accommodate all of us.

"It's on the news," Rose informed us as she and Susan joined us in the kitchen. Lifting a remote control, she turned on the small television on a kitchen counter.

"We have no idea, and it is more than frightening," a statesman with aboriginal ancestry told a reporter. "Nobody can get close, and there were a few hikers in the area that are unaccounted for."

"Do you think this has anything to do with the attack on Adelaide?" the reporter asked.

"I have no idea. Certainly no demands have been made. I will say this; my people are very concerned, as this is a holy place to us. The Prime Minister has asked for assistance from surrounding emergency departments, but I fear for Uluru's safety and that of those peoples living near it. We haven't been able to contact them since the explosion. Attempts to fly over result in blank images recorded, or the loss of the aircraft involved."

"Just like Peru," Opal sighed.

"Is it a standoff, then?" Anita asked.

"The Library isn't just going to let them walk in unscathed," Zaria said. "Remember the volcano?"

"What are you not telling us?" Opal frowned at Zaria.

"Something Papa Neff told me," she sighed.

"What's that?"

"That the Library is a record of everything—every person, planet, rock, tree, you name it. That's why it's constantly changing. Nefrigar thinks that rather than allowing itself to fall into the wrong hands, the Library may destroy everything."

My breath caught. How much power did this Library have? *Father, did you know this?* I sent a silent message into space.

"I really need to go to Kifirin," Zaria sighed. "I'll keep tabs on things here, but I have an idea that things here won't change—at least for a while."

"Need help?" Opal asked.

"Maybe," Zaria said.

"Then take some of us with you."

"All right. Morwin, would you and the owls like to come?"

"I want to go," Susan said. She had no idea what she was volunteering to do, but if Rose went, she wanted to accompany her.

"That's awesome," Zaria nodded to Susan. "Come on, I'll take you. Kiarra can handle things here for now."

"Madame hen," Tamp and Ilya appeared as if called. Tamp dipped his head to Susan. "You will come to our time. In the future."

I swear Susan squawked when she was folded away.

~

Foth Castle, Northern Reaches, Kifirin
Kordevik

I won't lie and say I didn't breathe a sigh of relief when Zaria, Opal and several others appeared in the castle courtyard.

In the distance, perhaps a mile away, Jayd's High Demon troops roared in Full Thifilathi.

"They're waiting on more troops to join them—Jayd wants to kill and trample everybody inside these walls," Zaria came toward me.

She looked tired.

"What's going on in Australia?" Lexsi joined us, with Reah right behind her.

"A standoff for the moment, between the Library and Liron's pet Ra'Ak," Zaria said. "Liron is likely in the middle of it, too, and I can't do anything about that without destroying the timeline."

"That doesn't sound good," Reah breathed.

"It isn't," Zaria agreed. "But there's nothing to be done there for the moment. We have to deal with this, first."

"My family," I blurted.

Zaria blinked at me, as if that had just occurred to her, too.

"Give me a minute," she said and disappeared before Opal could protest.

Warde and I wouldn't be the only ones on Kifirin with a death sentence already levied—Zaria would bring my Father and my brothers. Jayd would have a fight on his hands when he attacked.

"Pap's coming with the others," I informed Warde, who'd joined us.

"Good. We need them," Warde nodded. "Lady Reah, are you well?" he asked.

"I'm well enough," Reah sighed. "Lexsi and I will get past this—in time."

"If you wish to talk, I will be available," Warde offered with a slight bow.

"Thank you, that's very kind."

I considered that Kevis Halivar was one of Reah's mates, and would likely know best what comfort to offer.

She didn't say no, a tiny voice informed me.

Warde had offered; Reah hadn't said no.

Shaking off the tendrils of speculation, I clapped Warde on the shoulder and asked him to follow me. Morwin had come with the others, and he and I needed to plan an attack with the Amterean troops that had come earlier, courtesy of ASD Director Kooper Griff.

Morwin

"Master Morwin," Salidar DeLuca acknowledged me.

I hadn't gained that title. Hadn't even begun to work on it yet.

"Don't worry about it," Kordevik's hand dropped onto my shoulder. "What we have to do now is plan an attack, with your Amterean troops hidden in the tall grasses surrounding the castle."

"All armed with ranos pistols and rifles, I see," I responded.

"It's for the best, as you know," Salidar said.

"Yes. I do know."

"We need to pick off as many of the frontrunners as we can," Kordevik explained. "Jayd won't expect an attack outside the walls. We'll surprise them. He'll give orders to take the castle. There are probably enough High Demons out there to crawl over the curtain walls and parapets like swarming ants. I want to whittle those numbers down as much as possible before they get that far."

"We can certainly help with that," I said. "The troops are dressed in camouflage for the terrain, and have water and ration packs if needed. They know to move out of the way when the time is right, and how to survive in the wilds, if necessary, until the ASD arranges transportation afterward."

"Stay alive," Kordevik said. "Lexsi will take you inside her mist and drop you in strategic spots."

"Ready?" Lexsi appeared at Kory's side.

"Ready," I nodded. "Troops, remember your training. Shoot to kill. Protect your brothers."

"Yes, Commander." they chorused and thumped fists against their chests.

Pulling both ranos pistols from the holsters of the camouflaged gear I'd been given, I nodded to Lexsi.

We were airborne in an instant.

Lexsi

I dropped Morwin's troops, six at a time, at the locations Kory and

Warde indicated earlier. They fanned out quickly, in an arrow pattern, so their comrades wouldn't be in the line of fire.

I dropped Morwin and five others last, at the farthest point from the castle walls. Those six were now our front line of defense.

Stay safe, I sent mindspeech to Morwin, hoping he'd hear me.

If this Morwin died, too many things could go wrong.

We're here, Zaria sent as I misted toward the castle. A shiver went through my mist as I passed over the Amterean troops, hidden here and there amidst the tall grasses. It was too much to ask, I think, that all of them would survive.

Zaria

"We were prepared to help before. Let us help now," Rose stood stubbornly before me, arms crossed over her chest.

"They can help," Tamp said as he gripped my shoulders from behind. "Their owls are so small to a High Demon; they won't be seen as a threat."

"Mother Rose, you know this isn't your country or your fight," I reminded her.

"We know that, but if it weren't for Kory, Lexsi and the others, we could be dead already." Rose wasn't budging an inch.

"Fine. Same plan as before, except Morwin won't be with you," I relented.

"I'll go with Yoff," Esme volunteered. "To carry extra grenades."

"Good. Make them count," I sighed. "Go. Get ready. The moment they reach the wall, you fly. Morwin's troops will be out of the way by then."

"Susan," Rose turned to her friend. "Let's get this thing going."

I watched those two walk away—it was an unusual friendship between a hen and an owl, but I wasn't about to quibble.

Li'Neruh Rath

Jaydevik stalked back and forth before me, while I stood firm, a close, heavy shield surrounding me. Like him, I'd chosen my smaller Thifilathi for this meeting.

Smoke poured from his nostrils as dark eyes with fire in their depths narrowed in disgust.

He hadn't expected me to come.

"Stop this now, admit it is wrong and Glindarok may return to you," I said. "Use what wisdom you have left and save lives."

"My brother is dead." A cloud of smoke hid his face for several moments, until a northerly breeze blew it away. "Nobody saved his life."

"He was attacking innocents. His own son killed him, of his own volition, then killed himself. Be honest; Torevik was a victim of those filthy controllers you still possess. You've infected your own daughter with one, haven't you?"

"It's the only way they'll do what they're told," Jayd hissed around his fangs.

"Your daughters, or females in general?"

"Females. They're all the same." More smoke flew from his nostrils.

"Perhaps they're wiser and stronger, and you dislike that," I offered.

Flames were now licking about Jayd's feet and legs, setting the grass he'd trampled on fire. With only a thought, I extinguished it and laid a shield beneath his feet so he couldn't keep burning it.

"Wiser? Stronger? For a god, you have a lot to learn," Jayd laughed humorlessly. "You probably believe that quarter-blood trollop, Reah, will be a decent queen for Kifirin."

"She saved Kifirin," I pointed out.

"All she did was plant trees," he snorted. "Anybody can do that."

"But neither you nor anybody else thought of it, or put the work into it. You just took the money to pay off Kifirin's debts and support yourself in a lavish lifestyle."

"She is worthless," Jayd growled. "I'll die before I'll allow her to take the Queen's throne here."

"Call back your troops, Jaydevik. This is madness," I told him.

"There is still a glimmer of rationality in that warped brain—I can feel it. Go back to Veshtul, and I guarantee that your ills will be healed."

"What ills?"

"Those affecting your mind. You know that you've been affected. Admit it."

"I have been affected," he said. "I prefer it. It has opened my eyes."

"It's playing on your weaknesses," I snapped.

"Those weaknesses, as you call them, will keep Kifirin intact and strong. Independent. We don't need the Alliance or any woman telling us what to do."

"How do you propose to feed your people?" I demanded. "Much of your food and supplies has come from Alliance sources."

"We can skip, and we'll take what we want."

"Except that at the moment, there's a shield around the planet, and you can't skip anywhere—for that very reason."

"You did this to us." Jayd stopped pacing and turned toward me with clenched fists.

"What if I did? You know it's wrong to steal. You know it's wrong to overpower weaker beings. You know it's wrong to kill innocents. Yet you are planning all those things, are you not?"

"To keep my race alive."

"Your race will live if you give up these terrible plans. I promise it."

"Fuck you and your promises. I never accepted you as the deity Kifirin needs."

"Jaydevik Rath, you have led your people astray. I ask you one last time to set aside this madness and return to Veshtul." I unleashed a bit of my power and allowed it to vibrate about me.

"Fuck you. We take Foth Castle first. We'll see who survives and who doesn't."

"Very well. Never say I didn't warn you," I said and folded space.

~

Foth Castle
  Zaria

He didn't take well to reason, Hank's voice entered my mind.

You tried reason? Do you have any left yourself?

You know, not many would call me out on that, he admitted. *Jayd has some reason left. He knows what he's doing is wrong, but he'll never admit it. Not after it's gotten this far.*

Pride, fall, and all that?

Perhaps.

I don't understand this, I breathed a mental sigh.

Sweetheart, I know you're tired. We'll deal with that when this is over.

Right. Get in line. Val and several others say the same thing.

I'll be in that line. I'll also come if things don't go your way in this battle. At the last, of course, to face down the remaining army. That's my job.

My job is to keep as many of these alive as I can. Go get yourself a pizza and watch from the sidelines, bub.

I can supply a news crew so everybody can watch from the sidelines.

You do that. I have to go. War beckons and all that.

His voice disappeared from my mind as I stalked toward the tent covering the three-dimensional map of the castle and surrounding grounds. There, Nedevik, Aldavik, Fredevik, Kory, Warde and several others outlined their strategy.

I was ready to tell them that Jayd's army was on the way. I should have known that Jamie, Farin, Tibby and an entire news crew from Le-Ath Veronis would appear outside that tent, micro-cams ready to record.

Henry Hank Bell, your ass is in trouble, I grumped in his direction.

I refer you to Breanne. You and she can chew on said ass any time you want.

Sounds like a blast, I retorted while watching one of the news crew approach.

"Zaria, Bryan Riley," he held out a hand. "I hope you don't mind, and we'll be discreet and stay out of the way," he promised.

"Not a problem," I waved an arm at the Director of Media and Media Relations from Le-Ath Veronis. "I've got myself shielded. It's a cinch Jayd won't be watching vids while his army attacks."

He nodded, realizing that my words were more than half sarcasm.

"Do you have more of those ranos grenades?" Opal appeared beside me.

"I can get some," I said. "Why?"

"I run fast," Opal's smile was grim. "I can get far enough ahead of the Amterean troops that they won't be affected, and flee fast enough that the grenade will detonate behind me at a safe distance. Kell can do the same."

"A velociraptor and a vampire dropping grenades like Easter eggs?" I blinked at Opal.

"That's the idea. We're outnumbered at least twenty to one—in case you haven't noticed."

"I can help with that," Klancy joined Opal.

"I can grow enormous roots around the castle, hiding them in the tall grass to trip the front runners," Tamp arrived behind Klancy.

"You want to do this?" I asked all of them.

"Yes," they said together.

"Fine. Get to it. Don't die. It'll just piss me off more."

Klancy nodded, then winked at me before turning to follow Opal and the others. Bryan went with them; he'd already attempted to capture my likeness on his camera and discovered it didn't work.

Mr. Riley and I might have a word after this, if we were still able.

Jamie Rome

"I can carry a button camera, like before," Tibby offered. Farin, standing beside him, nodded.

"I can provide commentary on the images from behind the walls, if I have a monitor," Farin said.

"What sort of shifter are you?" Bryan Riley asked. I suspected he was vampire, like Kell and Klancy. He could smell that Tibby was a shifter.

"I'm a rat," Tibby grinned. "I can move easily outside the walls. All I have to do is avoid getting stepped on."

"Oh, my gosh, Tibby," Farin said. That hadn't occurred to her until now—that Tiburon could be crushed by stampeding High Demons.

"I'll be safe enough," Tibby promised. "Do not worry." He patted Farin's cheek.

"A button camera from that low will show the attacking High Demons as the frightening mob they are," Bryan said. "Mr. Rome, will you supervise the camera feeds and switchers?"

"Of course," I said. I'd done production work in the past. I'd get my feel for it again.

"Good. I'm taking a camera up top, into one of the corner towers. We'll have as many angles as we can get on this. Earpieces in, everybody; I can hear a rumble in the distance. It's show time."

Mutitjulu, Northern Territory, Australia
    V'ili

Morgett was so angry, even the twins kept their mouths shut and maintained a safe distance from him. They and I were prepared to fold space if he leveled his anger at any of us.

A few kilometers away, Prince Vantes and an army of Ra'Ak struggled to break through an invisible barrier surrounding the great, sandstone monolith named Uluru.

The fact that there was now a shield around it told Morgett that the Library was hidden there instead of Adelaide. The dwarf had laid a successful trap for us, and we'd fallen for it.

At least we hadn't seen what lay at the end of that trap; we'd folded space the moment Vantes and his army landed outside Uluru.

It was fortuitous; we had no idea what lay in wait inside the false Library. I imagined the High Demons waited to kill us there. It was no longer a secret that they'd allied with the dwarf to get their hands on the actual Library.

As it was, nobody could get close to it, now. Vantes had seen to that when he and his army had shown up in serpent form, seeking to break Uluru apart to reach the Library.

"Vantes is a fool." Someone new arrived.

He was tall and had wings—shining white wings that rustled at his back, as if he were displeased. I'd seen gods before. I hadn't seen this one.

"Liron, tell me what to do," Morgett turned toward the newcomer, as if he'd known him for a very long time.

"Use your skills, of course," the winged one replied with an indifferent shrug. "If you can't get to Uluru above the surface, then you must tunnel beneath it."

"Where should we start?" Morgett asked. He sounded as if he were desperate and begging.

"Here is good enough. With your power, you should be able to assess where and how deeply to build your tunnel, don't you think? If you hit the barrier at any time, either go around or under it. This way, you remain out of Vantes' sight. The Sirenali will take care of the rest for you."

"Of course," Morgett breathed, as if he should have thought of it himself. I wanted to snort. I didn't. If Morgett were bowing and scraping to this one, I should keep my mouth shut and my movements at a minimum.

Like before, when I'd seen other gods.

"Start now," Liron commanded and disappeared.

"What are you waiting for?" Morgett turned to snap at Deris. "Begin making a tunnel. If you need help, I will guide your power."

∼

Kent, England

Adam Chessman

"The Ra'Ak have drawn back for now, after repeatedly throwing their power and their bodies against the shield," Pheligar reported. "I imagine they fed before their arrival here, but it won't be long before they are hungry again."

"That means they'll attack the nearest food source, and that will be the surrounding towns," Kiarra frowned. "Are the authorities pulling everyone out of the area?"

"They are attempting evacuation, but there are some who refuse to leave," Pheligar replied.

"They'll be eaten," I said. "Is there a way to let the Australian Government know that this will be a massive attack, similar to the one in Adelaide?"

"I believe they've already come to that conclusion, although the Ra'Ak have successfully hidden behind their own shields," Pheligar said. "All they have is the information they constantly replay on their television screens—that of the giant hole in the ground outside the monolith."

"Have more attempts been made to send drones in?" Merrill asked.

"That was stopped after the last five were destroyed. By the Ra'Ak, no doubt," Pheligar said.

"Thanks for gathering information," Kiarra leaned against Pheligar's hip and put her arms about his waist.

"You are welcome, dearest," he smiled down at her.

What are we going to do? I sent to Merrill.

No idea. We'd need an army of Saa Thalarr to fight off that many Ra'Ak. There are thousands of them, he returned.

An army we don't have, I reminded myself. Merrill picked up my thoughts and silently agreed.

Northern Reaches, Kifirin

Opal

The last time I'd run toward an invading army, they'd been on horseback. This time, their feet carried them toward me, as fast as any horse could gallop.

I'd folded Kell, Klancy and myself to the grasses ahead of Morwin's small company. I was already changed when we landed.

Kell handed my velociraptor a batch of grenades. I nodded at him and we began to run toward advancing High Demons, their heavy footsteps shaking the ground beneath our feet.

Time to spread mayhem, I sent to my companion vampires, who'd fanned out on either side of me.

It will be a distinct pleasure, Klancy replied.

Grasses swished past me as I ran, keeping pace with both vampires. Kell tossed the first grenade in the air; we were far ahead of it when it hit the ground with a resulting loud explosion, knocking a running High Demon off his feet and causing several others running behind him to trip over his bleeding body.

Zaria

"Once they reach the wall, can you bring it down?" Reah asked me.

I turned toward her and chewed my lip for a moment until I saw her meaning. Reah and Kory wanted to set up their High Demon troops behind the wall, and if the wall suddenly disappeared, it could confuse the attackers long enough that it would give our High Demons the element of surprise.

"I can disintegrate it," I said.

"That would be wonderful," Reah said.

"Time to change," Kory shouted nearby.

Outside the walls, Morwin's dwarves were shooting High Demons as they ran toward the castle.

Other High Demons had tripped over Tamp's huge roots, until they learned to jump over the bulge surrounding the castle.

Opal, Kell and Klancy had some success in disrupting the attack, but there were so many High Demons in Jayd's army that the rest flowed around those who'd fallen and continued on their way.

Morwin and his troops were shooting as quickly as their pistols would fire, but had to clear out fast due to the speed of the invaders.

Still, they'd taken down a good share of the racing High Demons, and at least half of Morwin's troops had survived.

I refused to concentrate on our losses now. "Owls," I shouted. "Fly now!"

Sixteen small owls, each armed with two ranos grenades, took flight, with Yoff and Esme right behind them.

It was only seconds, but it felt like forever before the first grenades were dropped, sending shockwaves against the castle walls. It was nearly time to bring down the wall, as Reah asked.

"For Queen Reah," Wardevik's Thifilathi shouted and raised his arm in the air. Reah, whose golden Thifilathi stood next to Lexsi's silver, bowed her head before lifting her eyes to the wall.

I made it disappear and the two armies clashed with a great roar.

utijulu, Northern Territory, Australia
V'ili

Deris and Daris were sweating with the effort of expending power. Deris relocated rock and earth; Daris transported it to a pile at the surface.

I imagined we'd cleared at least twelve kilometers of tunnel, with forty-five or so to go—if we kept moving in the same direction. Should we be forced to move around a barrier shield, it would take longer.

I didn't point out to Morgett how lazy his niece and nephew had become—they were used to causing deaths and such, and stopped when they tired. Everything else they gained through someone else's actions.

Here, they were past tired, but Morgett compelled them to keep working. Surely he realized the tunnel would take more than one day to create?

"Stop," Morgett commanded. The twins were happy to oblige.

"I will take over while you rest," Morgett added.

I'd forgotten Morgett's Ra'Ak power. Another twelve kilometers were cleared and a firm tunnel created in less than two hours.

"We go slowly, so as not to alert Vantes," Morgett grunted as he cleared out more dirt and rock. "While he can't sense what I'm doing because of your abilities, those abilities only go so far," he informed me. "If he realizes he should be *Looking* for a tunnel, he'll find it outside your area of influence."

I hadn't thought about that. Morgett was right—I could only cover a small area with my power of concealment. I certainly didn't want the Ra'Ak Prince breathing down my neck in the next few minutes.

"How long?" I ventured to ask.

"We'll reach the edge of the underground rock tomorrow," Morgett grunted again, as if he were doing physical labor instead of employing power. "I hope there's a way to be found in or out of the Library past that point."

I sincerely hoped there was a way in, as I'd already grown tired of the closed-in stuffiness of the tunnel.

Anita

Sandra, Watson, Mason and I stood outside the tiny shack. One of the few remaining buildings of Mutitjulu that looked mostly in one piece, it was an improbable oxymoron of a structure. It should have fallen on its own long ago.

Somehow, it had survived the blast that mowed down the rest of the small town. Watson drew in a breath, sniffing the air.

"Somebody was here," he declared.

"No," I breathed my sarcasm. Power held the shack up; of that I was certain.

"Shall we?" Sandra jerked her head toward the small building.

"Careful, it could be booby-trapped," Mason warned.

"Yeah. If you guys smell explosives, get the hell out," I said.

"Not a problem," Sandra whispered.

"I'll go first," Mason volunteered.

"You do that," Watson said. "We'll be right behind you. At a safe distance."

Mason walked slowly toward the wooden door of the shack. "We should have told Kiarra we were leaving," Sandra nudged my arm.

"They would have stopped us," I said. "There has to be something we're missing here. If we need to go back, we will."

Sandra held her breath as Mason pushed on the door. It should have swung open. It didn't. That meant it was locked.

"Who would lock up a rundown shack?" Sandra asked.

"Stand back," Mason warned before kicking the door down. The rest of us cringed, waiting for an explosion or something. Nothing came.

"Look at this," Mason stepped inside the shack and disappeared.

"Come on," Sandra grabbed my arm. Watson followed us inside.

This was no shack. Inside was a luxurious home, albeit a small one. Someone had employed power to not only keep the structure standing, but to make it look as if it were rundown and abandoned on the outside.

Inside, it held a small living area with a sofa and television. Connected to the living area was a tiny kitchen and behind that, sleeping quarters.

It looked good enough for anyone to inhabit—except for the rather large hole in the floor's center.

Mason stared down that hole into darkness. "Somebody's building a tunnel," he lifted his eyes to mine.

"Three guesses where it's going," Watson growled.

"I don't need three guesses. Is it a straight drop?" I asked Mason.

"No. Roughly six feet down, it bends and then slopes gradually, I think. At least that's what I see from here."

He had vampire night vision, so of course he'd see that.

"Good. I'm going in," I said. "I missed dear old V'ili in Adelaide. I'd bet everything I have that he's at the bottom of this."

"No," Watson held out a hand as I dropped into the hole and landed on solid ground below.

"Come on, you wimps," my voice echoed. "Let's get this thing going."

~

Queen's Palace, Le-Ath Veronis

Lissa

"You should stay here," I said.

Glinda ignored me and pulled a long knife from a sheath to check the edge. The metal was black, the edge as sharp as Grey House could make it.

"Tell me why," she demanded, turning toward me.

"You haven't fought in a while," I pointed out.

"Jayd hasn't fought in a while, either."

"Glinda, you can't go against him. It'll destroy you, even if you survive."

"You think I haven't been destroyed already? He may as well have killed Jheri, shooting that filth into her neck."

"Then let me come with you," Denevik appeared beside me.

I won't lie; I sagged in relief.

"Denny, what happened to us?" Glinda's eyes filled with tears.

Denevik strode toward her and pulled her into a tight hug. "I think it started a long time ago, baby sister," he soothed. "Times changed. We didn't."

"Or most of us didn't," Glinda muffled against his shoulder.

"True. All it took was a little nudge from rogue gods, and the thin veneer of civilization sloughed right off," Denevik said. "We didn't fight to get it back. Li'Neruh Rath said Jayd and Garde could have fought for it. They didn't."

Garde.

I'd loved him. A part of me still did.

"I can't employ power for this, but I can still fight," I said. "I'm coming with you."

Glinda pulled away and stared at me in shock.

~

Foth Castle, Northern Reaches, Kifirin

Zaria

Blades clashed against blades; Kory's brothers had all shown up with their own arms. If they hadn't, they'd be forced to fight with fists against blades.

With what Foth had in his treasury, and the few swords they'd made that I'd reinforced, at least we didn't have faulty equipment to wage war.

I stood behind Bryan Riley in his tower, while he transmitted his camera feed directly to a room full of images that Jamie Rome and several others watched and sent immediately to Le-Ath Veronis and Wyyld. From there, they were transmitted to the Alliances.

The Alliances were watching a war first hand, and from close quarters.

I cringed every time I heard a death roar from a High Demon. Their blood slicked the courtyard at the center of the Castle, and I was too terrified to *Look* to see who lived and who died.

Interfering too much with this timeline could have disastrous consequences for the future; I knew that already.

And so I watched Kory's brothers fall through my tears.

At least Kory and Lexsi had their blades; they'd finally needed them.

Another roar.

Another fallen High Demon, his affiliation unknown.

We're here, Glinda, Denevik and I, Lissa sent.

Then haul your granddaughter away from her derring-do and get your mist on, I said. *I'm tired of watching Kory's family get slaughtered.*

On it, Lissa returned.

The first High Demon head exploded seconds later.

Kent, England

Adam Chessman

"Anita, Watson, Sandra and Mason are missing," Kiarra folded into the kitchen, where I was having a cup of afternoon tea.

My head jerked up at the news. "Where?" I stood, prepared to go after them.

"No idea. You know we can't find a Sirenali; that's their superpower."

"Then where do you think they may have gone?" I asked. By that time, Merrill was in the kitchen, listening carefully.

"I suggest looking in Mutitjulu," Pheligar appeared behind Merrill. "A few structures are still standing. All should have been knocked down by the force of the blast."

"We'll start there," Kiarra said, changing her clothing with a thought to deal with the heat of an Australian summer.

I didn't have time to do mine; Pheligar did it for Merrill and me before folding the three of us away with him.

"Here," I said, after sniffing about the small shack on the outskirts of the tiny town of Mutitjulu. "I smell both werewolves, the vampire and the Sirenali."

"Agreed," Merrill said.

"The door's still open and nobody's inside," Kiarra said after *Looking.*

"Shall we?" Pheligar transformed into a human-sized being and motioned toward the door.

I wasn't prepared to find a hole at the center of a nicely-appointed home inside the deceptive, shack-like exterior. "Somebody's tunneling their way toward Uluru," Merrill said, echoing my thoughts.

"The scent of our missing four is all around it," I said. "They're following the tunnel makers."

"Not good," Kiarra stared down the dark hole and shook her head.

"I will ensure that it will not collapse about us," Pheligar declared. "We will do our best to catch up to our knights errant before the timeline is damaged."

"I'll go first," I said and dropped into the hole.

~

Foth Castle, Northern Reaches, Kifirin

Zaria

Dearest, Val sent, *Father has heard from Pheligar. I'm afraid that Anita and three others are tracking V'ili and Morgett through a tunnel built by Morgett and the Blackmantle twins. They're attempting to reach Uluru underground.*

I slapped a hand over my face while High Demon heads continued to explode in the courtyard. *Is Pheligar following them? Please say yes,* I returned.

He, Kiarra, Adam and Merrill are following, although only Pheligar can employ his power. I have no doubt that any use of a Saa Thalarr's power will alert the Ra'Ak Prince to their location.

And chaos will surely come, I said.

Yes. That is my father's opinion, as well as my own.

When it rains, it pours.

Not always, dearest.

Honey?

Yes?

Now is not the time to be literal, okay?

I see your point.

Thank you.

What do you intend to do about this?

Honey, I'm thinking, I said. *It's not easy to do that, because High Demon heads are popping like Champagne corks below me.*

"Do what you must; I will watch here," Li'Neruh Rath's smaller Thifilathi appeared at my side.

I grimaced at him. He leaned in to kiss me. Energy slammed into me at the same time. I felt more alert afterward than I had in days. He'd given me strength to act and think, and I was grateful.

Plus, as a first kiss, it wasn't terrible and I told him so.

"Thanks, I think," he grinned around his fangs.

"I'll be back," I said and folded space.

~

Lexsi

Gran and I misted from one rogue High Demon to the next, misting in, expanding our mist quickly and causing heads to explode.

I could do nothing about the trail of bodies we left behind; those were piling up at an alarming rate. Still, they outnumbered us and more came.

Go to the back of the line and work your way forward, Gran instructed. *Hopefully we'll meet in the middle.*

Okay. I squelched a wave of queasiness at the growing mountain of bloody, headless High Demons below my mist and rushed toward the back of Jayd's troops.

Jayd stalked behind his army, uncaring that ahead of him, my grandmother and I had taken out so many High Demons already. Somehow, the anger on his Thifilathi's face let me know that he wanted his own hands on Lords Weth, Foth and Greth. If he could get his hands on me and Gran, he'd try to kill us, too.

Ignoring him for the moment, I misted inside the head of one close to him and blew out my mist.

Jayd barely faltered as the headless High Demon fell. He merely snorted clouds of smoke, as if daring me to kill him, too.

He was related, through my father. How could I kill him?

Forget him, a male voice sounded in my mind. Li'Neruh Rath had come. *Continue taking down the others,* he added.

Feeling somewhat relieved, I went back to work killing the others, just as Li'Neruh asked.

~

Reah

Edward and Gavril arrived. Edward's War Eagle screamed overhead before diving down and removing a High Demon's head with razor-sharp claws.

That's when several High Demons took flight to chase after him.

In midair, Gavril, as mist, exploded one head after another, raining bodies, blood, brain matter and skull fragments on the attacking High Demons below.

Edward and Gavril had planned this together. Jayd's rogue army was now threatened from above as well as on the ground.

Flinging out a wing, I knocked an attacker off his feet, then skewered him in the throat with my blade before he could rise.

Yes, it was nasty business. I killed them before they could kill me. That is the most basic rule of any war, and I'd been through more than enough battles in my lifetime. Slowly, these rogues were learning that my Thifilatha was just as seasoned (if not more so) than the best they could send against me.

My Grey House blade clanged against that of another rogue, who'd thought to come close as he attacked me. I punched him in the face while our blades were still crossed, then kneed him in the groin. While he doubled over in pain, I stepped back and relieved him of his head.

~

Near Mutitjulu, Northern Territory, Australia
Anita

They were digging as they went, if my supposition was correct. I and my three were following the easy path they'd created.

I figured V'ili had nothing to do with the formation of the tunnel; he'd be there to provide cover, only. Morgett and the twins would be tired from creating a tunnel so quickly.

Morgett wanted to get to the Library very badly.

As did the Ra'Ak horde covering the ground above our heads.

Sandra and Watson had turned to wolf; Mason carried their clothing in case it was needed again. Both werewolves followed the scent along the tunnel after Watson confirmed that we were on the right path.

Our quarry hadn't taken time to build misleading tunnels to trap or confuse any followers—likely because they wanted to reach their goal as swiftly as they could.

The question that kept niggling at my brain, however, was this; what did Morgett hope to gain from this? Did he think the Library was going to do his bidding or something? Would it give him an enormous amount of power—provided he could control it in some way?

Zaria's words came back to me, then. The words she'd said had come from Papa Neff—Nefrigar, Valegar's father and Chief Archivist of the Larentii Archives. He'd surmised that the Library could destroy everything.

I hadn't really considered that to mean *everything* everything.

Zaria imagined that rogue gods could be involved in all this, somehow.

"Oh, my fucking goodness," I stopped short to mutter under my breath. I was accompanied by two werewolves and a vampire. They could have heard my low voice from half a mile away.

"What is it?" Mason asked.

"I think we're all being played—to the bitterest end you can possibly imagine," I whispered.

"What are you talking about?" Sandra was human again. *Naked and human,* I reminded myself.

"On Kifirin, a planet so far away you can't see its sun's light from here, the High Demons are trying to destroy themselves, thanks to a bit of interference from rogue gods. Here, we have Morgett doing his best to get to the Library through this tunnel, and above our heads, we have an army of Ra'Ak, led by a Ra'Ak Prince who wants exactly the same thing. Who told them about the Library to begin with? I think the same rogue gods are playing both sides against each other. Why, you ask? Well, Nefrigar of the Larentii thinks that the Library could destroy everything, rather than fall into the wrong hands. What if this is the rogue gods' way to clean the slate? People, I think we're screwed."

"Clean the slate?" Watson pulled his shirt over his head, then blinked at me in confusion.

"Don't worry about it," Zaria said as she landed beside me. "Anita, Kiarra, Adam, Merrill and Pheligar are trying to catch up with you. Wait here for them, all right? You're not equipped to take on Morgett, you know. That's what they do—they fight Ra'Ak all the time."

"You sound like you're leaving again," I said, my hands going to my hips.

"Yeah. I think I have to. No, I can't explain it," she held up a hand before I could ask. "Just wait for Kiarra and the others. Besides, Pheligar can get you around and provide a shield so you won't be seen. Okay?"

"I'm all for not being seen," Sandra said right away.

"Fine," I grumped. "How long before they arrive?"

"Less than half an hour," Zaria replied. "It'll give you time to rest a bit."

"All right, but it's only because you helped me a long time ago," I said.

"Yeah. Don't forget that," she said and disappeared.

"What did she do to help you?" Sandra asked.

"It's a long story," I hedged. I really didn't want to explain my past to Watson and his sister. Not now, anyway.

"We have half an hour," Mason observed.

Fuck.

~

Zaria

So many things needed to be done, and those things crowded my mind, each clamoring to be the first.

Actually, there was something I wanted to do first.

Hank said he'd move mountains for me. This wasn't a mountain, and would require less effort on his part. Nevertheless, it would be inordinately more important to me than moving any mountain would be.

Except—I considered that for a moment.

Yes. I had two things to ask for, instead of just one. I sent mindspeech to him while he watched the battle unfold on Kifirin.

I waited. Seconds ticked by.

All right, he agreed.

Thank you, I replied and bent time.

The first thing on my list, after all, was getting a really good look at Morgett. I needed to know so many things about him, and seeing his face would give me that information. I suspected there were secrets he didn't want anyone else to know. Therefore, a volcanic eruption in Peru's past was my initial destination.

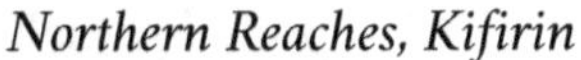

Northern Reaches, Kifirin

Lissa

At least I'd been well-rested before killing High Demon rogues this time. In the past, I was already tired when I took them and their Copper Ra'Ak allies on.

I recalled that I wasn't nearly as powerful then, too.

Come on, you fuckers, I sent mindspeech to Jayd's remaining army. Lexsi, Gavril and I had whittled those troops down, but still many thousands threatened Foth Castle and the High Demons fighting for Kifirin.

Gran! I heard Lexsi's mental voice clearly.

She'd sent a mental image, too.

Glinda had skipped to the back of the invading army, her White Thifilatha bowling straight into Jayd's Black Thifilathi.

Holy. Fucking. Hell.

I'm coming, I sent. Leaving my post would mean High Demons belonging to Weth, Foth and Greth would die without my help.

I had to leave them. Glinda had done the unthinkable, and would likely die from her actions.

Denevik, I sent. *Come and help.* I folded space to Lexsi's side.

Near Mutitjulu, Northwest Territory, Australia

Anita

"But," Sandra breathed.

She, Watson and Mason now knew my story. How V'ili and I were connected and related. How Esme was my sister and my cousin.

How she and I had died at V'ili's command, and then lived again—to hunt him. To bring his death if we could.

"Look, I don't know how it was done, but the powerful ones that bent time to pull us away can do it, as long as it doesn't upset the timeline in any way."

"That's frightening," Watson blinked at me.

"It was frightening," I agreed. "If Zaria hadn't come to reassure me and tell me someone was coming for us; it could have been much worse."

"There you are." Kiarra and her bunch had arrived. I pulled myself off the floor and brushed tunnel dust off my cargo pants.

"Zaria told us to wait for you," I said, feeling ashamed. I'd slipped away from Kiarra's home without telling anyone where I was headed, and had taken my three with me.

"Thank you for waiting, then," Kiarra sighed. "I hate to think what would happen if that Ra'Ak filth found you down here."

"We sort of figured that out," Sandra confessed. She looked as guilty as I felt.

"Your idea was sound and something we wouldn't have considered," Adam said. "I appreciate your ingenuity in this; it may allow us to get past the army above our heads and deal with the situation from another vantage point."

"If nothing else, we may be able to rescue any hikers left alive," Merrill said. "The news programs are listing names of the missing. Once the Ra'Ak become hungry, a feeding frenzy will ensue, you can be sure of that."

"I hadn't thought about that," I mumbled and hung my head. These —they understood all there was to understand about Ra'Ak. I'd never had dealings with any of them until recently. Of course the monsters would get hungry.

Humans were their preferred food source.

"Fuck," Mason breathed.

"Exactly," Kiarra confirmed. "Shall we?" I lifted my eyes to her as she gestured toward the open tunnel ahead of us.

"Yeah. Let's go," I agreed.

Tungurahua Volcano, Ecuador

Zaria

Shielded and invisible, I hovered at the outside entrance to the Library. Would it know if I went past the entrance? Somewhere, perhaps a quarter mile along that tunnel, Lexsi walked ahead and led our crew toward the Library's hiding place.

I could screw everything up beyond repair if I went in and the Library sensed me. While most anyone would never sense a Larentii's passage, the Library wasn't just anybody.

It held records of the Larentii, just as it held records of everything else. If I suddenly appeared in any part of the pathway leading to the Library, it could sense me and throw all the events that happened before into chaos.

How could I get in to wait for Morgett's arrival?

When it hit me, I wanted to shudder. I'd destroyed those devices. Now I needed one.

Badly.

Without another thought, I bent time again.

Northern Reaches, Kifirin

Lissa

I arrived just in time to watch Jayd shove Glinda aside and then swing at her, his huge fist connecting with her jaw. She went sailing, and crashed in a heap fifteen feet away.

He'd done damage—she was out cold and blood poured from her nose.

He wasn't done, though. He had a score to settle with the Queen who'd sought to replace him on the throne. His Thifilathi stalked toward her, kicking her in the ribs before I could consider what to do.

Denevik's Thifilathi landed in front of Jayd with a thump and a roar. *Get Glinda out of here,* he sent while throwing a punch at Jayd that connected with the asshole's nose.

I rushed to pull Glinda inside my mist. I doubted she'd appreciate the fact that I'd pulled her away when she regained consciousness, but she could argue with her brother about that—provided he survived a one-on-one with Jaydevik Rath.

Jayd wanted to kill Glinda. Denevik was now on his list, too. Jayd answered Denevik's punch with one of his own, connecting with a shoulder when Denny jerked his head out of the way.

That's when a horde of Jayd's guards got into the fight. Three swarmed Denevik immediately.

This was no longer anything close to a fair fight.

A rogue's head exploded. Lexsi was still on the job.

Get 'em, baby girl, I said, then sent Glinda back to Le-Ath Veronis with power and called for Karzac to tend her, before joining my granddaughter in the fray.

~

Paricos II, Pre-destruction
Zaria

"You need this, don't you?" I blinked at myself as I/she spoke. Yes, I was facing myself, and wondered what that self would tell this self.

She held one of the concealment devices in her palm.

"You may hold it for a moment, to record its construction," she floated it to me. "Remember, that information must stay with you always."

"Yeah, I remember, all right," I agreed and closed my eyes to study the object I pulled from the air. "I have it," I opened my eyes and floated it back to her/me. "Thank you."

"It is necessary, or we wouldn't be here," she shrugged. "Although your presence gives me hope for our future."

"You know I can't tell you anything," I said.

"No worries."

I bent time and folded space.

Northern Reaches, Kifirin

Morwin

Somehow, Yoff found me. I sat amid tall grasses, two dead owls in my hands. Not far away, a terrible battle between High Demons went on.

I'd shut it and the noise of it out of my mind and mourned for the fluff of feathers in my palms.

"I have to get you out of here," Yoff knelt beside me. I didn't have to tell him who I held—he already had the others safely tucked away in the mountains above Foth Castle.

Mother Rose and Leisa lay there, lifeless. Victims of High Demons who'd flown after them when the grenades were dropped.

Life was so fragile.

"How can I tell Chloe?" I choked on my words.

"Come." Someone else had arrived. He looked High Demon, although stars fell through his black eyes.

Without another word, he transported all of us to Chloe and the others.

ungurahua Volcano, Ecuador
Zaria

With a working device in my pocket and a sigh of relief when nothing happened as I landed, I surveyed the passageway halfway between Lexsi's crowd and Morgett's, who'd just encountered the last test.

So far, the Library hadn't taken action against my invasion, leading me to believe the device was doing its job.

Anybody else who folded inside the caves leading to the Library would have already been fried.

I'd read Morgett's Ra'Ak before, but then, I'd been focused on other things—the location of his allies' hideout, and the placement of who knew how many N'il Mo'erti.

This time, I needed to go into his past and learn his deepest secrets, and I needed more than the few seconds I'd had before to learn them.

The device would allow me to travel alongside him without detection, while I read every single thing I wanted to know.

That's when he and his bunch, V'ili included, rounded a bend in the tunnel, racing toward the light of the Library, which had beckoned Lexsi and the others in. I began reading everything in him, V'ili and the twins as swiftly as possible as they rushed toward me. Any bit of it could prove invaluable.

~

Near Mutitjulu, Northwest Territory, Australia
Anita

None of us knew what lifted us and propelled us forward.

Until later.

We'd been gathered as a group and whooshed through rock, dirt and everything in-between as we hurtled toward Uluru.

I saw what we flew through and passed, just as the others did.

When we landed (and we landed hard against a sandstone wall), we almost collided with Morgett, V'ili and the twins, who promptly ran before we could right ourselves.

Mason pulled me up after setting Watson and Sandra on their feet; he'd recovered first, although Adam and Merrill were up shortly after. Pheligar, though—he'd never fallen in the first place. He stood in a smooth, sandstone hallway, watching as Morgett and company rounded a corner and disappeared.

Like the cowards they were.

"What is this place?" Sandra gazed about her. Every surface was red sandstone, and as smooth as if it had been planed by the gods. Where the light came from to illuminate the space I had no idea.

In the distance lay the corner where Morgett and V'ili disappeared; opposite that was a set of steps leading downward.

Not a speck of dirt or dust motes had been disturbed by our sudden arrival.

"I cannot send mindspeech," Pheligar turned toward us. "We are cut off from everything."

"I believe this is the Library," I breathed.

"Are we trapped?" Watson asked.

"I can still sense the Ra'Ak above ground," Kiarra said. "They're furious for some reason."

"I shall attempt to discover why," Pheligar said. "Ah," he added after several moments.

"Well?" Kiarra asked.

"They were preparing to leave the area to feed, when a shield prevented it and something else happened, roughly the same time we were deposited here, if my calculation is correct."

"What happened?" I blurted.

"Uluru is now floating, in its entirety, a thousand yards above the surface. We are trapped and the Ra'Ak are trapped. I merely hope the Ra'ak do not find a path into the Library, or we may all be, in your terms, screwed."

"Morgett is here," Mason pointed out.

"But that is only one Ra'Ak. We do not wish for thousands more," Pheligar said.

"Yeah. We sure as hell don't wish for that," Kiarra confirmed.

"Might we ask the werewolves to lead us in the direction Morgett traveled?" Merrill suggested.

"I'm all for it," Watson agreed. I lifted his pile of discarded clothing after he changed, while Mason did the same for Sandra. Together, the werewolves put their noses close to the floor and trotted forward.

Tungurahua Volcano, Ecuador
Zaria

Before, I thought it was Morgett and his bunch that set the Library off. I was wrong.

You have returned, the Library spoke in my mind. I barely heard the impossible words it spoke afterward as indescribable pain engulfed me and knocked me against the cave wall.

I fell. As I convulsed on the floor, I could hear shouting from inside the Library, and a flash of light.

Just before I lost consciousness, the volcano exploded as the Library disappeared from its hiding place.

~

Northern Reaches, Kifirin

Lissa

Jayd must have called his army back to save his scaled hide; they turned away from the castle and came toward us in a run, because Denevik was gaining the upper hand.

Lexsi and I were stretched to the limit already, eliminating the High Demons who thought to attack Denevik while he fought with Jayd. Now, at least a thousand more were running in our direction.

Saying that time was no longer on our side could be considered the understatement of the millennia.

Gran, get as far away from here as you can, Lexsi's voice entered my mind.

Huh? Yeah, I wasn't particularly eloquent while blasting another High Demon head to bits.

Go. I've got this.

I wanted to say huh again, but decided to trust my granddaughter.

I folded space to the castle.

~

Lexsi

It promised fire if I needed it. I prayed it wasn't an empty promise as I made my request.

It is here, the Library replied. *Use it.*

Visions of flames engulfed me. Not the flames of normal fire, though. This fire burned with the heat of a sun. This fire would kill High Demons; I knew it without asking. If the fire didn't kill the rogues about me, the percussion from the blast surely would.

And the Library's voice?

It didn't sound quite the same. All the others times—I considered that briefly. Was it only a few times, or had it been more than that? I distinctly recalled that this wasn't the voice I'd heard before, no matter how many times it had been.

Trust me, it whispered.

I didn't have time to reply; Jayd's army was bearing down on us.

I was filled with so much fire from the Library that it pained me. I became corporeal and my Thifilatha dropped to the ground.

I turned myself toward the advancing High Demons, closed my eyes and lifted my arms.

Fire!

❧

Lissa

If I hadn't shielded Foth Castle and those few of ours remaining outside it, it would have been destroyed, too.

You'd have thought that Lexsi released a ranos bomb with her fire. The explosion that accompanied it created a crater nearly half a mile across, and could be seen easily from the ramparts of Foth Castle.

"Where is she?" Kordevik skipped to my side and asked.

He was covered in cuts, some of which leaked blood. His blades were still in his hands, too; he hadn't realized he could set them down.

He was beyond weary, and he was asking about Lexsi.

"I don't know," I admitted. "Jayd and Denevik—I don't know about them, either."

"Fuck." Kory skipped away. He was heading for the crater. I followed.

❧

Lexsi

"I didn't mean to kill him, Grampa Denny."

He and I sat at the bottom of the crater I'd created. I felt like a small child as my Great-grandfather cuddled me in his arms. Tears dripped down my cheeks. "I didn't mean to kill Uncle Jayd," I croaked.

"Hush baby. If you hadn't, I would have."

"Grampa? Lexsi?" Mom had arrived and now stood over us.

"Jaydevik is gone," Grampa Denny told her.

"Just as well," she sighed and turned in a circle to examine the crater I'd made. "Baby, he went mad. I don't think there was anything left worth saving."

"Queen Reah?" Wardevik arrived and dipped his head to Mom. Concern filled his face and his voice.

"Baby?" Kory came next, with Gran. I blinked up at him before bursting into tears.

"She's upset because she feels responsible for Jaydevik's death," Grampa Denny said as he stood and handed me to Kory. "Let's go back to the castle and take stock. Too many have died this day, unless I am greatly mistaken."

~

Beneath Uluru

Anita

It was almost too easy to follow Morgett's trail. Ahead of us, through what appeared to be endless, brightly-lit corridors, Morgett, V'ili and the twins had begun running. Morgett still hoped to command the Library after reaching it first.

"This place is a maze," Mason said as he trotted beside me. He and I were at the back of our group; Adam, Kiarra and the others ran behind Watson and Sandra.

"I hate mazes," my words sounded choppy as I spoke while running.

"I can't say I'm fond of them myself, but we're following Morgett, remember? We're not chasing anything else."

He was right. Morgett, V'ili and the twins were our goal. I didn't care if I ever saw the Library again. And, if it could destroy everything, I sure as hell didn't want to come near it again.

I also felt as if we'd been running forever. I was no vampire or werewolf, but I considered myself in good shape. I worried I'd begin to tire soon and be left behind. That was the last thing I wanted.

I wanted to see V'ili die. I wanted to watch the light fade from his eyes—as he'd done the same for my sister and me. He and his grand idea of taking the Larentii homeworld had effectively destroyed our world.

Those of us who'd objected or argued with him ended up dead.

The rest of our race died when the Larentii retaliated—except for V'ili and a handful of others, chosen by rogue gods to continue a quest to destroy their enemies.

"Hmmph," I snorted as I ran.

"What?" Mason asked.

"Nothing."

"Right."

Watson yipped. We were almost upon our prey. I allowed my claws to form first, and then my scales as clothing ripped and dropped away from me.

This time, V'ili would die.

Foth Castle, Northern Reaches, Kifirin
Lissa

"I don't want my sons' bodies mingled with those of Jayd's rogues," Nedevik Weth sighed.

He'd lost almost half of his children to this fight. Foth and Greth suffered heavy losses, too. All of us were weary. Many chose an alcove or hidden place to release their tears.

Brothers and comrades had fallen. Grief had come as it always does after a terrible battle, settling like a smothering weight over those left behind.

"I will send Kifirin's heroes to Baetrah."

I jerked my head up as Kifirin appeared.

"Honey?" I said.

"Avilepha, I worried it would come to this." He held his arms open and I went to him.

"Baetrah will receive them," Lord Weth nodded to Kifirin. "Thank you."

"Will you come with me?" Kifirin breathed against my hair.

"Yeah."

~

Reah

"Dearest, I will do this for you, if you wish it," Nefrigar arrived. Kory, Warde and several others had gathered around me to discuss disposing of the bodies of our enemies—those that survived Lexsi's fire, anyway.

"Will it not disturb you to do it?" I blinked at my Larentii mate.

"No, dearest. The disease has been cut away. It should be disposed of properly, without leaving any shrine or place to visit behind it."

"I hadn't thought of that," I said, allowing my shoulders to sag.

"Kifirin was created with inherent flaws, my love. Those flaws are now excised. The High Demon race will choose its own path from now on."

"We have so much work to do," I said.

"I know this. I also know that you will have the support you need, and a worthy heir when you tire of the throne."

"You're right."

"Shall we?" Nefrigar held out a hand.

"Yes. We will separate the particles of our enemies together," I agreed and placed my hand in his.

~

Kinvalles, Amterea
Morwin

"This is my father's home—and mine," I explained to the Hiboux family. Li'Neruh Rath had transported us here and left, taking Mother Rose's and Leisa's bodies with him.

I had no idea what his intentions were, but I wasn't important enough to argue with a god.

He'd assured me they'd be kept in stasis before he left, but that was all he'd said.

He wore a worried expression, too, and that, in turn, had worried me. I didn't want to transfer that worry to the owl family, who were grieving for their loved ones and needed comfort.

"There is a small pub nearby," I said. "Food and drink will be available there, and we will talk."

"I think we need it," Jim agreed. "Come, owl brood. Follow Morwin."

~

Uluru

Anita

Watson rounded a corner, then yipped again, and it sounded as if he were afraid. Mason and I almost tumbled over him and the others as we rounded the corner, too.

The floor had ended.

Just like that, with no warning, it stopped, creating a high precipice. Over that sudden cliff, I couldn't see a bottom.

Opposite us, on another precipice that had also ended just as abruptly, stood Morgett, V'ili and the twins.

Morgett had turned; his Ra'Ak now hissed at us from his perch.

Curved walls surrounded us, now.

Massive, curved walls, lined with shelves too numerous to count.

This was the Library's other home.

Except—the shelves were empty. The Library was missing.

"What the bloody hell?" Adam mumbled softly.

"You have it," V'ili tossed an accusation toward us.

"We fucking don't," Kiarra snapped back.

Morgett's Ra'Ak wanted us dead—he hissed venom at us this time, although it didn't reach us, falling into the chasm between us instead.

I listened for the fluid to hit the bottom with an acidic hiss.

That sound never came.

"It's bigger than six football fields," Mason breathed beside me. Sandra, whose wolf had leaned against Mason's leg, whined her confusion.

The Library in the volcano hadn't been this large. The shelves, however, were the same general size as those in Tungurahua.

What the hell was going on?

Kinvalles, Amterea

Morwin

"Try this, dearest." I'd ordered a berry ale for her—an old favorite of mine. Our server, a cheeky, older dwarf, smiled encouragingly at Chloe.

She'd been informed that we'd suffered a loss in the family, and the pub was doing everything in their power to see that we were taken care of.

More people wandered in from the street and took a table near the window. They'd come here after a day's work, to relax. The owl family watched the new arrivals, as well as the servers and bartender.

"They're all—like us," Chloe turned toward me and brushed a stray tear off her cheek with a shaking hand.

"This is my home, love," I leaned in to kiss her forehead.

"You never felt out of place, did you?" Jim asked softly from the other side of the table.

"No. This is normal. You will find good and bad here, like everywhere else, it's just that here—you would easily fit in."

"I wish Gran could have seen this. And Mum." Two more tears rolled down Chloe's cheeks.

"My love, don't cry," I pleaded with her.

"I can't help it," she buried her face against my shoulder.

"I know. I'm here," I whispered and held her close.

~

Campiaa

Tybus

"The war is over," Dormas placed a comp-vid on my desk. "I've had mindspeech from Teeg. He says there are massive losses, and Veshtul was practically destroyed before Jaydevik's army left. He says, too, that bodies of the remaining humanoids in that city are scattered in the streets, bloated and rotting."

"I was afraid it would come to that," I said and touched the comp-vid to power it on. "Many of those High Demons were alive when Le-Ath Veronis and Harifa Edus were attacked long ago. They did nothing, then, to help us against the Ra'Ak. All the dark worlds were destroyed, while Lendevik and his closest cronies watched from a distance."

"And so comes payment due," Dormas shook his head. "Teeg says that only a quarter of the High Demon population survives."

"Vampire and werewolf races were rebuilt from less," I pointed out. "Others failed to survive at all."

"I wish I had the information you hold," Dormas said. "You remember so much, while I only recall that which occurred during my lifetime."

"Most only know that much, and some much less, because they believe it unimportant."

"Have Jaydevik's daughters been informed?" I asked.

"Not yet. I was hoping a family member would arrive to tell them."

"Family members are in short supply," I said.

"We know what one of them did when she heard her father could be dethroned. I shudder to think what could happen when they learn he is no more."

"Transport them to Kifirin. Let them see the destruction their father wrought."

"Belen," I rose and dipped my head to him.

"We will do as you ask," Dragon, Crane, Drake and Drew arrived, all nodding to Belen. Winkler and Martin joined those four quickly.

"Dormas, gather our guests," I instructed. "It is time to take them home."

~

Uluru

Anita

I suppose someone was listening, and had become weary of us trading insults and accusations with Morgett and V'ili. The chasm lay between us, and neither party could bridge that gap.

Power had been eliminated in some warped and perplexing way. Even Pheligar could do nothing about our predicament.

"I will kill you again," V'ili shouted across the distance at me.

"Fucking try it," I shouted back.

That's when the walkway moved beneath our feet, pushing both platforms toward one another. I realized that they should have been connected all along, and whatever sentience remained in the empty Library was correcting that problem.

Morgett's Ra'Ak roared; the walkway moved again, closing the distance and bringing us nearer.

We couldn't form a shield against his venom, now. Another roar; another jolt forward.

"Move back," Adam turned and motioned for us to obey. I learned why quickly—Kiarra became a giant white unicorn. At least that ability hadn't been taken away from us. She'd been created to do battle with the Ra'Ak. Lowering her head, she pawed the ground with a hoof, sending a challenge to Morgett.

The walkway moved forward again.

"Wait," I hissed as both crouched.

"No," I shouted as the unicorn and Ra'Ak leapt across the remaining distance. I think I screamed as the unicorn's horn skewered the Ra'Ak, who dusted, sending his chunks toward us.

We were knocked off our feet when the walkway moved again,

connecting one end to the other above the falling body of a selfless unicorn.

The twins attempted to flee; Adam and Merrill were on them immediately.

V'ili, however, strode angrily toward the rest of us, casually swiping his claws against Watson's wolf as he attempted to bite through black scales.

"Get back," I shouted at Mason and Sandra. "This is my fight," I added.

Somewhere in the distance, I heard Daris scream before it was cut off.

One twin down.

I grinned at V'ili as he approached, showing him my full set of pointed teeth. "Come on, brother," I hissed. "It's time I paid you back."

❧

Veshtul, Kifirin

Lissa

Dragon, Crane, Winkler and my Falchani twins arrived with Glinda's girls and Reah's eldest daughters.

Belen had asked us to hold off clearing Veshtul's streets of the dead until those eight young women arrived with their husbands.

Here, the humanoids had no power or recourse against High Demons gone mad. Some of the dead were children, who'd perished beside their parents.

Every structure in the city was damaged. Many were completely destroyed. In the background, standing tall and forbidding, was the High Demon palace.

Tybus had designed it long ago. He'd never intended for it to witness such horrors.

"Why does it smell so awful?" Jheri asked.

I wanted to snort. I didn't. Obviously, she'd never seen the dead, before. Had never come close to a corpse left baking in the sun for two days or more.

Tara and Raedah had medical training, however. They weren't surprised at all. "They've been dead at least two days, Jheri," Tara said. "This can happen quickly, when the temperatures are higher."

At least Reah had insisted that her girls get additional schooling. Jhase and Jheri had gone straight into marriage after they reached twenty-two years of age, after finishing their studies with tutors at eighteen.

"Glinda is sleeping." Karzac arrived—probably after Drake and Drew sent mindspeech. "This will produce a pestilence if it isn't cleaned up quickly." Karzac surveyed the dead with a critical eye.

"Why is Mom sleeping?" Jhase walked toward Karzac, her husband right behind her.

"Because your father attacked her," Karzac handed her unvarnished truth. "He broke several bones in her face and ribs. If my Lissa hadn't been there to send her back to Le-Ath Veronis, she'd have died at his hand. This," Karzac swept a hand toward bloated bodies, "is also his handiwork."

Jheri's hands went to the back of her neck as she blinked at Karzac. "Mom's all right, isn't she?" She walked toward Jhase and Karzac.

"Your mother is healed of her physical trauma and is now resting."

"Where's Daddy?" Jhase's words were whispered.

"Dead, after attacking Glinda and your uncle Denevik," I said. "He led an army against Foth Castle, and only a quarter of the High Demon population is now alive to tell that tale."

"That can't be true," Sara, one of Reah's last set of twins, breathed.

"It is true."

Reah had come, with Wardevik, Nedevik and Denevik with her.

"Here's your chance, Jheri, to sneer at Reah because she had dirt under her fingernails after tending the gishi fruit groves," I said. "Look around you. Every death here, and every death at Foth Castle was brought about by your father and your uncle Garde. Yours is not the only loss, here. I lost a mate and a son. Tara, Raedah, do you not acknowledge that your father is dead, too?"

The tears that refused to fall before were falling now. For my son, and the daughters who didn't recognize him as their father.

For Reah, who'd saved Kifirin and was belittled and ostracized for it.

"It's all right." A large, blue hand dropped onto my shoulder from behind.

Except that it wasn't completely blue.

It looked as if the blue were covered in gold glitter.

It wasn't gold glitter.

I blinked at Zaria through my tears.

"I will *Change What Was*, now," she said, and lifted her arms.

CHAPTER 18

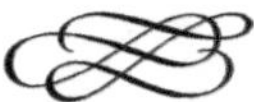

Queen's Palace, Le-Ath Veronis
Lissa

Zaria didn't rebuild the city, or remove the dead. The High Demon palace was cleared of the curse infecting it, however, and Reah's six, who'd long thought of Glinda as their mother, dropped to the street where they'd stood and wept—at the loss of their father and the plight of their mother.

Kory and Lexsi had shown up shortly after, and joined Reah to walk into the palace. Already the Reth Alliance was processing Kifirin's application to rejoin the Alliance, under Reah's rule as Queen.

Glinda and her daughters were offered Council positions, so they could assist in shaping new laws for Kifirin. Glinda accepted immediately; Jhase and Jheri with less enthusiasm.

All of Reah's daughters were now on the Council, although Lexsi, as Reah's designated heir, held a higher place.

Nedevik and Wardevik Weth, along with Kory and Denevik, served as the Prime Committee of personal advisors to the new Queen. That position would no longer be held by a single person, and I was grateful. Together, they added proper representation from the humanoid population, so all of Kifirin's inhabitants would have a voice and a vote on the Council. Roff smiled when I delivered that news to him.

As for Zaria, she'd disappeared as swiftly as she'd arrived. It left me wondering what else she'd had to do to set things right.

~

Revalus

Anita

I'd killed V'ili inside Uluru, while the Ra'Ak horde surrounding that monolith disappeared in a rain of sparks that dropped to the ground.

Images from Old Earth show Uluru slowly lowering to its normal spot on the ground, with not a scratch to be seen.

None of what we'd seen or experienced inside was ever revealed.

It wasn't until later that I learned the truth.

Yes, I'd killed V'ili, there inside Uluru.

Adam and Merrill had destroyed the twins. Kiarra's unicorn killed Morgett, before she fell to her death.

Those things happened.

And they didn't.

I learned something, there.

I still have no idea how it was accomplished.

V'ili was there, in Uluru.

He was also elsewhere, ahead in the timeline. As were the twins. Kiarra, too; placed there by Zaria, in an effort to keep the timeline intact. I hadn't known what dire consequences could come from destroying the timeline.

Not then.

I do, now.

Lexsi was the one to tell me. How she knew it, I have no idea. I visit her on Kifirin now and then, with Watson by my side. Queen Reah, her mother, always makes us feel welcome.

Somehow, too, the twins and V'ili's other selves didn't recall meeting one another, or attacking Earth with Morgett.

"I think they were taken from before," Lexsi reasoned with me one day.

"Before they'd met?" I asked.

"Yes. It doesn't sound logical, but it is. Zaria had to maintain the future she'd already participated in."

"That gives me a headache, just thinking about it," I'd replied.

Watson and I had been given a home on Revalus, although once or twice a month, a werewolf with the talent would arrive and transport him to Harifa Edus, to run with a wolf pack there under one of its six full moons. That's where he was, now. I sat on our patio, thinking of the past and listening to birds in the trees around our home.

"Anita?"

I stiffened. I knew that voice.

"Zaria?" I turned toward her. She'd come to Revalus.

Finally.

"I have something for you," she held out a hand.

"What is it?" I reached out to take what she offered. It was a tiny chip to fit my comp-vid.

"V'ili's final death," she smiled at me. "And Vardil Cayetes', V'ili's latest criminal cohort."

I hadn't lived on Revalus long—because it hadn't existed before. Somehow, Zaria had achieved that miracle and brought many Sirenali to live here, alongside the pod'l-morphs.

"Is it fitting?" I asked. My fight with the Uluru version of V'ili had been vicious and bloody before I gained the upper hand and sliced his throat.

"I separated his particles, I'm sorry to say. I don't do fights or torture," she added.

"I sort of get that about you," I said. "Thank you for this," I held up the chip. "I'll wait for Watson to get home and we'll watch it together. Want to stay for dinner?"

"Thanks but no. I have a few errands to run," she said and disappeared.

Errands could mean buying shoes or saving worlds, where Zaria was concerned. Honestly, I'd been afraid to ask which it might be.

≈

SouthStar, Avendor

Morwin

"Tea," Chloe set a cup at my elbow as I read a student's report. "Gran and Mum are coming for dinner, and bringing Susan, Tim, Georgia and Sarah with them. David isn't coming; he's out with the reptanoids, tinkering with the hover-tractors."

"I think Mother Rose and her family like vacations at SouthStar," I said, setting the comp-vid down and smiling at my wife.

"I think Gran likes flying with your Avii students," Chloe laughed. "They love Mother Owl."

I'd never told Chloe that in our past, her grandmother and mother had died. Zaria, whatever she'd become, had brought a miracle to the owl family. I was grateful.

"I'll be pleased to have dinner with your family, dearest," I patted Chloe's hand.

"That's your way of saying run along so I can finish my work," she teased.

"I would also be pleased if my students learned proper punctuation," I declared. Chloe left my study with a chuckle.

"I made a promise."

Two ranos pistols were set on my desk. I looked up to find Zaria standing there.

"The only promise I recall is that of telling me who killed my father."

"And that's why I'm here," she said. "Come. Bring your pistols. It is time."

≈

"Morwin, I understand you have a score to settle."

I'd taught this one. Quite shrewd was Rylend Morphis, King of Karathia. "Their power has been removed," Rylend rose and nodded to Zaria, who stood by my side in the King's study.

"Which one?" I knew about the Karathian Court trials. Deris and Daris Blackmantle had been found guilty of crimes too numerous to list.

"Deris killed your father," Zaria said.

"I don't do executions," I said, my voice sharper than intended. The pain of my father's death still disturbed me, even after so many years had passed.

"I know that," Zaria said, patting my shoulder. "Why do you think I brought both your pistols?"

"So. You match a rusty, old soldier against a known killer?" I studied Zaria's face.

"You don't like those odds?" Rylend asked, his voice soft.

Zaria's gaze pierced me. I wish I could say that it didn't make me uncomfortable after a while, but it did.

"I will allow you to choose your weapon," she said. I blinked for a moment before lowering my eyes.

"I find that acceptable," I agreed.

"Dad and I will come with you, as witnesses," Rylend said. "To close the books on this, I hope."

"Where is Deris?" I asked Zaria while Rylend sent mindspeech to his father, Erland Morphis.

"Deris and Daris are scheduled to be released on Evensun shortly. We will arrive to greet them."

"I'm ready," Erland arrived. "Shall we?"

Zaria transported us to the penal planet of Evensun.

Evensun

King Rylend Morphis

Zaria arranged for us to arrive just as Deris and Daris walked off the transport ship. She'd shielded us, too, so the Campiaan Alliance ship wouldn't know we were there. The transport lifted from the ground and flew away, leaving the two prisoners behind.

That's when we were revealed to the twins.

"Come to rub it in?" Daris sneered at me.

"I don't have to. I can leave anytime I want," I said. "You, on the other hand," I shrugged.

"You are filth and have no right to the throne," Deris snapped. "If our grandfather were still alive," he didn't finish.

"If Hegatt were alive, he'd be standing here with you, stripped of power," Dad said. "That's a dead argument and not why we're here."

"Then why are we here?" Deris demanded. "And why did you bring that dwarf with you?" He pointed rudely at Morwin.

"Well," Morwin said, "Long ago, you killed my father."

"Ah. That. I killed many people. You can't expect me to answer for all of them, can you?" Deris laughed, as if it were a joke to him. Daris giggled, amused by her brother's words.

"I'm not the one sentenced to a penal planet," Morwin observed.

"You came here for something," Deris became serious quickly.

"Yes. I came here to challenge you to a duel."

"What if I choose not to participate?" Deris lifted an eyebrow. Already he was sizing up Morwin, and considering that he held the height and the upper hand in the matter.

"Then you get to walk into the general population, who are no doubt heading this way, intent on stealing your clothing and killing you if you resist," Morwin explained.

"What do I get if I win the duel?" It was a fair question.

"You get to keep the weapon you choose," Zaria said. "To fight off your attackers and establish yourself here on the planet as someone to be obeyed."

"A weapon? What sort of weapon?" Deris was now interested.

"Choose." Zaria held out a hand and a variety of weapons appeared on the ground between the twins and us. Swords, knives, guns, even ranos pistols lay there.

"This is a ranos pistol?" Deris stepped forward and lifted the weapon.

"Most definitely a ranos pistol," Morwin nodded.

"Then I choose this," he waved the pistol and stepped away from the other weapons.

"Morwin, you must now choose your weapon," I said, expecting him to choose the identical ranos pistol.

"I choose Zaria," he said.

~

Morwin

Zaria was Larentii. I suspected that she was other things, too, but I wasn't going to point that out to Deris.

He didn't wait, either, for the rules to be explained or to follow any protocols of a normal duel.

He fired at Zaria, almost the moment her name left my mouth. It was his intention, I think, to keep the weapon no matter the cost.

When his particles separated, they were red instead of the usual gold. I'd seen a Larentii separate particles before, in Queen Lissa's Council Chambers. This was like nothing I'd ever seen.

"You will never be reborn, Deris Blackmantle," Zaria breathed as the last red spark disappeared.

The ranos pistol dropped to the ground.

"You bitch," Daris hissed and dived for the pistol. The moment she attempted to fire it at Zaria, she also disintegrated into red, dissipating sparks.

I think I knew then that I'd overstepped my bounds, as Queen Lissa often said. Zaria had done so many things for me, and I'd used her as a weapon.

"It won't happen again," her gaze locked with mine. Instead of blue eyes, her eyes shone gold.

"I and my family owe you," I bowed to her.

"Yes. You do." Her voice was flat. "Rylend, I trust you can take Master Morwin back with you? He'll have to ask for transport to SouthStar from Karathia. I hope he isn't late for dinner."

Zaria disappeared.

~

Royal Palace; Veshtul, Kifirin

   Lexsi

It has taken three years to rebuild most of Veshtul. Mom and I stood in the arboretum at the top of the palace, looking over the city. In the distance, more construction was in progress.

Schools had been built; more were planned. The humanoid population was beginning to believe they had rights and that their votes counted. Kifirin was a member in good standing of the Reth Alliance, and trade in Gishi fruit was the best it had ever been.

Sunset is the best time to visit the arboretum, as the last fingers of sunlight bathe Veshtul and turn its multi-colored streets to gold.

The sun was setting, now, and we'd just finished a long day of Council meetings.

"Want to come?" Zaria appeared between Mom and me.

"Come where?" I asked, turning to her. She looked like Zaria instead of a Larentii sprinkled in gold today.

"Oh, a short trip to the past," she sighed. "Just something I want to see, to remind me why I am."

Her words were odd, but I didn't question her meaning. I was tired from a long day of dealing with High Demon Council members and politicians from the humanoid cities.

All had a voice now, thanks to Mom.

"I'll go," Mom smiled at Zaria.

"Yeah. Me too," I agreed.

Zaria landed us on the streets of Veshtul. The sun was setting, still, but I knew this wasn't the Veshtul I'd been gazing upon from the arboretum.

This was a Veshtul in another time.

"Is that?" Mom placed a hand over her mouth as a comesuli walked out of a wine shop and closed the shutters on the open window.

"It's Roff," Zaria said. "It's all right to talk—we can't be seen or heard."

Roff went back inside.

A few moments later, I gasped. Kifirin appeared, with Gran.

"It's Lissa," Mom breathed, her hand beginning to tremble.

Kifirin called out.

Another comesuli stepped outside the wine shop and bowed to Kifirin.

Toff.

Only that's not how things happened.

Not that I remembered.

Toff, grown and smiling, went back inside the shop and then returned with two bottles of oxberry wine for Kifirin, who paid.

"This didn't happen," Mom choked out.

"It did. And it didn't," Zaria replied. "Come. I will show you more."

We landed at the edge of a massive crater. All around us, the ground was burned and blackened. In the distance, I could see Foth Castle. It lay in ruins. Everywhere, amid the rock and charred grasses, lay the bodies of the fallen.

High Demons, dwarves, humanoids—all sorts. All dead.

All. Dead.

None had survived this battle.

"When?" Mom's voice sounded strangled.

"It did. Then it didn't," Zaria said. "Shall we?" We were transported again.

"It's Peru," I gasped, my breath catching in my throat. It was the only thing left that thrived; all around it was devastation. N'il Mo'erti guarded the borders, but there was nothing left to guard it against.

We drew closer.

Fields of drakus seed, as far as the eye could see, grew in that country, tended by humanoids who appeared as automatons, picking the seed pods and placing them in large baskets.

I couldn't bring myself to ask where Morgett was, because he was surely there, at the root of all this evil.

"They're all there," Zaria said. "And they're not."

We moved again.

I gasped as we hung in the air above the burning remains of the cruise ship. Morgett and V'ili had undoubtedly found Morwin and the others there. Blinking back tears, I watched as the smoking, broken hull rolled and disappeared beneath the waves. There were no lifeboats floating in the water; all aboard had perished.

Zaria moved us.

"Where is this?" Mom asked. We'd landed inside some sort of structure built of smoothed red sandstone.

"Uluru," Zaria answered.

"There are people, wait, is that Kiarra?" Mom asked. She sounded terrified.

In the distance lay two walkways, separated by a chasm. Morgett's Ra'Ak, accompanied by V'ili, Deris and Daris, stood on one side while Kiarra, Anita and others stood opposite.

A rumble shook the structure; only then did I seen the massive, curving walls of empty shelves surrounding us.

I heard screams and jerked my head toward those on the walkways.

I will always find it difficult to revisit those images in my mind, as all were consumed by a terrible, red fire.

None of them had survived in this scenario.

"They died and didn't," Zaria sighed.

We moved again; I found that we were suspended above the space that should have contained Earth. Only a massive, red sandstone monolith floated there, barren and lifeless. The sky around us was black and empty of stars. I choked and couldn't speak; so many questions needed an answer and I couldn't voice any of them.

Then, I found myself back in the palace arboretum, just as the sun dropped below the horizon.

"Why did you show us that?" I wiped tears off my cheeks. Mom was too overcome to speak, and chose to pull me into her arms instead. We both gazed at Zaria, horror surely written into our features.

"You hold a copy of the library, as does Kory," Zaria reached out to wipe a tear off my cheek with a thumb. "In the past, it has either destroyed everything, or chosen this one or that as a catalyst or a weapon. It chose you and Kory, there in Tungurahua."

I blinked at her while more tears blurred my vision.

"Don't worry, sweetheart," Zaria wiped more tears from my face. "It will never speak to you again. Or control either of you again."

"What happened?" I sobbed. "How? Why would it?" I begged.

"It attacked me when I went back there," Zaria shrugged. "It thought to take me, too. I fought it for a very long time. Once I had the upper hand, it took even longer to control it properly," Zaria blew out a breath. "But it is controlled, now. It actually understands, now. Before, it didn't feel. Now it does."

"You hold the actual Library?" Mom asked.

"Yes. All those metal books inhabit my cells in a miniature form. I won't say it happened without a great deal of pain, either."

"So, my memories of how things happened," I began.

"Is just one of the ways—the last of those ways, that things really happened."

"May the Mighty be merciful," Mom sighed.

"The Mighty? That's between you and them," Zaria said and disappeared.

"Dearest?" Wardevik's voice interrupted.

"Warde?" Mom turned toward him. Their wedding would take place in a moon-turn. He was good for her, and it was fitting. Those two on Kifirin's thrones would ensure the planet grew and thrived.

Thanks to Zaria.

Larentii Archives

Nefrigar, Chief Archivist

"These are the only prophecies associated with the Vhanaraszh that are contained in the Archives," I nodded at the massive books lying before the pod'l-morph.

"This isn't everything," Phrinnis Tampirus lifted his eyes to mine.

"Hmmph," I made a noise at him and turned my back. Those records the pod'l-morph desired would never be placed in his or anyone's hands, although he was mated to the Vhanaraszh. The answers he seeks lie within Corinnelar, whom most name Zaria.

She bore the weight of it—not in actual weight, but that of responsibility. She'd told me once, when I asked, that it was like carrying the reset button for everything. "Lather, rinse, repeat," she'd added. "Control, Alt, Delete."

～

Zaria

Even my white wings are dusted with gold when I employ them. Quin stands on the balcony outside the royal suite at Avii Castle as I fly toward her.

She is smiling as I approach.

"Hello, daughter," I land beside her and offer a hug. She wraps her arms about me and laughs because I am there.

The End